PRAISE FOR
DRAGON INK

"In *Dragon Ink*, an appealing young heroine wins a future "bestie," or perhaps a "beastie," through her courage and concern for others. Dragon lovers will find much to swoon over in this interspecies adventure."

—LINDA WATANABE MCFERRIN, author of *Namako, Dead Love,* and *Navigating the Divide*

DRAGON INK

Dragon Ink

Tami Casias

OOMM Books

OOMM Books
Dunsmuir, CA, 96025, USA

February 2023

ISBN: 978-0-9829735-4-7
E-ISBN: 978-0-9829735-5-4
Library of Congress Control Number: 2023901902

Publisher's note:
This is a work of fiction. Names, characters, places, and incidents either are the product of the author's imagination or are used fictitiously, and any resemblance to actual persons, living or dead, business establishments, events or locales is entirely coincidental.

Cover tattoo art by Jaime Meredith at Olde Thyme Tattoos, Dunsmuir, CA.
Dragon sketch by Haley Kvasnicka.
Photographic Design by Benjamin Casias, Inertia Pictures.
Front cover image © rawpixel/123RF.com.
Back cover image © dundanim/123RF.com.

Cover and Interior design by Tabitha Lahr

To my great friend Ellen.
Thanks for letting me use your name all those times.

To my husband Glenn, who supported my need to
talk about dragons for a decade.

To my dear friend Shana Rose Abela, who was there
in the beginning but didn't make it to the end.
Hope your e-reader is eternally charged.

CHAPTER 1

Even the sun gave up on Ellen, slipping toward the rooftops of the souvenir shops and sending long shadows over the cobblestone sidewalk. She paced in front of Big Mark's Tattoo Parlor, already late for her appointment. Spurts of adrenaline pinballed through her body. She exhaled in a long push, but the fear couldn't escape the thick coat of dread she'd worn for months.

Her once flowing career, blocked. Her exciting young life, frozen in a dark place.

Her agent's call had been final. No extension on the third extension to finish her book. Ellen would be in breach of contract in three weeks if she didn't get back on track.

Off the rails, she barreled through a new territory where life didn't come easily anymore, afraid the stories had dried up in the same ironic twist that had hit her love life.

She'd written a plan. As usual. A daring idea to restart her life. The last-ditch effort had a severe flaw. She could break through her fear but still be blocked.

The glass door of the tattoo parlor burst open in a frenzy of bells.

Big Mark filled the frame. His curly red hair was moussed into two spiked cones. Inked pythons twisted around his thick arm muscles. The tail of a rattlesnake circled the base of his neck. The only visible straight line on his body was his mouth. "Are you coming in this time or not? I need to feed my cat."

Tension dropped out of her shoulders, sending her backpack straps sliding down her arms. She tugged the bag back in place. Tomorrow might be a better day to start. "If you have to go, we can do the tattoo thing another day."

He crossed his bulging arms and stared.

She chewed on her top lip.

"Look, kid." He wagged a long finger in front of her. "You've rescheduled once a day for a week. Maybe a tattoo isn't in your cards."

"I'm going to do this. I have to." *I need my life back.*

"Your mouth keeps saying that, but your running shoes avoid this threshold." He turned back inside. The late afternoon light glinted off the chain that ran from an ear pierce to somewhere below his leather vest. "You're not ready."

The door clanged shut. He flipped the *Open* sign to *Closed.*

Ellen released the death grip from her backpack straps and shook out her hands.

Big Mark glared at her through the window. He selected a pencil, then rubbed the eraser on the page of his appointment book with the exaggerated flourish of a double-dog dare.

"Son of a..." She forced her bowed shoulders straight and tugged the noisy door back open. "Hey, I'm . . . I'm ready."

"I'm closed." He grabbed a broom and swept forward, forcing her back to the door. Photos of Big Mark's specialties filled every inch of display space with snakes, crocodiles, and dragons. A sign near the register read: 'I don't do dolphins or butterflies. Don't even ask.'

"Haven't you ever had one of those years where so many things go wrong, you're afraid to do anything?"

"Nope."

"I'm having one now. My entire once-amazing life's a mess. I've missed my deadline for grad school, and my publisher is threatening to drop me. If I lose that gig, I can add my home to the growing list of things I earned early and lost quick."

"Don't you have any little playmates you could tell all your crap to?"

"That's on my list. Today, aside from a couple of bartenders and a neighbor fixated on the correct shade of grass, you're all I've got."

"A tattoo isn't for everyone." Big Mark propped the broom against the wall and traced a finger along the length of one of the snakes that wound down from his shoulder in a spiral of colors. "It's a manifestation of the life within each of us, showing the world our true selves. It takes bravery to allow others to see us clearly."

Ellen slapped her hands together then held them up, palms facing the ceiling. "That's my problem. The tattoo is connected to the fear bone. The fear bone is attached to the working bone. And the working bone is fastened to the roof over my head. If I can get past this suffocating fear, I can take at least some of my dreams back."

Big Mark arched his eyebrows, raising the metal studs an inch on his forehead. "You know you're weird, right?"

She nodded. She'd heard that same thing on her first day of college at sixteen.

"A tattoo was the scariest thing you could come up with?"

"I'm afraid it's going to be the easiest thing on my list."

Big Mark yanked a curtain open to reveal a black padded chair. “Sit.” He flicked a switch, and a low buzz filled the room. “I need to be out of here in thirty minutes or Little Spot will shred the good couch.”

CHAPTER 2

The shadows betrayed Welglen, stretching his tall outline to the building's edge. He pressed against the bark of the fruitless tree and fixed on the windows, grimy fingerprints reflecting against the harsh angles of sunset.

The veil rippled, then stilled. The human lingered.

The stringent scent of her fear dissipated. He unclenched long enough to brush the rusty leaves off his tight shoulders. His hot muscles craved flight—escape from old compulsions. But the girl had reawakened the beast and drew him to her.

He pretended that he waited only to discover why the voices had returned. He pretended he could leave at any moment.

Broken bells sounded as she pushed the door open. The shopkeeper followed her out and slid a key into the lock.

She tied her hair into a spiky blond bun, a rare smile widening across her face. "I can't believe I really did it."

The man shook his head. "Neither can I."

The pair walked toward the corner, the female bouncing, her pace light, animated. The man's arms pumped with each brisk step, his muscles poised and prepared for action.

Welglen stepped into the last of the sunlight, ready to return to the heat of his nest.

At the corner, the male waved goodbye. The female continued alone.

She crossed at a diagonal and walked along the shops on the opposite side of the park.

Defenseless.

He followed.

CHAPTER 3

Ellen pushed through the double doors of Britta's Brews and pulled down her pants.

Just enough. She pointed an exposed hip across the bar to Britta, her favorite brew guru. "Badass, right?"

Britta walked around the end of the long, empty bar, tying a black scarf around dark curls that matched her dress and her fingernails. "Hold still." She gazed down at Ellen's side, then squatted for a closer look. "What is it?"

"A tattoo. Ninety thousand tiny pinpricks that prove I have the courage to face pain, and a lifetime of potential regret."

"Tattoo, huh." Britta angled her head to one side. "I mean, of what?"

Ellen dropped her backpack into the booth closest to the door. She twisted and ran a finger around the tender outline encased beneath a clear wrap. "Dragon scales."

"I thought you wanted the whole dragon."

"I like to think my inner dragon has emerged."

"Writers are weird." Britta walked behind the bar and held up a coffee mug and a beer glass. "Still going ahead with your crazy plan?"

Ellen pointed to the glass, stretched her yoga pants back into place, and slid into the booth. "I need to prove my bravery."

"I've seen your list. You might want to rethink swimming with sharks."

"Go big or go home." She did everything quickly. She'd graduated high school and college early. She'd snagged a three-book deal on a family of dragons. She'd tackle her grief and get her life back by running headfirst toward anything that scared her.

Britta carried the drink over. "You know the other option."

"I promise I'll see a therapist if this doesn't work." It was going to be hard to explain to a mental health professional that she missed the imaginary family of dragons that had abandoned her dreams.

She pulled her laptop out of the backpack.

A sensation of being watched breezed over her. She turned to the door then scanned the room. Empty except for Britta, dozens of antique coffee pots hanging from the ceiling, and a row of stainless-steel beer vats behind the bar. She pushed her things across the scarred wooden table, then scooted around the booth, facing front.

She opened the project page on her laptop to chapter thirty.

For the umpteenth time.

Her characters had waited months for her to write them out of danger. And dragons could be a little needy—especially the big ones.

She cracked her knuckles and held her hands over the keyboard. She paused for an idea to formulate in her brain and radiate down the network of nerves to her fingertips. She'd always been good at tuning out the world to write.

Today would work. She'd ignited her plan. The creative juices would flow.

She waited.

Her formerly responsive digits hovered.

Minutes passed. The muscle in her right pinky twitched.

Nothing.

And only weeks left until she found out how fast breach-of-contract would pull her house out from under her.

Shit. Why do I want the very thing I'm told I can't have? I'm going to lose everything.

She forced her mind back to the plan and whispered, "Don't go there Ellen." Twenty minutes in a tattoo chair while Big Mark jabbed her with needles and his cat's latest dental surgery story was only the first item on the long scary list designed to restart her life.

Laughter erupted outside the empty bar. She sipped her drink and gazed beyond the bright *Open* sign on the front window to the sidewalk. A group of guys in blue Sonoma State Seawolves jerseys stopped and vaped. The fire-breathing rookies managed to create a hazy cloud of tear-inducing smoke that coughed out the mouths of all but one, a taller guy standing alone.

The loner's mouth closed tight, the tension creating an angry frown as he forced smoke from his nostrils. Dark brown hair curled to his shoulders. The chiseled chin, freshly shaven. The tavern sign blocked his eyes, adding a mysterious element. She might write him into a thriller—the stranger who saved the world.

An unexpected wisp curled out of his full lips.

Ellen sucked in.

She exhaled at the subtle fall of his muscular chest and tried to match the pattern of his breaths.

His rhythm continued at a slow, even pace.

Increasing awareness shortened her breaths into pants.

At each exhale, smoke swirled from his nostrils.

No vape pen or cigarette touched his lips.

He smoked.

In an instant, he ducked below the sign, staring back with bold, green eyes.

Then, he simply disappeared.

Ellen searched past the sound of her pounding heart for a rational explanation that didn't involve teleportation or apparitions.

Nothing.

The guy had vanished.

CHAPTER 4

A soft breeze rolled over Welglen's body but didn't cool his anger. The quick enhanced spell hid him from the human's dazed eyes, though she still searched, mouth hanging open. He froze and waited for the human's belief system to repair the damage.

She'd seen him.

After centuries of masquerading, his powers weakened. He had to know why.

The female leaned against the table, raised one hand to shade her eyes from the hanging light, and squinted forward. Her voice carried out the partially opened door, "What the hell?"

Two young males walked into the tavern, trailing the burnt scent of ganja. One turned in her direction and asked, "You okay, dude?"

She shook her head, short blond hairs escaping from a loose knot. "I just saw a guy disappear. There, then . . . gone."

"Probably wind. We're supposed to get a few gusts."

Her attention moved from the window to the young male's face. "You think the wind blew someone away?" She slid back into the booth.

The other male spread his arms wide. "Once the wind lifted me and carried me home."

The tavern keeper blocked Welglen's view and addressed the woman. "Do I have to watch you tonight?"

"I'm fine. I guess." She scanned for the young man Welglen had been a few minutes before. Not until she returned to her tasks and her drink, did he allow his flight muscles to calm.

Oblivious to the real world, her thin body relaxed into her seat. She drank in deep pulls. The surprise of her direct gaze continued to charge through him like the after-effects of battle. His wings strained against his disguise. He yearned to take off, but he'd have to endure the torture of waiting until he knew what drew him to her.

A faint scent of industriousness rippled from her direction. Her face morphed from one emotion to another while her fingers flew across the keys at a pace that he guessed barely kept up with her thoughts.

Fear registered first. Power erupted in the slight movements of her shoulders. Her head ducked from imagined attacks, nearly knocking a fresh drink over.

He understood the role of the chronicler. Storytellers served an important role in all cultures. Did she use her skills to teach and entertain? Or did this human mix her facts with fiction in the way of sorcerers?

He kept watch. If the spells weakened, there wasn't much time left. He needed to find the warrior. First, he had to serve his basic instincts.

The shield of males next to him moved away. He envied their herd. He hadn't been born a solitary creature.

She stared absently around the small room. She raised the glass again to her lips and searched over the rim in his direction.

He was her prey.

He preferred the reverse.

CHAPTER 5

Ellen raised the last of her drink to the monitor and toasted the first new scene she'd written in months. It wouldn't help her finish the book she'd already been partially paid for, but they were new words. Her words. All about the disappearing guy.

It was the first time she'd journaled a hallucination.

Britta waved her hands in front of Ellen's face. "Hello. Are you in there?"

Ellen shook her head. "Sorry. Deep in thought."

"I guessed that." She held out a fresh pint. "I killed the keg. Want the last?"

Ellen debated the rare third beer for about three seconds. She nodded. "Cut me off after. I wouldn't want my fairness fairy to get out tonight."

Britta laughed. "Like the night you got between those two idiots fighting and ended up on the floor covered in lime wedges?"

"My alter ego can be a little embarrassing, but she means well."

Ellen sipped the beer that tasted of citrus and procrastination. She listened to the two guys at the bar debate prime causes of climate change and waited for her imaginary courage to arrive in time for her last challenge of the day.

She lifted the waistband away from the slightly puffy red skin surrounding the teardrop-shaped tattoo on her hip. Even in the dim bar light, the colors matched the exact imagined shades of the scales on Ashamoor, her youngest dragon character.

She needed back into that story.

Britta called across the bar. "Want me to call for a ride? It's getting dark earlier."

"I'm good. My walks home are great thinking time."

At the bottom of her pint, she stood and dug out cash for her drinks. The act released the alcohol into her system. She clamped her hands around the edge of the table to allow her brain to slip back into gear and decided on a quick trip to the bathroom. She stopped at the ladies' room doorway and looked back along the narrow bar to the front window for the guy with the green eyes. The group of guys climbed into a car.

No invisible man.

Too bad. Her fairness fairy would like to meet him.

Ellen splashed water on her face and returned to the booth. She loaded her backpack—ready to make the call and work her plan. She was the author of her own story.

And on her way to drunk.

The cool night air tingled Ellen's warm cheeks on the walk across the street to the Plaza Park. She scanned her options. She chose the well-lighted diagonal sidewalk that cut through the center. Ducks gathered under the lights along the pond's edge and watched her pass.

A lone mallard, green neck feathers reflecting in the limited light, stood in the middle of the path, and stared. At her.

She stepped around it onto the grass. Playing chicken with a duck was a bad idea.

She hit her hand on a leaning park sign. "Ow!" She shook her stinging fingers. A coldness gripped her. She jerked to her right.

A large shadow darted behind a tall sycamore.

Ellen's flight mechanism froze.

She estimated the distance back to the safety of the bar and intertwined her keys between her fingers. She stared at the tree, only a dozen feet away.

Nothing moved.

Adrenaline forced her a step forward.

A trickle of sweat rolled in a chilling track from her temple to her neck. She examined her defense—silver points of keys in a small hand in bad need of a manicure.

No hero's weapon.

Ellen prepped her cell phone, ready to punch in 911.

The lights of a car circled the plaza and highlighted the shape of the tree trunk.

No one.

A gust of wind rustled the branches above her. She kept an eye on the tree and walked toward the edge of the plaza. At the corner, she took one last look backward, then jogged. She stayed in the middle of the tree-lined street, avoiding the dark shadows on her four-block run.

Ellen cut across the angled driveway to her small house. She leaped over the three steps onto the tiny porch, unlocking and opening in one movement.

A package that had leaned against the door fell into the house. She kicked it inside, slammed the door, and hurried in the dark to the front kitchen window to prove her imagination ran wild, again.

He stood across the street.

The same tall, broad-shouldered guy with the green

eyes, hands in his pockets. He stared at her door for half a minute, then walked down the street.

Ellen debated calling the police or her ex-boyfriend Josh. What would they say? 'You're a woman. You can't be out at night without a man, or the boogeyman will get you.'

She tossed her phone onto the counter, stretched across the top of a sink of dirty dishes, and struggled to open the window latch to give him a piece of her mind. She wanted to fight. And if middle school counted, she had experience.

"Why are you following me, jerk?" she yelled at the closed pane and bounced like a boxer warming up, the buzz from the beer mixing with adrenaline. "I don't have to take that. I can beat your ass with my baton if I want to. I'm a state champ!"

Ellen swung her fist in a large punch, tripping into the hallway over the box she'd kicked in. She landed on the floor, hard. "Uh!"

The long, narrow shape under her legs provided the only sign she needed.

Rising on her knees under the light of the microwave clock, she ripped the tape and peeled back the cardboard flaps to reveal a dark, wooden box secured with leather straps. She unbuckled the ties, lifted the lid, and gasped at her first sight of the twenty-four-inch sword she'd designed from a lifetime of dreams.

She slipped her hand around the body of the dragon that created the hilt and lifted the solid weight. The tail curved over to protect her knuckles in a perfect fit. The high cost for the mold had been worth every cent. She might lose her home, but she'd have her sword.

Ellen slid off the black sheath. A glint caught on the sharp edges of the double blade. She turned on the light and posed in front of the hall mirror, admiring the reflection as if trying on a designer dress.

She'd wanted this sword for years.

It arrived exactly when she needed it.

It would be all she required to make her point.

He didn't need to know that she didn't know how to use it.

Ellen slipped back outside. Her pulse calm. Spine straight.

The weapon clanked against the concrete steps.

She scanned the road. Would "I'm a writer" be a sufficient explanation for carrying a sword in public to any police officer in the area? She shrugged and tilted the blade forward. At the sidewalk she managed a lopsided jog, keeping the seven pounds of lanky steel from impaling any of the trees that lined the street.

She searched for her stalker, ready to turn the tables.

Her internal fairness fairy had volunteered for neighborhood watch.

CHAPTER 6

Welglen hesitated at the corner, struck with the sensation of a shift in his universe. A physical burn ignited in his stomach and expanded into his shoulder blades. He tamped down the desire for flight and ran ahead through the lamplight.

The secure sight of his nest calmed him—the green door closed tight. No sign of disruption along the stone walls.

His senses had been amiss all day. The intensity of the day's pull should have signaled a potential near-death experience. Welglen had given in and gone to her side, but it ended before it began. He would try harder to resist tomorrow.

When her door had closed, the female hadn't followed her custom to turn on her light, due certainly to ale over-indulgence. Her wits could be dulled, though she had seen him. If an inebriated human had spotted him, the spell weakened.

He walked between the hedges along the short path toward the porch, his thoughts on the lives of those he protected.

A small voice slurred. "Stop! Don't move. I'm armed."

He swirled to see a flash of reflected light.

In front of her face, the tiny human held the base of all his hopes and fears.

The Sword of Srekums.

"Who sent you?" he boomed, the muscles under his skin poised to explode in a battle to protect his charges. "The devil, Nilrem? Are you a Warrior of Death from the Old World?"

"Huh? I'm from Omaha." The metal glistened at the top of the sword that waved precariously near her nose before she re-pointed it at his heart. "You followed me tonight."

The last time he had seen this sword, it had been covered with the blood of the Great One. He hadn't imagined he would ever see it again. Yet it waved in the shaky grip of this human whose presence had tormented him.

Two possibilities erupted.

The first, a trick. He held her gaze and didn't offer any words.

She pointed her free hand at him. "I saw you following me in the park. I'm tired of worrying about where I walk." She stepped back, caught her foot on a shrub and stumbled.

He steadied her with one hand on her shoulder and grabbed the weapon with the other. She reached for it. He held it out of her reach. "I want to walk wherever and whenever I want. I don't want to be disturbed. I'll stand up for myself! Give me my sword."

The little female who'd brought him the Sword of Srekums stepped onto the stones at his doorway—the first human to ever notice the existence of his nest.

Would the sorcerers have sent such an inept warrior?

Desire to confirm his charges' safety combined with the thought of keeping this enemy close. He made his choice.

"Oomm Enran." He stood on the walkway and chanted the spell designed to control her thoughts with the powers of honesty. Once he learned what he needed, she would return to her life with no memory of their meeting. "Oomm Enran."

"What?" she squinted at the light from the street pole.

"Oomm Enran," he chanted and touched her shoulder. She flinched.

She should be standing erect and ready to answer questions. Instead, her eyes squinted into angry slits, the skin on her cheeks reddening in the limited light.

"What are you babbling about? Wait, don't answer. I don't care. Hear me. Following people, especially women, is creepy. Don't do it again!"

She grasped the Sword of Srekums. He let her take it from his hand, though he continued to block the narrow walkway leading to the street.

This human held the sword that could change everything.

She couldn't leave.

"I fear you have misunderstood my actions." He tipped his head in a practiced move to appear docile. "I often walk between town and home. When I see a weak one, I am inclined to follow to ensure safety."

"You protected me?" She snorted. "That's a new one."

He turned to allow her the feeling she could pass freely. "It is true. I walk the same direction as you. No hardship on my part."

"You're quite a character. What is your name?"

He took a moment to determine where, and if, to begin. "I am called Welglen."

She relaxed the sword to a less-threatening angle. "I'm Ellen. I run this street every day. Weird I don't remember seeing your house before. It's unusual—a sweet little stone cottage." She cocked her head slightly and gazed at the dwelling. "A rounded door, a sloping roof . . . right out of a storybook."

"It is a small old beauty. You are a female, already on alert in the presence of a strange man, so you would probably not feel comfortable entering. However, I would be happy to give you a tour."

Her eyebrows shot up. She squinted at him and drew a cell phone out of her pocket.

"Hi, it's Ellen. I wanted you to know I'm going to be at a new address for a little while in case you need me. I don't see the number, but it's across from 727 Claudine. I've met a guy named Welglen, and he's giving me a tour of his old house. It might make a great setting for my next book." She pointed the Sword of Srekums at his middle. "Yes, I'll be careful."

CHAPTER 7

The strange guy disappeared into the dark room. Ellen squeezed her sword hand tighter around the hilt and wrapped the other behind her as she staged her entrance. Low red coals glowed in a fireplace across the small room.

"How about some light?" she called from the porch.

The strike of a match sounded, and the flame illuminated his face. He touched it to each of three wicks on a short, fat candle that sat on a wooden table, bringing the room into view. Racks of thin-cut meat stretched over a pile of hot coals. A pair of doors in front of her were both closed. The opposite side of the room included a large carved chair, a pile of blankets, and a stack of leather-bound books.

"You're off the grid, huh?" Ellen glanced at the walls and ceiling. No lamps. No overhead lights. "Way off."

"That is accurate." He waved a hand toward the single chair. A man without visitors. "Would you like to come in?"

Ellen's gut rumbled. Her instincts to run cried out for attention. The smart move would be to hurry home. The call to Britta's voicemail would only be helpful in locating her body parts. Yet the oddness of the room filtered through the alcohol in her brain with a sense of déjà vu. There was a story here. She'd soak in the scene and the character for a few minutes, then go. She stepped into the room. "You're quite the renaissance man. No apparent electricity and cooking on an open hearth."

"Please sit." He backed away between the table and fire, though he didn't take his gaze off the weapon. He squinted in the flickering light. Thin wrinkles appeared on the sunburnt skin around his eyes. Probably mid to late twenties, six two or three. "Though I didn't believe so in my beginning, time passing without learning and evolving is without merit. I find many of the modern inventions too fast. I see no benefit in rushing."

Ellen pushed the door fully open and backed toward the chair. He didn't move. The sword pulled against her thin wrist. She pointed the tip upward to center the weight.

"How did you come by that sword? It's unusual."

She leaned back to settle in the chair, but it was too high. Her opposite hand on the arm, she hopped into the seat, the blade swinging past her nose. She cleared her throat and pushed back into the seat. Her feet dangled from the massive piece. She snorted at the image of little people in big furniture, then coughed to stop the impending giggle fit. She straightened her shoulders and raised her chin higher. "I made it. Had it made, really. Isn't it a beauty? I plan to use it for work. I'm a writer."

The stranger leaned against the oversize table. "What is it you write each day?"

Lately, a lot of nothing. "Books about dragons."

His voice boomed as he stepped around the table. "What do you know of dragons? And how did you acquire the Sword of Srekums?"

Ellen jumped, brandishing the sword—her eyes on the

still-open exit. Adrenaline cut through her beer buzz and sharpened her focus.

He held his hands toward the ceiling and backed away.

She sidestepped toward the door and tried to recollect stories with a happy ending that started with a girl going into a stranger's house. Nothing but Hansel and Gretel. Ellen needed to change her brave character to one who knew when to run. She reached the doorway.

He lowered his hands. "I'm sorry for my outburst. To be truthful, I have seen this sword before, though on a somewhat larger scale."

"That's impossible. I had it made from my imagination. Every part of the design came from a recurring dream."

Welglen's broad shoulders slumped slightly. He rubbed a hand across his forehead before moving to sit in the chair, increasing the gap between them. From the threshold, the murmur of a neighbor's television and the footsteps of someone on the sidewalk across the street added a comforting background. She could be out to the curb screaming in seconds. "I believe we must start anew. I'd like to understand the source of your courage. You are a storyteller. Would you tell me what you know of dragons?"

"I could talk about them all day. It all started with my childhood dreams. My mom got me into journaling, so the dreams turned into stories. I know, or at least have imagined, more about dragons than anyone."

He sighed and leaned back against the chair. "I see. You are not from the devils."

She adjusted her grip on the sword, stretching her aching hand muscles. "That's the strangest statement I've ever heard, but no. I'm not from the devils, though if they exist, I can't exactly guarantee I won't be heading that way. Who are you? What is all this?"

Welglen held his hands out to his sides, palms up. "I consider myself quite an expert on dragons as well. And you are in my home."

"Nice place," she pointed the blade past the pile of blankets to the two wooden doors. "What is it? One bedroom, one dungeon?"

His green eyes darkened.

She tried on a stronger character and faced down his stare. "Are you attempting to frighten me?"

His eyebrow lifted. "Don't I?"

Ellen stretched to her full below-average height and tried to look casual. "Yes."

The corner of his mouth twitched in a quick smile. "As you should be, in the home of a stranger. No harm will come to you at my hand."

He rose and walked slowly toward her, stopping at sword's length.

"It would go a long way to know why you were following me."

Welglen shrugged. "I wish I knew. It appears you need protection."

"Nice. Or what every stalker might say."

"I didn't stalk you. I followed to protect you from those who would do you harm."

Ellen chuckled. "Sure, real believable. Guys must do that all the time."

"Men do not do that all the time."

"We agree." She moved the point of the sword up a fraction of an inch. "I should go."

Ellen scanned the room again, securing descriptions to journal. Kitchen for eating, chair for sitting. A pile of blankets and fur evidently for sleeping. No TV, appliances, or family photos. She motioned him back toward the fireplace wall. After he slipped behind the table, she walked to the opposite wall.

"Out of professional curiosity," she touched one of the two doorknobs on the back wall, "bathroom?" Without giving him time to answer, she turned the knob.

A burst of wet heat opened the pores on her face and blew back her hair.

At the bottom of an aging stairway rested dozens of eggs in a glowing nest of orange coals.

CHAPTER 8

Welglen launched between the door and the woman, shutting off her view. She stumbled back; her hand still raised knob height, and in his tight grip.

Her voice stuttered. "Wh-what are those?"

"Oomm Enran, Oomm Enran," he chanted, keeping hold of her hand. The Sword of Srekums dangled; its tip touched the floor. The human opened her mouth to speak again, then fell silent. Her lips didn't fully close. "Oomm Enran, Oomm Enran."

He held her gaze. Her pupils dilated. The spell worked at last. Perhaps his powers weren't weakening. Dire circumstances had forced these tactics. The danger for humans was the occasional loss of all memories. No council to answer to, but the protective instincts were hard to break. "Oomm Enran—"

"Will you please stop that nonsense?" She jerked her hand away and sat on the edge of the chair, waving the weapon in chopping vertical moves. "I need to think."

Welglen stepped forward and leaned over her, hands on the arms of the chair, the point of the sword catching on the fabric stretched over his chest. Even in the poorly lit room the blade's sharp edge shone. "You have gone too far to turn back. I must know who you are. You carry the sword of a warrior. What brings you to the home of a strange man to challenge him? Is it courage or stupidity?"

"Beer." An expression crossed her face that he didn't understand, though it was not fear. Perhaps confusion, frustration, or curiosity. "When I drink too much, like tonight, I become outraged at unfairness. I'll follow the outrage until I either correct the injustice or sober up."

"Or die."

"That's not a possibility I like to think about." She angled the tip of the sword to touch the fabric of his shirt and forced him backward as she stood. "Why were you following me? And skip the kinky stuff."

Welglen raised his hands to remove any perception of physical threat and backed to lean against the table. He had much to learn from this human. "I did it to protect you."

"How often have you followed me?"

She wouldn't care for the answer. "A fortnight—two weeks."

"I know what a fortnight is. Why? If you wanted to meet me, why not introduce yourself, you know, like a regular person."

"Regular is not my strong suit." *If impervious to spells, whatever she learned here couldn't be erased.* "The truth is I am not sure why I followed you. For reasons beyond my control, I'm compelled to protect you. I've saved you more than once."

Her laughter was laced with suspicion. "What are you talking about?"

"Two days ago, while you ran on the bike path, a rabid mountain lion stalked you. I chased her into the hills and ended her suffering."

"What?"

"And the first night I was called to your side, one of the young men from the tavern, wearing the black shirt, followed you with what I assume to be, in your words, kinky intentions. I persuaded him to leave you alone."

A slight nod of her head proved she remembered the drunk who had pestered her for attention. "If that's true, thank you. I still don't understand why you feel you have to follow me and why you would admit it. The state has lots of laws against this sort of thing. I have rights—and a sword."

"Indeed." Welglen remained still, afraid to scare her out the door. She couldn't leave yet. His actions were limited. He longed to converse with the ancestors for guidance. If he chose poorly, all hope would be lost. "Tell me more about how this sword came to you."

"First, explain why you have ostrich eggs in your basement."

She stared at him intently. Though unsmiling, her face held the small lines about her mouth created by happiness. Her eyes were more alert, the ale's effects wearing off. The spells didn't work on this one—so different from the great warrior he had imagined would arrive one day.

She had the sword. But not the knowledge.

He would have to explain much. "They are not from ostriches," he whispered, the decision made. "They're dragon eggs."

CHAPTER 9

"Best hallucination ever!" Ellen cried out, her free hand slapping the side of her forehead. "Let's pretend for one minute I believe you have dragon eggs in your basement. How'd you make the ground glow?"

Welglen backed against the door. "Geothermal, and an added spell. The Earth has geysers and vernal pools in the area. The nest has been carefully placed to ensure year-round warmth. The rocks retain the heat and provide light."

Sort of believable. At least the part about hot underground water. Ellen had played tourist at the local spas and soaked in the warm waters. Half of the valley made a living connected to them. "But how could this kind of house have been built here? This is the same city that cares about the historical shade of their red roof tiles."

"The house simply already existed. Though no human, until you, has been able to see it."

"Let me check them out again." Ellen stepped closer. He tightened a grip on the doorknob. His eyes were his tell. They deepened to a deep emerald. He doesn't trust her.

He muttered something she couldn't understand, then spoke up. "You are a most unusual human."

"Thanks." She waved the point of the sword toward him. "Can we go down?"

"Your belief system is working faster than mine. Tell me, what is your honest reason for wanting to see the nest?"

"I love dragons, duh." She transferred the sword to her left hand and tugged her waistband down to display the blue, purple, and green tattoo of tiny dragon scales. "Know anyone else with one of these?"

He stared at her hip for an instant, then back to her face. She tugged her pants up and shifted the sword back to her dominant hand. "I'll take you down. Though not without a warning. If you threaten my nest, I'll do whatever I can to stop you."

Ellen should be afraid. If she were watching a horror movie, at this part of the film she'd be screaming at the girl not to go down into the cellar. But she was ready to beg to go beyond that door.

She needed to be smart. She raised the sword upward in a confident pose she'd write for one of her dragon-warrior characters. "I have my own condition."

The green eyes narrowed.

"You go first."

Ellen followed the stranger into the dark basement. Drawn to the glow below, she noted her rapid heartbeat and the wet, dripping, dirt walls and dark overhead beams to write later. She reached out in the darkness to steady against a railing or wall but found neither on the staircase suspended between her old reality at the top and fantasies at the bottom. "This can't be happening."

He walked slowly in front of her, making it more of a procession than a movement. The air warmed. The humidity grew the lower they moved. At the bottom, she stepped onto the rocky surface of the ground, glowing in reds and oranges with countless eggs nestled in small clusters.

"How did you create—"

He swung to face her. "You didn't die?" his voice more question than statement. "The old spell should have killed a liar."

She pointed the sword at his brow and tried to deepen her voice, but she couldn't wait to check out these eggs. Giggles peppered her speech. "Hey! I'm the one with the sword here. Let's stop talking about the dying thing."

Welglen stepped further into the room. She kept between him and the escape route, unable to look away from the eggs.

Close up, the mythical creature containers were shaped like oversized breakfast food—large at one end and tapering to a smaller point at the other. About the size of footballs. Too big for ostrich eggs. She leaned over and examined one.

Not plastic or papier-mâché.

Tiny pits and ridges covered the off-white surface.

Ellen rested her open palm over the top of one of the eggs. Heat radiated into her skin. "Where did these come from?"

Welglen stepped deeper into the space, lighted only by the glow from the ground, and swept his arms wide. "The gods created the cradle from the Earth's heat, and the ancestors laid the eggs in love and hope. I only moved them here. I created nothing, save the path and the spell that keeps this sight from humans."

He squatted in front of a cluster and reached out to stroke one with a light touch, glancing back at her repeatedly as if expecting her to disappear.

The heat in the room generated sweat that trickled down her cheeks and sides. "I'm not saying I believe or not, but how can I see them? I'm human."

"The elders have shared prophecies about the one who can help save all. One destined to have the strength to see injustice and the courage to fight." He circled between her and the stairs and lifted a large hand to wipe away a strand of cobweb from above her. "Though the Sword of Srekums has come to you, I cannot believe the one to save us could be such a tiny warrior. Let alone, a human."

"If I didn't think you were nuts, I'd be insulted." She straightened her spine to appear taller, but wobbled, overwhelmed with possibilities. She allowed her knees to bend and slipped back to the steamy rock-covered ground. "This is so detailed for a dream. Maybe I'm wasted. Am I slurring?"

Welglen knelt before her and shook his head. "I need you fully conscious for the question I'm about to ask of you. If it's true, your presence signifies that change approaches, which means a fight. I need to know if you can be counted upon. You said you battle injustice. I'll tell you a story. When I am through, I'll ask you to fight beside me. If you choose not to, you will leave, never to return." His emerald eyes, dark in the muted light, searched hers. "Are you prepared?"

Ellen nodded and stood, her body agreeing before her brain knew the question. "If these are dragon eggs, that's a story I have to hear."

CHAPTER 10

Welglen brushed aside the rocks in a small circle away from the escape route. He waved one hand in a flourish, offering her the seat. She moved one sword's length around him and sat on the steps.

He rubbed the aching itch at the back of his neck and searched for a gentle place to begin. "Dragons were created by the gods with a single purpose: to protect humans."

"What a great storyline!" She raised both hands, the sword swinging as her volume increased. "There could be like an entire security company comprised of dragon bodyguards that protected rock stars and political figures. They'd be an elite force, uh . . ." she gasped, "the 'D team.'"

He crossed his arms and stared down until she stopped talking. "May I continue?"

She shrugged.

"In their infancy, humans had to learn how to find food and create shelter. The dragons kept them safe from predators with fire during this period. They taught them how to hunt and to cook the raw meats to prevent disease. Humans trusted the dragons. Dragons cared for humans."

"I'm totally picturing cavemen times." The woman looked past him to a dark spot on the rock wall. "Or even in like the 1800s and a female archaeologist unearths what they think is a dinosaur skeleton covering the bones of a small child. At first, they guess the animal had killed the child, then been killed by something larger. On closer scrutiny they discover the child was being cradled, protected. And they couldn't match any of the gene sequencing that had been recorded for dinosaurs."

He breathed in deeply and held a single finger to his lips. The female opened her mouth to speak again. She gazed into his eyes, and settled back, without saying a word. "Dragons would watch over the same tribe, protecting small children while their parents hunted, guarding against attack from others. This care extended to the afterlife. Dragons ferried humans high into the heavens, past glimpses and messages of love left by those who had passed before. Once the soul absorbed the messages, dragons flamed the bodies into ash that drifted back to the earth to be reborn as plants or animals—while the souls of the good returned to new forms."

She raised one arm, waving a hand. "Can I just say what a fantastic storyline? Much better than the selfish dragons with their hordes of gold and jewels."

He leaned down, inches from her face. "Stay focused. This isn't a story. This is real life. Dragon life. If you'll be quiet, I'll tell you what you need to know."

She pressed her lips together. He waited a moment. She remained silent. "This life continued for thousands of years until the birth of sorcerers. The humans, more educated in the ways of the wild, lost the memories of how they achieved their independence, and forgot the importance of their protectors. Sorcerers took advantage of this loss of memory and instilled fear, claiming dragons were evil. Manufacturing mistrust, they created drought and famine and blamed it on dragons. They drove wedges between the human tribes, ensuring people wouldn't band together against the true threat."

The nails on Welglen's fingers bit into his palms. He shook his fists loose and struggled for calm. The human's eye didn't leave his face. The words tore out of his throat with a searing heat. "Humans turned against dragons. They plotted to turn humans into dragon killers because a dragon, created to protect, couldn't—wouldn't—fight back. Sorcerers who led kingdoms gave large entitlements to any warrior able to kill a dragon. The numbers fell, and the powers of the sorcerers rose. However, the sorcerers knew they would never have complete control over the humans until the death of every dragon."

She rocked slightly, her head nodding. "What could they do? How could they survive?"

"The dragons banded together to protect their existence. The five strongest were chosen to flee to the far corners of the Earth." He knelt and faced the nest. "Each would carry a clutch of eggs, entrusted with the survival of the entire species. Three succeeded."

"Awesome. It could be the start of a series that wouldn't ever have to end. It's so fresh, and yet believable. My stories have always placed the dragons in the good-guy roles, but this backstory pulls everything together into a great tale."

"Hear me, human." Welglen's voice charged against the walls of the nest. She stood and backed a step up, her eyes wide. "This isn't a story I tell to entertain you. These are facts you'll need to know. The Sword of Srekums has made its choice. You'll have to make yours."

"What are you talking about?"

Welglen glanced at the overhead beams and backed four feet away. "The three who survived included a female, and my brother."

"Brother?"

Welglen opened his arms wide. "You see before you a man. I am a dragon."

A brief laugh escaped her lips. "Surely if dragons existed, we'd know about it."

"A human response." Welglen kicked off his boots and pulled the shirt over his head. The internal burn ignited. The skin on his back tightened.

"Wait a minute!" She backed up a step. "I didn't come down here for this."

"See me." Welglen's voice deepened. He dropped his pants to the floor and scales erupted from his skin. He rolled his chest upward and inhaled in a gasp.

Wings broke free in a loud crack that echoed across the close walls. He rose off the surface, touching the ceiling and glared down at the human.

He'd expected her to soil herself, break down into tears, or run screaming from the nest.

She smiled.

CHAPTER 11

Ellen collapsed hard onto the wood step, wincing at the sharp sting of her tailbone, and overwhelmed with an intense desire to take notes. The sword slipped out of her hand and clanked against the rocks below.

In the dull light of the cellar, thousands of tiny scales shimmered in deep greens and blues, down a strong back to thickly muscled legs.

Large black wings moved in tiny increments, holding him inches off the ground. The undersides flashed a white leather that rippled in a feathery pattern like the wings of an angel.

Two straight horns swept back, threatening to tear into the wood subfloor above. His angular head ended in a squared-off snout, and rows of pointy teeth glistened behind the curtain of his steamy breath.

Ellen pushed against the surface to stand on wobbly legs, drawn toward the embodiment of all her dreams.

He backed away.

She held up her hands, palms forward. She'd need a lifetime to write the story lines flooding her brain. "It's okay. Dream or truth, this is the most wondrous, marvelous moment in my entire life. May I touch you?"

Welglen jerked back and glared, a slit of black in the large green rounds dilated. *Yes,* his voice penetrated her thoughts.

"You speak?" her voice squeaked.

I speak directly. His deep words entered her head, calm. *Human vocal cords are not needed for a dragon.*

"I understand!" She stretched on tiptoe, curbing the desire to jump up and down and squeal. "Thought transfers, of course. I suppose your throat is full of fire anyway, so speaking could be dangerous."

You are well versed on dragons for a modern human. His great eyelids blinked. His head dipped slightly. *You may touch.*

Ellen grazed his warm side, slippery between the sweat of her palm and the humidity. She'd always imagined the scales to seal together like the bony scutes of an alligator's back. In this reality, individual plates of thickened glass layered in bold iridescent colors.

Under the canopy of a silent outstretched wing framed in a series of geometrically designed bones, a vision of Leonardo da Vinci's flying machine sketches flashed through her mind. A soft musky smell of muscles in use blended into the wet room.

"I see you. I feel you. And unless I'm totally nuts, I'm meeting a dragon." Her vision blurred. She wiped tears away. "You're not a myth. You've been here this whole time, right under our noses."

There is truth in that, though not many have made it to this land.

"Where were you from?"

Our territory originally spread through the land of fire and ice. I was born in the rocky hills you would know as Northern Scotland. When we were first hunted, many died defenseless, not believing the danger. We fell back to the ancient nesting grounds in the hope of saving those we could. Intent on destruction, the humans crossed the great bodies of water by ship to finish us off.

Ellen slumped near the outstretched claws of his feet. Each long talon moved independently and curved into a pointed black hook. "Please tell me more. I have to know everything."

You will need to know of the last battle. The time when all had been lost. It's when our stories may have collided.

She leaned forward, hugging her knees to her chest. He hovered, filling her view, in no apparent hurry to restart his tale. He waved his massive head, twin curls of smoke twirling out of his nostrils. The first link to her memory of the guy she'd seen outside the bar window. He lowered his gaze to match her eyes. She sunk into the green depths as he spoke. *The battle surrounded us in blasts of hot air from flaming boulders. The aim of the human weapons would have taken me down if not for Tacoma's warning call.*

"Tacoma?"

She was to be my mate. We hadn't seasoned yet for offspring. A valiant fighter, she could often best me in scrimmages, though my male stamina would carry me longer. The battle was fierce. She didn't survive.

Ellen touched his extended leg. He recoiled; a thick tail that tapered to a fan of spikes wrapped around his body and waved her off.

"I'm sorry. You don't have to talk about it if you don't want to."

Welglen's silence stretched out.

She scooted back, allowing him space. "How did you become a man?"

After Tacoma's death I was called to the elders. I didn't respond at first. I couldn't stop fighting, even though my efforts only slowed their progress. We couldn't win or escape. Duty outweighed anger when our leader directed me back to the nest. Slatetail couldn't be ignored.

I had never been so close to him and will never forget the sight. Half again my size, and twice my age, Slatetail's scales glowed a rare deep ebony. He'd sat before the tremendous piles of eggs, and his tattered wings folded in self-defense across his chest. His voice deep.

'We have lost this battle,' Slatetail had said. The depth of the great one's despair startled me more than his words. I answered, 'I fight to the death.' He replied I had earned the right, though he couldn't grant the request. He needed each of us for something far more dangerous. He opened his wings with a gasping breath to reveal the hilt of a sword, buried deep in his chest.

"Sword?" Her precious weapon lay discarded in the dirt.

Even at these words, so long after, the old scents of blood and decay return to haunt me. Though there were others, he looked to me to remove it. I gripped the dragon-shaped end in my mouth and tasted the life pouring from him. The sword and our leader dropped to the ground.

'This is the Sword of Srekums,' Slatetail gasped. 'Forged from the stones of this mountain, our home. Blessed to protect the humans from the sorcerers, then turned against us. It will be turned back. Another will come who will find this weapon and use it to end the tyranny of the sorcerers. Goloo Glem Niks Kukar.*'*

Slatetail breathed a burst of flames that glowed blue on the metal. He coughed; a dark drool dripped from his jaw. He pushed himself to his full height and fired. His flames turned the sword a fiery red that morphed to orange and yellow as the metal melted into a silvery liquid slipping into the cracks of the rock. He declared, 'The Sword of Srekums is again part of the Earth, flowing through the hot core until it is reforged by the one destined to save us all.'

Ellen held her breath. The metal near her feet reflected the orange glow surrounding the eggs. "My sword killed your leader?"

Welglen closed his eyes. His chest heaved in several deep breaths. His wings moved in small flickers. *We listened in helpless silence to his last words. 'The sorcerers have bewitched the humans into believing we are to blame for every lost sheep and child. Even the horns on the tops of our heads are man's symbols of everlasting pain and agony. We cannot blame the humans for their ignorance—they don't remember the truth of our dedication. The sorcerer who kills the remaining dragons achieves immortality and will never live in fear of another sorcerer, because without dragon hearts, a new sorcerer can't be created. Our last act cannot be to protect ourselves—we must protect the humans. By sheltering the last of the eggs, we keep hold of our future, and humans safe from domination.'*

"The last thing you wanted to hear."

I tried to understand what he charged. 'You want us to run?' I'd asked. 'To live when all of our sisters and brothers lay dead and dying?' Slatetail commanded we each take an equal share of the remaining eggs to different corners of the world to protect until safe to live again as dragons. The sorcerers would have easily found us in our natural state. They know of every dragon's location the instant of its birth. Slatetail had a plan. We would live among the humans as one of them.

"Not your first preference."

We had no choice but to follow his strategy. Until the birth of the eggs in an unknown future, we would live as men. At their hatching, the war would restart with our fated warrior. Slatetail believed the future held a chance for our survival.

Ellen rubbed at her chest and exhaled deep enough to breathe out some of the building emotion. "Condemned to centuries of loneliness."

Welglen nodded. *A spell had been cast on the eggs, not to hatch until one arrived who would fight alongside dragons against the sorcerers. The prophecy foresaw only one with an understanding of both humans and dragons could end this war and return our lives. I didn't believe this possible.*

"The sorcerers survived all this time?"

Only two sorcerers remain that I am certain of.

"How can you be sure?"

I can't. I know of two who fought against us. They were alive when I left. There were likely others.

"How did you choose this town? Why Sonoma?"

I flew to the edge between land and sea searching for an area containing the necessary incubation element: rivers of deep and hot underground water. I found it here. Ages passed before humans arrived. Though languages and customs differed from the humans I'd known, your thoughts are similar. You continue to identify yourselves by what makes you different from one another. Perfect targets for a sorcerers' will.

"I'm not like that," Ellen stood under one wing. "I'd never hurt a dragon. You're magnificent."

No one can say what they are really made of, until they are tested.

"What can I do? How can I help?"

You have brought me the sword. Are you the warrior?

"Whoa. I write about heroes. I'm not one."

A long, slow hiss of smoke wove across his teeth and into the room. *As you are young, perhaps your role was to bring the sword back into existence. Leave it here and go. I pray the spells to erase our meeting will work better than my other attempts to control your thoughts.*

Ellen picked up the sword. "This isn't something I can just walk away from. For sure not without this."

You must. Go. If you are not here to fight, your continued presence places the eggs in danger.

Ellen chewed on her bottom lip. She ran her fingers over the sword's hilt, trailing the length of the steel dragon. She gazed over the field of eggs, then back to Welglen. He was beautiful. Her dreams had come true.

There was no other ending worthy of this moment.

She placed the sword below his claws. "I'll do what you ask because I believe in you and want you to win this battle. But I hope your spell doesn't work. I don't ever want to forget this night."

A loud pop echoed against the walls.

Ellen jerked back and covered her ears. Welglen moved over the cluster, his wings wide, his head down, his focus on one below him.

A long crack split the surface of one of the eggs.

CHAPTER 12

A tiny square muzzle poked through the white shell below Welglen. The small jaws dragged against thick strands of mucus to display two miniature rows of young dragon teeth. The hatchling stretched its neck against the suction of the yellowy-white matter, then drew back inside.

Conscious of the beating of his heart, Welglen startled at the light touch of the human's hand on the tip of one claw. She stepped between the eggs and sniffled against the tears that rolled down her cheeks.

The newborn widened the crack to free its head in one large thrust. The protective membrane coated the eyes closed, but the jaws worked free.

A crackly squawk announced Welglen wasn't the only dragon anymore.

Welglen stretched his dragon's feet down to touch the great transmitter of the Earth for the first time in centuries.

The time of hiding had passed.

A larger piece of shell fell away from the hatchling's side and the first sticky, wet wing pressed free. The little green dragon rolled sideways to open the other. Both wings stretched wide to dry, batting the remaining case to the side.

The new one rolled awkwardly from side to side before balancing on short legs jeweled with long sharp claws.

Instinct pulled Welglen forward. He leaned close and licked the egg's salty residue away from the hatchling's face. He'd witnessed the birth of a dragon only once when quite young, a mere sixty or eighty years old.

The first layer of eyelids opened, leaving the second to adjust to the light. Welglen continued to clean until the eyes opened fully to reveal a green color a few shades lighter than his own.

"He's so beautiful." The human's soft voice startled Welglen. He'd forgotten her presence. "The scales are glowing the same color as his eyes!"

She's so beautiful, Welglen corrected. He couldn't remember what beauty was, until this new life appeared. *And yes, her coloring is most unusual.*

The green female bent and licked at the scales on her chest that shown brighter with each layer of mucus removed.

"What do we do?" the human asked.

Once she's cleaned and rested, I'll need to find food for her. She'll need her strength for what's to come.

"What's that?"

Welglen lifted the dragon out of the nest with his mouth and settled her on the ground. He'd need to find a way to hide one adolescent dragon and a nest full of eggs from a world of sorcerers and demons.

That's partially up to you.

The human uttered a few words, but the explosion of sounds in the small space deafened.

Multiple eggs cracked and rocked against each other, determined to come into this world all at once.

The second muzzle shone in dark blue tones, near black. Before this newborn could free itself from its shell, another egg broke open to reveal scales of the deepest red.

He cleaned the eyes of the second dragon—a black female—conscious that another waited blindly for his help, other eggs were opening, and the green first-born stumbled hungrily across the rocks.

The human knelt next to him and reached out with a layer of her clothing. The young one hissed and snapped at the smell of the fabric. "It's all right, baby." The young dragon calmed at her tone. "Let me clean you off."

The hatchling allowed the human's touch, cleaning his body and wings in slow and tender movements.

Welglen moved quickly from dragon to dragon, clearing their view to a new world. The human followed, helping clean away the remains of birth. She worked from one newborn to the next—wiping and soothing.

Squawks gradually replaced the chaotic cracks and popping sounds as twenty-six eggs hatched. Twenty-six small dragons wobbled and climbed among the debris of their birth.

The smallest egg remained.

The human collapsed next to Welglen and allowed a dozen newborn dragons to climb over her lap, shrieking in a noisy crescendo. She stroked their backs, her gaze on the single still egg. "Maybe that one needs more time."

Something has determined that today all the eggs in this nest will open. There could be no purpose for all to arrive, and one to stay behind. It is unlikely it will survive.

The human gasped.

It is the way. Nature determines who is strong enough.

A choke sounded in her throat. "It's not fair. To come through all this time and not make it to the end. Isn't there something you can do?"

Welglen shook his head. Her tears rolled unchecked. She released a long breath, then reached out to hold the tip of his wing. "Oh, little one. I'm so sorry."

She rubbed her other hand across the last dragon egg.

A thin hairline crack ran end to end over the smooth surface.

She jumped back and clapped. "It's alive! It's going to make it."

The dozens of squawking dragons silenced.

The hush jarred Welglen to his core.

The egg lay motionless for several minutes.

"What's wrong? The others broke free quickly."

This one lacks the strength of its brothers and sisters.

"Let's open the shell."

Young dragons require strength from their first breaths. It would not be a kindness to interfere. To be strong enough for birth, is to be strong enough for life.

The human shook her head and leaned over the egg. "Come on little one," she whispered. "You can do it. I won't let anything happen to you."

The crack widened slightly, revealing dark multi-colored scales.

"That's it," the human coaxed. "Poke your head out and take a breath."

A small muzzle nudged out of the shell at her command. It slipped back in.

"I'm Ellen. I'm here for you. We all are. Your brothers and sisters wait." The small jaws cleared the shell again in tiny pants, in search of strength. The crack widened.

The human reached to pull away the shell. Welglen batted her away with a flick of his wing. *It is the way.*

"Your way sucks."

The hatchling chipped away miniscule pieces of the tough shell to release a dark head.

"Great job, baby," the human said. "You can do it."

The head ducked down. Soft tones vibrated inside the egg. The hatchling pushed up and in one motion, the wings broke free. The newborn rolled into the open. Her scales sparkled in the dim light in an iridescent rainbow of purple, blue, and green.

Identical to the mark on the human.

CHAPTER 13

Ellen crumpled into the middle of the squawking baby dragons. The last newborn rested on its unsure legs, claws grasping at the rocks, wings spread for balance. The multicolored scales matched the shades of her tattoo.

The colors of her favorite dragon character had arrived in a dream.

Only it hadn't been a dream.

She'd been living one.

Welglen gently licked the little one's eyes open. Ellen reached out to clean the shining scales. The baby dragon rubbed against the cloth, unafraid.

Ellen exhaled a long, slow breath. "Dragons have been with me all my life."

Welglen nodded. *A clear connection links you to these infants. You have brought the sword, and at your presence, the eggs hatch. We must look deeper. Do you know of other humans strong enough and trained in warfare? Perhaps someone to whom you would gift the Sword of Srekums?*

An image of Josh holding a sword against anyone popped into Ellen's thoughts. She shook her head. He couldn't even keep an argument up with her. He always looked for peaceful resolutions.

If I could remember back to the time before I'd stopped hoping for this miracle, I'm certain I'd not pictured a human warrior. Yet here you are with the sword, and by the touch of your hand you invite the smallest of dragons out of her shell—a dragon with the colors of your own mark. If you're not a warrior, I don't understand why Slatetail has gifted these stories of our existence to you.

"Neither do I." Ellen rubbed her face. A slightly sour smell of dragons filled her nostrils. Shocked, thrilled, and on nervous overload, she tried to process. She craved a caramel macchiato double espresso. "I need to wash up, and I'm hungry."

You'll find meat and human washing supplies above. You're welcome to all I have.

She pictured the meat at the fireplace next to the door that led back to a life where the line between fact and fiction remained anchored in place.

I hope you will return to help us in our quest.

"This mind-reading thing and you in your dragon suit are more than I can handle right now. Do me a favor and the next time I see you, look human."

At the top of the stairs, she walked to the front door and stepped outside.

The early-morning sunlight hit the tops of the trees and the sound of downtown traffic rumbled. Her laptop and her real life were only minutes away. And they didn't include actual battles beyond paying her bills. Behind her lived a den of dragons where she'd witnessed the miracle of birth—rebirth of a dragon nation.

Ellen went back inside. There was a reason she was here. She had to figure out what that was. Saving dragons hadn't been on her bravery list, but she couldn't let them down.

The pipes groaned into action. She let the water run over her hands and rubbed at a bar of soap until its outdoorsy scent returned her illusion of humanity. Any ideas of literary grandeur dissolved with the soap bubbles. She wasn't a creative powerhouse. She hadn't written the stories. She'd been granted glimpses of dragon history in her dreams. She was a stenographer.

A small oval mirror hung on the wall. The tired and haggard reflection looked slightly familiar—dark brown eyes and the small bump on the bridge of her nose she'd inherited from her mother.

Something about the way she looked—inside this new reality—appeared alien.

She'd already changed. This image knew dragons were real.

Her stomach growled at the sight of the long strips of meat that lay on drying racks above a cold pile of ash. She reached for one of the smaller pieces and nibbled. Simple but tasty. She finished off the strip, then chose two others and glanced down the staircase. Welglen stood dressed at the bottom, a man.

She descended to his side and handed him a piece of the jerky. "Thought you could use this too." He chewed while they watched the babies tussle and screech. "I'm not ready to sign up for any battle or to admit I understand what's going on, but I can't deny these little ones are real and I can tell they need me. I'm in. For now. What's next?"

The squawks grew louder, and two of the young ones nibbled at her shoelaces. The smallest, the last born, took short, tentative steps away from the ruckus of the others.

"We need to feed them."

"That I can do. I can run to the store and get whatever we need. What do they eat—baby food or Kibbles and Bits?"

"Live meat."

A shiver rippled through her. "Yuk."

"I'll need to leave you to watch over these hatchlings while I hunt. It should only take a short while. I don't like trusting you to stay and protect these young ones, yet I have no choice," Welglen said.

"Hey, take it easy on my self-esteem. Remember I'm the one who just learned dragons are real. What am I protecting them from anyway?"

"Other humans. Larger animals. Sorcerers."

"Sorry I asked." She sat and stretched out her legs, beckoning the smallest dragon to her lap. "I'll name them while you're gone."

"These are not pets, human! Dragons choose their own names at maturity."

"Whatever." It was difficult to jump at the sound of his bark after she'd witnessed the tender care he'd shown the babies. Besides, belief in the existence of dragons meant they were here to protect her.

He climbed the stairs and Ellen tried to process her situation.

She spoke to the baby dragon who chewed on her shirtsleeve. "My life's a book pitch. A writer is babysitting twenty-seven newly hatched dragons while one very large dragon living in the body of a man hunts for live meat to give them enough strength to fight in a war against sorcerers. And they're missing the warrior destined to save everyone."

Ellen pulled her phone out of her pocket for a sanity check.

The smallest dragon nudged at one hand.

"No offense, but I need to talk to a human." She punched in the first digits of Josh's number, then snorted at an imagined conversation that would start with 'I'm hanging with a roomful of dragons and thought I'd give you a call.' *Yeah. Great talk.* Plus there was a conversation they needed to have. A question she needed to ask. Either way

Josh answered could be a problem. His denying her terms for getting back together might not be the worst outcome.

The reasons she'd bailed on their relationship didn't matter anymore—she didn't need him to support her if she could kick-start her writing. He wouldn't need to worry about children cramping his Peter-Pan style.

But he would love her. And she really missed sex.

She opened a text from Britta asking if she was okay after listening to last night's voicemail. Ellen replied that she was fine.

The small dragon that matched her tattoo climbed to Ellen's shoulder and tried to nest at the hair escaping her bun. "You're Ashamoor. Don't tell the others, but you're my favorite character."

She didn't know if a dragon chose a human to protect or the other way around. She chose Ashamoor.

The larger infants waddled, flapped their wings, and squawked around the room, hopping over rocks, and digging through shell fragments. Three chewed at her clothes and two had curled on her lap.

Welglen had counted eleven females and sixteen males. Each had a different color, many in shades of deep purple, blue, red, green, and two in gold and copper.

They resembled chubby lizards. Cold to the touch—they were tiny glass-like versions of Welglen. Several hatchlings tousled together, puppy style. When they ventured close enough, Ellen used what was left of her jacket to wipe away remaining mucus from their faces and bellies.

The hair on her arms lifted at a noise from upstairs, and she rushed to the bottom step. A large silhouette, barely visible at the top, shrank to the recognizable size of Welglen. Ellen turned away as he dressed. He carried a large canvas bag down.

The bag wiggled.

She didn't want to ask why.

Welglen scanned the room, his head bobbing slightly, counting—apparently satisfied she hadn't lost any. He passed with his live load. He dropped the bag in the center of the twenty-seven hungry dragons keenly interested in what squirmed inside. They danced around it. No one dared to creep closer than a foot. "You may want to climb a few steps. I wouldn't want you caught in the first kill."

Ellen jumped three stairs. "What is in there? Or do I want to know?"

"Simple vermin. They will provide what is needed. A dragon must learn to hunt from the first meal or starve." He leaned down and untied the top of the bag. The dragons bounced in place.

Welglen dumped the contents to the ground.

Dozens of white mice, lizards, and a few snakes spilled out. A few froze and tried to catch their bearings. The others scattered in every direction.

Movement and sound took over in a blur of pouncing dragons and panicked creatures. The green female caught a mouse in her teeth. She raised her head and gulped the mouse into her throat. The mouse's tail whipped across her face.

"Ew!" Ellen leaped two more stairs and covered her face. "Gruesome."

The space quieted. Ellen slid her fingers away from her eyes. The dragons had swallowed the last of their food. All their tiny bellies were rounded in digestion, except for one, Ashamoor.

Welglen scooped the little one into his arms and cradled her near his heart. He turned over a rock at his feet and grabbed a lizard by the tail. He held the wiggling reptile over Ashamoor's mouth. She gulped it down.

Ellen smiled at his fatherly attention. So much for the big bad dragon.

Welglen motioned for her to climb the stairs while the dragons huddled into a pile. "They'll sleep for a day or two. We have much to do before they wake."

The ground beneath the cottage shook.

Ellen cried out and threw her arms wide to balance near the top step. "Earthquake?"

I fear not. Welglen tilted his head, listening. *A sorcerer comes. We don't have time to find another warrior. You're our only hope. You must use the Sword of Srekums and kill him.*

"I'm outta here!" She ran for the doorway and pressed against the front door frame until the rumble stopped. Power lines and tree branches swung. A few car alarms sounded in the distance.

The babies' squawks escalated and drew her back into the basement.

Welglen bent over the newborns, calming them with his touch.

Ellen slumped onto the ground next to the babies piled in a safe multicolored litter. "You've turned my world upside down."

Welglen placed one hand on her shoulder. Heat radiated into her muscles. "The world has always tilted at this angle, human."

"The name is Ellen." She gulped in air. A slight sulfur smell added to her new point of view. Impossible to rewind. No going backward. She couldn't see past the safety of the baby dragons falling to sleep next to her. "Sorcerers cause earthquakes by searching for dragons?"

"If you mean the shaking of the core, then yes." He sat next to her, also facing the little dragons. She studied his profile—creases around his eyes, the tan skin of an outdoorsman. No smile lines at his mouth. "The Earth continues to change while the heat of the center moves about, radiating toward cracks and imperfections in need of healing. The movements make the necessary alterations. The lava flows create new soil, and with it, eventual new life. Sorcerers can absorb and blend with this energy. The flow moves in all directions, seeking the only beings that keep the sorcerer from eternal life and rule. When eggs are found, the sorcerer will follow. The searching has intensified during the past few generations, warming the Earth as the lava cycles increase."

"Global warming? I know a lot of people who would be interested in this theory." Ellen massaged her forehead to blend the two realities. "The other eggs and their dragon caretakers... what happened to them?"

His voice rolled on slowly. "I don't know for certain, though I fear that those sisters and brothers of mine who chose the warm island climates have long since been killed. The volcanic activity in those areas has been tremendous and survival would be difficult, deep within a nest."

In the soft light of the basement, Ellen couldn't see his eyes. "Are you the last of the dragons that saved the eggs?"

He let out a heavy, slow breath, trails of smoke circling out of his mouth.

"I have long sensed a brother to the north, though I could never risk leaving the nest to confirm. My powers to protect the eggs only work when I'm in this valley. Now that the infants have hatched, I need to find him. His closeness in this hemisphere places a target on him and his eggs."

"How can you be sure he's there?"

"Humans. They tell their stories and share their lives daily. Once their skills at communicating reached across the world, I watched and listened. Many years, nothing happened I couldn't attribute to the natural process of the Earth and of life—until I saw the signs. When humans focus only on the goal of killing those unlike them, the force behind a sorcerer grows, and the more difficult it will be for a dragon to stop."

A sharp, quick jolt knocked her into his side.

He wrapped an arm around and drew her into his chest—covering her head with his own until the ground stilled.

A sprinkle of dust drifted down from the subfloor.

"Aftershock." She sneezed three times. After several years in California, earthquakes were a semi-normal fact of life. Basements, however, were for tornadoes. "We need to get upstairs. This isn't safe."

Welglen directed his gaze toward the baby dragons, his head bobbing in another silent count. He stopped and looked down, his arms still shielding her. "I need you."

"What?" She stepped back and tried to find stable emotional ground. His view of a world where sorcerers controlled humans blurred at the edges. His story and the earthquake had combined to rock her world. "What can *I* do?"

"The night's actions have proven you're worthy. You have been chosen for a role to save the dragons."

"Chosen one? We've been through that. I'm not a hero. I'm a writer. I'm only brave when I'm buzzed." The whine in her voice freaked her out. "Either way, I could never kill. Even the good guys end up with PTSD, and I'm not strong enough to survive that."

"We'll have to unfold your role a little at a time. I must travel north and follow the prophecy. As war approaches, the remaining dragons will need to band together for the fight. If my brother has survived these years, he is close enough his eggs may also hatch. I cannot take these young ones. They can't transform until their first moon and it will be days before they can fly. If I wait, it could be too late for the others."

"And . . . if the sorcerer arrives before you return?"

“That will likely not happen. According to the elders’ stories, it would take the sorcerer’s lava days to find us, then days more for the sorcerers to travel. I’ll return in two days’ time, before the hatchlings’ next feeding.”

“Can you wait for me to run home and grab a couple of things?”

“There’s no time. You have sustenance here.”

“Forty-eight hours of jerky and water?” Dragons or not, staying inside a dark basement sucked. Ellen had no idea how long Welglen’s incredible journey would take. She couldn’t do battle with anyone or anything. The baby dragons would starve waiting for her to find, catch, and transport enough creepy critters for their next meal. “What if you don’t return?”

“Pray for the salvation of us all. Many will die and those who survive will be enslaved.”

Her sense of indignation called her to a purpose. “That’s not right. We can’t let that happen.”

He picked up the Sword of Srekums, removed his shirt, and polished the blade before handing it over.

The metal picked up the minimal light in the room and reflected the beaded sweat on his chiseled chest. She tried to refocus on the sword. “I forgot all about that in this craziness.” She slipped her hand into the hilt.

“The sorcerers are mighty, though they cannot easily harm a human who fights for what is right. You’re strong when you sense injustice.”

She raised the sword, admiring the craftsmanship. Would she be able to call on her fairness fairy at will? “Do dragons believe in fairies?”

“It is not for me to believe.”

His words and the sword combined into an odd sense of possibility. “What if the bad guys beat you here?”

“Fight.”

So not what she wanted to hear. She preferred a happily-ever-after. “Let’s be clear that I don’t know how to use this. Are you leaving a spell or another weapon of some sort?”

“You’re the weapon.”

CHAPTER 14

Welglen pumped north against the frigid air, forced to zigzag between clouds to avoid the few humans living along the icy streams that cut through the snow-covered mountains. At dawn he'd stopped touching down to leave his scent; he couldn't draw attention away from the hatchlings, only to aim danger at his brother.

A quick slice of warmth lifted his aching muscles and offered hope. He adjusted course, slipped lower on the current, and searched for the source of heat over the dense forest that rolled up and down the hills below.

A mist rose in the trees ahead. Too thin for smoke, it held the scent of wet, burned wood. Before rising back into the cover of clouds, he scanned the area. No roads or trails for miles. He darted through the dark, billowy clouds.

Part of an old roofline with a spiraled rock chimney poked through the pine trees. Welglen circled high. The other half of the structure had collapsed into rubble. No sign of humans or dragons. A bright yellow color in the foliage drew him closer. Peppers and tomatoes lay among the debris of a garden. This structure had been occupied recently.

A wave of heat rolled past, under his left wing.

Steam wheezed from a hole still under the protection of the small cottage.

Welglen forced himself to circle back. He dropped to transform into human form in the shelter of a thick grove of pine trees. He couldn't run directly into trouble.

Except for boots, the pack of clothing he carried did little for his thin flesh. His heart pounding, he plodded through the snowy brambles into a clearing.

Glass from shattered windows littered the steps to the front door, hanging open on broken hinges. Welglen stepped inside. The left side opened across burned beams to the forest. The remaining half of the house held a table and a fireplace.

And the smell of death.

On the hearth, in a pile of blankets, lay a slender old man with a wild white beard and skin the color of a buttercup.

The old man opened sapphire eyes to Welglen and rasped. "What an ugly human you make, my brother."

Welglen dropped to his side to better hear the old man's soft voice.

"If this is you, Roglir, you are by far the least attractive human on this planet." He leaned over his older brother and enveloped his hands to warm them, only to find them already burning. "Am I too late?"

"For some." Roglir coughed. "Not for others." He motioned to the blanket covering his legs.

The tattered rag lifted to reveal three eggs lying among the tangled remains of his burned calves.

Bile filled Welglen's throat. Anger pulsed through his core. "The sorcerers."

"Aye—their lava, at least. It licked through the Earth's rocks beneath the nest and killed all the young, save these. In an instant, the heat surrounded us. I had to run through the liquid fire to get out, which left me too injured to transform or flee. The sorcerers will be here soon to finish the job. You must take these to safety until the time of the prophecy."

"It has begun." The words he had waited centuries to share caught in his throat while he watched the last of another great warrior. "Twenty-seven hatchlings have survived entrance into this world."

Welglen's brother smiled, teeth yellowed and cracked. "We've made it. How did you leave them? Are they with you? I'd love to see one more dragon. Life has been lonely without another soul."

"I've left them with the warrior." Welglen placed a cool hand on his brother's forehead. "The earthquakes have begun. I needed to warn you. I should have flown faster."

Roglir raised an unlit pipe to his mouth and thin wisps of smoke escaped his nostrils. "It is as it was meant to be. Tell me how you found the warrior."

"She found me."

"A female?" Roglir chuckled, which morphed into a cough. Puffs of dark smoke escaped his lungs. A tiny red spot of blood appeared on his chin. "How interesting."

"A human female."

Roglir's eyes widened slightly, then collapsed to narrow slits from the effort. "That is a surprise. I had expected no less than a god. We must keep our faith in Slatetail that the chosen one will save us."

Welglen didn't share his fear surrounding the human's lack in size, skill, and strength with his brother. He slid the pack from his back to pick up the eggs. "I will take you outside first. I'll create a carrier to accommodate you and the others."

"It's too late for me." A hacking cough forced blood out of the wounds on Roglir's legs. "I'm to join our flight in the after."

"I haven't endured centuries of loneliness only to lose you. Transform and I'll heal your wounds."

"Though we were meant to join before the fight, I haven't the strength."

"There's nothing we can do in battle. We rely on a warrior who may not be enough. It's all we can do to run and hide."

"There is something more." Roglir coughed in a chain of gurgling phlegm. "Before I left our home, the elders tried a spell to pull the light from the sorcerers to render them again human. Remember the old stories?"

Welglen nodded. "Did it work?"

"I don't know. I left with the eggs as they flew into the last battle."

"What's the spell?"

Roglir shook his head, causing another burst of choking coughs. "Ask the ancestors."

"We'll ask together. Let's leave."

A sharp tremor knocked small chunks of ceiling down on Welglen's back. He curled over his brother.

Grief tightened in Welglen's breast.

The world stilled. Before the dust settled, Welglen loaded the remaining eggs into the pack. Time couldn't be purchased, though if the fates would lend a few moments, they had a small chance.

Roglir's faint voice rippled in the filthy air. "Hurry. Save the young."

Welglen turned back to argue, only to face a still brother. Roglir's life had ended without another sound. Welglen had no time to tell him that he couldn't remain alone in a world that didn't want or understand him.

The old man's skin erupted in deep gray-blue scales. His head morphed to his true shape; eyes closed in death. Dark wings beneath him.

Roglir shared all the same memories of the time before the great battle. He'd taught him to hunt. He'd trained him in fighting from the air. He was there when he'd been matched with Tacoma.

Welglen was alone, again. Long-held illusions he'd spend remaining years with family evaporated. He had a new herd and needed to hurry back.

He transformed to dragon and pulled his nestmate outside. While he couldn't save his brother's body, his soul would receive a proper finish.

He slipped his head through the tie in the pack, wriggling until the eggs nestled between the blades of his wings. He beat hard enough against the cold still air to lift off the shaking ground, clutching the weight of his brother. He held his snout to the sky and shot straight up.

In a final show of love, he would carry his brother to the afterlife. His heart would not be left to the sorcerers to consume for immortality.

The cold air burned Welglen's nostrils. He climbed toward the light of the fathers on his first journey and allowed instincts to rule.

Soul, energy, and flesh.

The positive force of every soul flowed eternal while negative energies jerked through voids. Heaven was revealed in a joyous rebirth where souls reconnected before the life energy returned to Earth.

Hell, a void where the negative energy couldn't find new life.

Energy circled Welglen.

Enveloped in the light, the load lightened in Welglen's claws as his brother's soul joined the others who had gone before.

Welglen longed to go with him.

The brightest of blues from Welglen's memories left his brother's scales, and his energy returned to Earth to be reborn as whichever creature fate desired.

Welglen leveled off, released his grasp, then flew down through the cool air a measure behind.

With all the love he had for his brother, and a degree of envy, he let his fire turn the body to ash.

As his brother's next life rained down to nurture the world below, Welglen called out to the ancestors. *Hear me. The last war has begun. We need the spell to pull a sorcerer's light.*

He circled in the cold current, straining for a sign or the words that could save his young dragons.

No response. No spell. No direction.

A dead end.

No more time for loss.

Welglen had to save the eggs, the hatchlings, and the human.

She could be trusted to care for the charges for two days, no longer. Smart and strong of heart, she would defend with everything she possessed.

Defense wouldn't be enough on the third day.

She'd have to fight.

CHAPTER 15

Ellen's cell phone died in the middle of a long note, abandoning her in the dim kitchen with an extreme desire to write, and time to kill. Stories erupted in her brain and pushed against her skull for the first time in months. But she couldn't record them.

Beams from a distant streetlight filtered through the small window. She checked down the stairs at the dark pile.

"Sure, you can sleep," she called to them. "I'd kill for something to write with." She gasped at her word choice. She might be called upon to literally kill.

She'd already searched the house. Welglen kept books. No pencils or pens. She added a small log from the dwindling wood pile. It caught quickly and brightened the space. Thanks to the heat rising from the basement, she didn't need it for warmth. Just comfort.

Ellen drew the poker back. A thin line of charred ash marked the wooden floor. She dug the iron rod back into the back piles at the fire's edge and tried to write out a note. The thick tool required multiple reloads for each letter. She checked her handiwork. It looked more like a cave drawing by a trapped writer than an actual word.

Welglen should be here in a few hours if his time estimates were accurate. If she could hold on to her sanity a little while longer, she'd be back home on her laptop soon.

Prepping for her basement shift, she placed a cup with water and some of the dried meat at the top of the stairs, and drug over a deer hide blanket. Alternating between a bizarre basement and a room with a view of human life helped settle her mind during the past day. She stepped out onto the quiet front porch, inhaling the cool air.

The sparse lights added shadows to the dry leaves tumbling down the street in the gusty fall winds. A television illuminated a window across the street. Someone else couldn't sleep. Or perhaps they prepared for their day—going to work to fulfill their career or just to pay the bills. They had a direction.

She was circling.

Maybe her purpose revolved around caring for these magnificent creatures and writing about them.

If she had something to write with.

Ellen recalculated the time it would take to run home, grab her laptop, a change of clothes, cup of coffee, toothbrush, and portable charger. It was the same fifteen minutes she'd figured out before. She wasn't going to be one of those babysitters who'd leave the kids alone for 'just a minute.' She couldn't leave until Welglen returned. She wanted to talk to someone—tell them about the new reality. Welglen hadn't said to keep his story a secret, though no one would believe it. She'd made her choice when she'd killed her phone battery taking story notes.

She washed her hands again, found the tub of ointment from Big Mark that had rolled out of what was left of her jacket, and checked the tattoo. Dark red surrounded the black outline. The clear bandage already puckered at the corners. She rolled it back far enough to coat it with the soothing gel, then recovered. This wasn't the most sanitary of locations to heal.

She carried her supplies down the shadowy stairs. She was on her own, as usual. It wasn't on purpose. She hadn't planned to live a life alone. College friends had moved back to distant homes and Josh had wanted something different. New relationships had always been a distant possibility, but a writer's life didn't include many social opportunities. She'd already spent so much life in fiction.

Now the stories *were* her life.

The deer hide took the bite out of the rough rocks. She stretched out and started a yoga routine designed to take her mind away from unwritten outlines. She hadn't slept for more than twenty minutes at a time since Welglen left.

Renaming the yoga positions, Ellen rolled from ceiling-beam salutations to downward dragon.

A strange sound rippled through the basement.

She froze, her body on high alert.

The pile of dragons remained still. Their cuteness dulled a little over envy of their ability to sleep through anything.

They made no odd sounds. There were no new earthquakes. But the warm air thickened with a new layer of strangeness.

Unable to place the source, she gathered an assortment of weapons including a pile of the warm rocks, and the Sword of Srekums. She dashed upstairs and added the fireplace poker to her arsenal.

None of the items were likely to bring down a sorcerer. She had no idea how to fight in a real battle. She could imagine anything, except that she could save all mankind against a force rising to power by forcing humans to do their bidding.

She jogged in place to increase the flow of blood to her legs.

The Earth shook in a tiny movement. She stumbled, spreading her stance wide to balance.

A rough jolt slammed her to the floor where a sharp jab pierced her ribs.

"Oh!" Ellen bounced against the rough surface springing like a trampoline. Debris fell from the ceiling and the wooden staircase creaked against the force of the Earth.

She bridged over the pile of babies. Rubble pummeled her back. She braced for the ceiling to collapse.

The rocking stopped.

Coughing, she inched away and tugged her shirt up over her mouth.

The dust settled, offering a new view of the room. A few small pieces of splintered wood had fallen from the floor joists above. She circled the pile to check for injuries and clear away anything that had landed on them.

They slept, unaware.

She lay down on her right side, focusing on breathing in a slow pattern.

A drip rolled across her ribs. Lifting her shirt, she watched a small trickle of blood ooze from a ragged gash. She stared at the wound and evaluated her feelings.

Utter calm.

Then she freaked.

"Holy crap, I'm bleeding. This isn't normal. I'm in a basement with dragons. Earthquakes are trying to kill me. Think, Ellen. Get upstairs."

Ellen rolled the sword and other weapons into the blanket and carried the bundle to the top step. She hurried down, debating the merits of picking up sleeping dragons.

Halfway down, a light shake swung the staircase into undulation. Ellen spread her body over the moving steps and wrapped her arms around the wood.

She didn't understand the words at first. Or that they were words.

"I feel the birth of my eternal life." The disembodied voice rippled below her in a small echo, a soft contrast to the jarring movements. Male, deep, and likely the final sign she'd lost her mind. "I have waited a long time. I shall come for you, little ones."

Ellen searched the glowing rocks below her for the source of the voice. A slit had opened near the back wall. Unlike the glowing ground around it, the opening was dark and deep.

Steam sputtered out.

The ground jarred again as the Earth spoke with the voice of her every nightmare. "I shall come for you soon."

CHAPTER 16

Welglen sped south by instinct. Thick, dark clouds below blocked his sight while a cold downwind helped anchor the pack along his spine.

The image of Roglir's burned-out nest flashed through his mind in a blur of loss and waste. The sorcerer hadn't minded killing so many, knowing there were others.

A half-day's flight would reveal if leaving twenty-seven hatchlings alone with a human had been worth saving three eggs.

He pushed harder.

His flight must move. They were most vulnerable before they could fly. If they survived until mature enough to transform, they could scatter across the world and hide in relative peace.

Dragons could never live openly among humans again. The old days were gone. Life continued to change. Welglen would have to determine how much more change he could take.

The bag shifted at his spine.

Welglen glided, wings still, and waited.

A tremor rippled along his backbone.

The tiny movement sent shock waves through his core.

They were hatching.

The last three dragon eggs from Roglir's nest rocked against him and the bag slipped from his back to the joint of his right wing.

Welglen dipped left to reel the pack back to center.

He slipped into the wet clouds and sunk lower toward the Earth, straining the muscles at the back of his wings against his precious load.

He had to land, or they'd fall through the simple flap at the top of the pack to their death.

The strong smell of wet grass drew Welglen down through a driving rain. A lush green field stretched below, dotted with grazing cows. A thick forest at the far end could provide the cover he needed.

The distinct rumble of humans started at his left.

A dark truck moved toward the animals. One male rode in the back, covered in black rain gear and a large white hat. He pushed bales of hay out in a line as another drove across the field.

Welglen flew higher into the clouds, aiming for the forest's edge.

The cracking of an egg pierced the air.

The pack slid to his side.

A dragon fought to escape his shell and the dark leather bag.

Welglen angled his wings to create a cup and turned to re-center the pack. He had to make it past the humans unseen.

The bag jerked. The contents squirmed in a panic-induced state. If the newborn slipped out of the pack it would fall to its death and leave an opening for the other eggs to follow.

Rest easy. I'll free you in a moment.

Forced out of the safety of height, Welglen dropped just above the surface. He wove among the black cattle for cover.

Focused on the feed coming from the truck, the animals ignored him. A brown dog circled around them, nipping at their hooves to pull them back together and toward the truck.

The dog spotted Welglen and whipped into a barking frenzy.

The truck engine roared, angled between the herd and the forest.

Directly in Welglen's path. Out of options, he soared over the hood of the truck.

The brakes squealed, sending the truck into a crescent spin. The male in the back fell to the bales and grabbed the metal side.

The truck jolted to a stop.

Welglen dropped into the trees and transformed before he hit the slick ground, cradling the pack in his arms, and tumbling forward.

He glanced back. The driver stared into the sky for a flying dragon. He wasn't looking for a man running naked into the trees.

Welglen dove into the scratchy brush.

The men's voices cut through the trees.

"What the hell did you do that for, Jerry? I think a tooth is loose."

"Didn't you see that? A giant bird flew right in front of me."

"Giant bird?"

"More like a flying alligator or something. Bird wings. Long nose."

"You're losing it. I didn't see anything. I was working, not bird-watching."

"It just appeared."

"So where is it?"

No answer from the driver.

"How could you see anything through that windshield of yours anyway? Between the bugs and the rain, you're driving blind. It was probably an eagle. Let's finish up. I want to get back."

"Strangest eagle I've ever seen."

The truck engine revved, then grew distant. Welglen moved further into the cover.

He hung the long straps of the pack between two trees near a small spring and opened the wiggling pack. The squirming mucus-covered hatchling stuck out his turquoise-blue head, scratching to get free. Two other eggs remained, still.

He transformed and hovered to keep from alerting the Earth to his presence. The nest was too close to draw attention.

I'm sorry your first moments were frightening. Welglen cleared the young one, taking time to calm the panicked mass of scales and mucus with slow licks and caresses. *I'll protect you.*

The hatchling settled the instant Welglen scooped him up.

Welglen caught a small newt among the damp grasses and held it below the newborn. The gray male chomped on his first meal.

You should be hunting for your meals, but I can't afford your energies on the Earth. You've been born at the start of a battle. Our only strength lay in our ability to hide.

The baby dragon curled in the pack as if still inside a shell. He watched Welglen through drooping lids.

The two remaining eggs were still.

His flight had hatched all at once, save the smallest who had waited for the human's touch. Perhaps there would be time to carry these eggs back to the others. The dragons needed to band together, for the best defense.

Anxious to fly, he cleared the shell fragments out of the pack with his teeth. He'd need to transform again to secure it tight enough to ensure the newborn couldn't escape.

A crack sliced across an egg.

Welglen hovered, ready.

The egg wiggled, then stilled.

The gray newborn drifted to sleep, curled against the unmoving egg.

The rain stopped. Clouds drifted in the remaining sunlight as the hatchling chipped tiny pieces of the shell away, in no apparent hurry to join the world.

A burnt-orange head finally peaked out.

The third egg rocked against it. A green and gold head popped out through a wide crack. He escaped his shell before the orange.

Dual squeals carried further in the quiet of the forest.

Welglen cleaned the pair. He settled them into the pack to leave his hands free to hunt for their first bite. Impatient, they crawled to the edge, determined to follow.

Forced to transform again, he gathered their hungry wiggling bodies into his arms and carried them near a pile of rocks where the smell of reptiles lingered in the shadows. They picked up the scent of food. Long thin claws scratched at his chest.

"Calm, young ones. I need to hunt for you."

Welglen caught a small lizard. The orange snatched it by the head. The other snapped into the tail and pulled.

The lizard's tail broke free. The green-gold dragon slipped out of Welglen's grasp and rolled onto the damp grasses, sucking in the pointy tail.

A distant rustle of trees rolled toward Welglen. He grabbed the newborn and ran back to the pack. The ground swayed and knocked him onto his back.

The hatchlings shivered. He huddled the infants to his chest to generate a calming warmth.

A crack pierced the air.

A large branch swung down over Welglen's head. He rolled out of the way and lunged at the pack. He tied the flap down over the frightened dragons and transformed.

Settle, young ones. We must hurry.

The sorcerers headed south.

Welglen had to reach the human and the young ones before the slaughter.

CHAPTER 17

Ellen circled her pile of babies, looking for a safe place to start. Dust from the latest aftershock drifted from the overhead beams and covered their brilliant colors in the same dull gray.

'Don't wake a sleeping dragon' was the type of advice usually found tucked inside folds of baked cookie dough. It sounded better than waiting for the scary voice to return from the ground or for the top story to collapse on her head. The little babies had been friendly before they fell asleep. She'd carry them upstairs, closer to the exit.

Armed with a plan, Ellen knelt beside Ashamoor, the smallest dragon she'd helped bring into the world.

"Hello, baby. We need to leave. I'll pick you up gently." She reached out and continued her 'everything's going to be okay' voice. "We're going— " Ashamoor snapped at her hand. "Ahh!"

Ellen rocked back. Her tailbone slammed against the rough surface. She shook the hand the infant had nipped. A crescent of small indentations covered the knuckles of two fingers. "You were supposed to be the nice one."

Ellen went back upstairs and paced between the open basement and front doors. The slight sulfur smell intensified. She fanned the deer hide toward the outside.

A car stopped across the street. The teenage girl driver waited while an elderly neighbor came out of her house rolling a large suitcase and faced Ellen. The older woman looked familiar. Perhaps she'd seen her on her runs or at the grocery store.

Ellen waved, excited for human interaction. The woman looked through her. An invisible house must cover her too. If no one could see her stand in plain sight, anything could happen next, including a vampire attack or a zombie apocalypse.

A light aftershock rolled under her feet. Competing car alarms blared in the distance. She rode it out in the doorway.

The neighbor froze on the sidewalk and screamed. The young driver held onto the sides for balance and circled to help the older woman inside. Branches scraped down the side of the house and scratched Ellen's arms. She squatted, covering her head with the hide and struggling to remember if it was safer under the table.

"This is insane."

In the seconds after the quake ended, she ran to check on the babies. Her last footsteps on the staircase had been covered in dust. But the beams had held. The little ones were alive. She collapsed on the hide. The deer skin had sheltered her against the falling debris. It protected her from the sharp rocks. If she could figure out a way to carry the babies in it, she might not lose a finger.

She raced to the fireplace for the small shovel. On the way back down, another tremor hit.

The open staircase undulated.

Ellen tossed the shovel to the bottom and scooted down the steps, hands tight on the wooden planks.

Halfway down, a large jolt knocked her to her side.

She yelled at the crack near the wall. "You didn't get me that time, weirdo!" Another sharp shift whipped her back against the wood. Her head smacked the surface. Pain exploded, ringing in her ears, and adding a brief sparkle to her vision.

"Are you kidding me?" She touched the tender blood-free lump. The temperature rose to a sweating, suffocating high. She slid to the still ground.

A bright orange glow filled the room from the direction the voice had come.

The color intensified with the heat, lighting the room in flickering shadows before a narrow trickle oozed out. She didn't remember a lot about high school science, but the regular kind of lava would have already killed her.

Either way—bad stuff.

Ellen turned back toward the stairs for the exit she should have taken hours before. But stopped for a last look at the miracle that had waited so long to come to life.

The thickening steam shot out between the rocks.

"Is that you, crazy guy? I don't care how long you've had to wait. You can't have my babies." She rushed to the pile of newborns.

The flow inched toward the hatchlings and ignited pieces of shell. She threw the hide next to the heap and scrambled for the shovel. She scooped gently under the pile closest to the scary globs. Two dragons pulled free. She rested them on the hide. One dragon rolled on his back without waking. The other snapped.

Ellen flipped the edge over and caught them in a roll. She raced up the stairs and gently deposited them on the fur rug near the door.

"Stay!"

At the bottom third of the steps, a wall of heat blasted her face. She sunk below the building heat trapped at the ceiling and crab-walked to the bottom.

She shoveled several more babies into the roll. Four or five dragons were the most the deer hide could cover and keep her skin protected from sharp teeth.

Ellen lugged the load up one step at a time, scooting butt to wood. From the view at the top of the stairs, the orange globs oozed closer to the sleeping pile. She squinted against the harsh vapor and moved back down into the heat to wrap another batch.

The dragons struggled to reposition in their disrupted pile. She scooped several over to the hide, then reached for the next.

The dragon's eyes flashed open. Agitated and afraid, it bit her outstretched arm.

"No!" Ellen covered the stinging bite with her hand and came away with a warm, slick trail of blood. "Like I don't have enough on my plate?"

She forced her thoughts into automation and clutched the roll of babies. She hauled them to the others near the front door, prepared to escape.

Four new jets of hot steam whistled open from the back of the room at her next trip down. A fifth opened inches away from the dwindling pile.

She threw the hide over the vent and grabbed a tangled mess of baby dragons. The armload of teeth and claws poked against her skin. If she couldn't make it, a few bites wouldn't make a difference.

Steam thickened to a smoke screen and poured out of the basement into the top floor. A fire was about to start.

Seven dragons still slept in the basement.

Ellen tied the tattered remains of her jacket over her head and slid back into the dark abyss, counting each step.

Kneeling on the low ground, she searched for a line of sight through the smoke.

Her eyes stung against the harsh air and clamped shut. No time to adjust, she crawled over the rocks toward the pile by muscle memory.

She tapped at the hot surface for the last dragons. Her hand found a slippery tail. Connected to teeth. It whipped around to nip before she could grab it by the back of the neck. She peeled her shirt away from her sweaty body and forced her lids open enough to gather the remaining dragons into the fold, praying she hadn't lost count.

They squirmed against her skin. Her knees screamed against the heavy load.

A blast of heat lighted the room in a bright orange.

The heat and thick smoke intensified with each inch forward.

Halfway up, the heat against Ellen's skin tripled. The bottoms of her shoes pulled against the wood. Her lungs burned for oxygen. She charged toward the open door, her shoes disintegrating into floppy mounds.

The steaming fibers threatened to become part of her skin.

The voice called from below. "You cannot hide. I am everywhere."

The walls of the house sweated in the intense heat and threatened to ignite.

CHAPTER 18

Hazy daylight forced Welglen to land blocks away from his nest on a secluded dead-end street. Fire alarms deafened. The acrid smell of smoke filled his nostrils.

In the steps between landing and running, he tugged on his pants and transferred the swaddled hatchlings to his bare back.

Neighbors clustered in the few clear openings, in nervous conversations around a crew of orange-vested workers keeping everyone away from a downed power line. A curl of black smoke rose above the middle of the next block. Welglen darted around the power trucks.

Two trees crossed over each other, blocking the road to his street. He climbed through the scratchy limbs and raced ahead. His heart dropped with each sprint forward. His curved roofline should show in the distance.

Wisps of gray smoke rose above the treetops.

Welglen stumbled to a stop at the tangled charred branches lining his front walk.

Only the curved outline of the door and the stone fireplace remained.

From the top step of the charred ruin, he stared past the pile of rubble into the large hole where once the hatchlings had waited for his return.

He'd been chosen to protect. He'd failed.

Welglen collapsed to his knees. He hadn't protected Tacoma. He couldn't save the young dragons. He'd been too late for Roglir.

The pack of life on his back wriggled against the drop. Generations wasted. After all the years of sacrifice and effort, only three remained.

All males. Dragon future eliminated.

The human hadn't been enough.

Neither had he.

Two women passed, one carrying a small crying child. They didn't notice the burned remains of the house or the man in agony with a pack of infant dragons on his back.

The spell had outlived the structure.

Unable to roar and flame in grief, his human form tightened against his organs, squeezing emotion into his chest. His breaths heaving, he leaned his face into his hands.

The last of the dragons rolled slowly against his skin.

Welglen still had a job to do. He turned his back to the nest.

The hatchlings would need a safe place to mature enough to stand a chance in a fight. Perhaps the east. His small flight could still be carried. He would fly until his wings dissolved in agony to keep the younglings off the Earth.

There was a chance, however unlikely, another miracle occurred, and the other eggs ferried to another part of this land had survived.

Hard to believe in miracles while standing in ash.

Welglen pushed against the walkway to force his body forward. Debris caught his eye.

A shoe.

He examined the melted remains.

The human's shoe. On the outside of the nest.

Welglen ran down the street. He rushed against the doubt created by centuries of living alone.

He pushed the limits of his human body to reach her dwelling.

He froze at her door. The blinds were closed.

No sound came from within. He reached for the knob. Locked.

Welglen burst shoulder first into a narrow hall littered with books and ceramics jostled from floor to ceiling, shelves empty.

To his left, a sight brought the first sense of joy he'd experienced as a human.

Ellen crouched at the large brick fireplace. She pointed the Sword of Srekums between him and a pile of sleeping dragons.

He held his hands out, palms up. "It is all right, human."

She dropped the sword, lunged, and gripped him tight.

Over the top of her head, he counted twenty-seven dragons.

CHAPTER 19

Ellen panted against his slick chest. Her arms tightened around him. His skin was bright red at the shoulder that had rammed through her locked door.

She'd thought it was the sorcerer.

"Thank God it's you," she whimpered, anxious to pass the weight of responsibility to someone stronger. Her tears tangled with the musky sweat rolling down his body. After the intense days alone, she desperately needed relief from someone who understood dragons, and sorcerers with world-domination issues.

His rapid heartbeat sounded against her ear. She bit her tongue against an impulse to run it over the nipple to her left.

She tightened her squeeze on his shoulders, then ran her fingers down his arms.

He held them to the sides. He didn't hold her. He allowed her to lean. She needed to get a grip.

She sniffled against the back of her hand and stepped away. She dried his chest with her sleeve. "Sorry, I don't usually . . . no, I never do that. I thought I could handle earthquakes, but they were never this scary. When the sorcerer's voice came through a crack in the ground, I lost it."

"A voice?"

"He's coming for his eternity." She stepped across the debris to the fireplace to create a little distance between her rusty libido and that chest.

The man-dragon rubbed his hands over his mouth, bringing them together in a small child's prayer. "Nilrem."

Ellen stroked the backs of the baby dragons. "What's that? A dragon swear word?"

"The name of a man who hated me."

"What did you do to him?"

"I saved his son."

"We are *so* going to have to talk about that later." Ellen stretched, arms reaching overhead. "I'm having trouble putting everything that's happened into some type of sense. What do we do first?"

He looked from her to the pile of life sleeping behind her. "We reunite the flight." He slipped a pack off his shoulders and opened the flap to reveal three baby dragons—a turquoise, a gray, and a yellow.

"They're beautiful." Each about the size of the others, their scales held a more iridescent quality. "How did you find them? Where did they come from? Did you find your brother?"

Welglen lifted them out one by one and nestled them into the pile. "I'll tell you everything." He cleared a spot on the couch next to him. "After I hear your story."

Ellen pushed another pile of books off the end and sat apart. "The ground cracked, and something that looked like lava flowed out toward us. A terrible, creepy, seductive voice called out. I had to get everyone out. I didn't know if the aftershocks would drop the house over our heads before the explosive heat in the nest burned us alive. It took forever to carry them to the front door in small groups. I thought I wouldn't be able to save all. I almost didn't make it out with the last. I recounted them for hours."

She gasped, then held her breath to calm down. She willed her voice to steady while reliving the moments in the basement. "The flames started downstairs and climbed into the kitchen. I dragged our babies out over the front steps. I had to leave them for long enough to run for my car. I couldn't risk anyone seeing me carry the dragons home."

"You've already saved us all. For the first time."

"I can't deal with that." She exhaled while falling back into the cushion, rubbing at the tension seeping out of her head. "And your brother? Did you see him?"

Pain darkened his eyes. "He was injured when the sorcerer burned the nest. He lived long enough to pass these three on to me."

Ellen squeezed Welglen's hand. "I'm so sorry. To have waited this long, only to lose him." She crushed the impulse to cradle his head against her chest.

"He followed his path and saved those he could." Welglen slipped his hand out of her grasp and shifted to the fireplace. "He is one with the elders. There is no more I can do for him except protect his charges."

Welglen moved one of her batons and restacked a pile of books knocked out of one of the bookcases at the right side of the mantel. Only a couple of novels from the shelves remained. Her treasures of a lifetime reduced to unimportant clutter.

A rustle in the fireplace drew their attention to the pile of dragons, adjusting in a sleeping pile. He stroked the back of one of the silver babies. Watching his care lowered her anxiety. Her breathing slowed and the panic lessened with each of his strokes. She suspected the little ones were his therapy too.

"Is the entire town under a spell? The people I saw on the streets focused only on the earthquakes. They didn't notice a house on fire, even when it was right next door."

"The spell enchanted the nest to be something so simply average as to be invisible to humans. To fade into the background. Whatever happens in the nest ends at the edge of the spell. The fire wouldn't go out into the community. Nor would a fire outside of the spell harm the nest."

Ellen had a question to ask, she didn't want to know the answer to. She'd enlisted her fairness fairy to help her save the little ones when the fear of being nearly burned alive evolved into a huge case of pissed off. "Will there be many days like today? I'm not sure I have much more gumption to draw on. The last hours were pure adrenaline and terror."

One of the three new dragons, the yellow, whined in his sleep. Welglen ran a hand across the shiny scaled head. The newborn quieted. "I fear today was merely one battle in a large war."

Ellen's cheeks puffed out in a long exhale. "How much time before the next?"

"Not long. We'll have to act quickly. Assuming you're signing on with us."

"I'm ready to defend these guys. I might even fight. But I'm telling you, I'm no killer. Where do we start?"

"We hide."

"Where?"

"In plain sight."

CHAPTER 20

Welglen picked up an odd metal bar, fringed at the ends, and pushed away enough of the larger debris to form a path through the house. His brain required movement.

Thirty dragons would be much harder to care for than thirty eggs. Even without the impending sorcerer threat, the young ones needed protection. They touch the Earth, so their lives aren't a secret.

The human had risked her life to care for his charges. Perhaps she might tip the scales in their favor.

He found another bar buried under books. They could be used as weapons. He leaned them both against the wall near the front door.

Welglen paced, from back bedroom to living room, over broken crockery, and picture frames. The home was much larger than his nest. It needed cleaning but was in good repair, except for the lock he'd broken. "We'll stay here."

She sputtered a response, her voice rising into a tight squeak. "My house? It's only blocks from yours. They'll find us in no time. We have thirty baby dragons. Both the sorcerers and my neighbors are bound to notice."

The stakes were high. They needed a plan. One of the young ones scratched against the wood floor, hunting in his slumber. They would wake soon, famished for the next kill. Instinct would keep them close if they were fed. "The hatchlings are too young to transform. I'll have to conjure enough energy to shield them. To do this, I'll relinquish my abilities and remain human until they are safe. I'll be a man, and they will be small humans."

"Babies?" Ellen waved her hands. "Are you kidding me? Do you know how hard it would be to care for thirty babies? The number of diapers, food… and the crying? I'd have Child Protective Services at my door in an hour."

Welglen studied the pile on the fireplace hearth. "I could sustain the transformation of another small creature. A dog perhaps? Humans appear to care for them."

She shook her head. "Almost worse than babies in this town. Sonoma people care deeply about dogs. If they found dozens living in this small house, we'd be arrested."

"What would work here?"

Ellen stood at the window; her red, swollen eyes drooped in her reflection. She stretched, checked her scratched arms, and swore. He followed her to the kitchen, pieces of an old ceramic mug crunching underfoot. The water from the tap sputtered to a flow. She soaped her arms. "Would they be safe in any form other than a dragon?"

"As long as they are transformed, they're as secure from the detection of the sorcerers as we can manage."

She splashed water over her face, then rubbed her cheeks with a towel, and broke into a smile. "One thing I am zoned for might work. Of course, it's a little crazy. But crazy is relative."

"What do you suggest?"

"Chickens."

"The meat we live on?"

"Ironic and perfect!" She pointed out the window. "There is an old chicken coop outside. We can fix it up in a couple of hours with a trip to the hardware store. They can live outside. No one will think anything of it."

A possibility, though no plan guaranteed success. "Once they transform, I won't be able to fly or hunt as a dragon. We'll have to fend for these hungry creatures together."

"You'll live here?" Ellen stared at his chest. "Hmm . . ."

CHAPTER 21

Ellen perched on the edge of the now dirty tan couch, not allowing her back the comfort of the cushion. Muscles and brain matter had been running on overload for more than two days. She couldn't risk falling asleep and missing a front row seat to a miracle.

The babies slept on the hand-me-down hearth rug from her aunt in Denver. Dragon drool probably wasn't going to wash out.

"How do you make chickens?" Ellen asked as her temporary roommate stepped up to the infants.

He didn't answer. Instead, he chanted in a low, deep voice. The rhythmic pattern clicked and hummed. "Kukar Oomm Ayer. Kikar Oomm Ayer."

The backs of the small dragons moved in a slow ripple. Ellen stared at their beautiful scales and slowly rocked to the rhythmic pattern of Welglen's chant.

Her chin dropped to her chest and startled her awake. "Uh." She rose for a deep stretch. The little dragons were still little dragons. "I guess even magic has its limits."

A green-red dragon puffed into a fuzzy ball of feathers.

Ellen gasped. "Oh my God!"

The elongated snout shortened into a black beak. The tail into a spray of green. The front legs curved into a breast. Sage-colored feathers matching its original color started at the head and traveled down the back. Deep crimson covered the wings.

The little dragon bird shifted in the pile but didn't wake up.

Ellen dropped to her knees and pushed back against the couch. The pile popped into a flurry of brilliant color.

Downy brown plumes sprouted from some heads. Others sported crowns in reds, purples, and whites.

Ashamoor's patchwork coat started gold at the head, then rippled into purples, blues, and greens.

One by one, the mystical pile of dragons turned into a fantastic mass of sleeping chickens.

In her living room.

And other than a slight stir in readjustment, not one eye opened.

"I've never seen poultry like this." Amazed she could think at all at this point.

"What did you expect?"

A vision of two ratty birds trying to pass themselves off as prime organic chickens in a television commercial passed through her mind. "You know, white feathers, orange beaks."

"It's less energy to retain portions of their natural state. These would blend with the chickens of my time."

"How much longer will they sleep?" She yawned. Pain mounted between her shoulder blades and along the edges of her scratches.

"A day, no more. We must plan."

"I'm sure I won't be able to sleep, but I'm going to close my eyes for a few minutes." Ellen stretched on the couch and faced the babies. "After, we'll fix the coop into a dragon-chicken palace."

Ellen awoke with her head on Welglen's smooth, bare chest, her stiff neck testifying she'd slept deeply. The pain in her head had lightened against his heartbeat. His muscles were firm and comfortable. Not a bad start to a new adventure.

Welglen's light brown right nipple stood in her view of the transformed dragons. Instead of moving, she froze in place and tried to identify his smell—musky toasted marshmallows or syrup-dipped bacon.

She was seriously hungry.

Parts of Ellen's dream slammed back into her mind. She'd carried a large sword and battled a tall, cloaked man. It was a familiar battle she'd tried to include before in one of her dragon stories but hadn't found the place for yet.

She never saw the end of the dream, to know if she'd won or died.

She stretched out one leg to reach the floor and lifted off Welglen's body.

He exhaled a lovely moan, as if talking in his sleep.

If only he were a man.

She tiptoed to the sword she'd tossed aside when Welglen returned.

Cold and heavy, it provided security. She admired the dragon on the hilt she'd thought she'd designed to guard the back of her hand. The long-necked creature shared the slender qualities of the little babies, with long necks and talons. The face fierce, though without Welglen's dual horns.

Ellen spun the sword over her head, then whipped an X in front of her. The weight compared to the tournament batons she had used to act out battle scenes. Little did Dad know all the years of jujitsu he'd made her take might start to pay off.

She stood in the hallway and admired the pile of feathery babies in front of the fireplace, and the topless guy stretched out on her couch. If she possessed enough strength and bravery to protect these creatures, she would. More likely her character would run in the face of a fight.

Saving the babies from the flames had been pure maternal instinct. Even if he were an evil sorcerer, sticking a sword into a man required a killer's instinct.

Welglen had explained her skill with the sword was a last resort, which was good considering she didn't have any skill. She needed more information, though she hesitated to ask. There were still parts of this fantasy that hadn't completely absorbed into her reality.

The doorbell rang.

Welglen sprang up, startled awake. He knocked the couch cushions to the floor and focused on the ringing unit that hung on the wall. "What is it?"

Ellen waved to the front. "The door."

"What does it mean?" he cried, battle-ready, bare chest heaving, pectoral muscles expanding.

"It means someone wants in." She placed the Sword of Srekums at the baseboard. "Haven't you ever had a visitor?"

He shook his head, still wary.

"It'll be fine. I'll get rid of whoever it is." She crept into the hallway still littered with broken pictures. She pulled the front door open to Mrs. Delalo.

"Can I come in?" In an assault of heavy perfume, Ellen's neighbor stepped over the box the sword had been packed in. "My son made me stay over at his house last night. He wouldn't let me come home to check on the house until now. Thanks to all the earthquake putty and strapping I used, hardly anything fell over. I worried about you with half the power off in town. Well, hello!"

Mrs. Delalo stopped at the sight of Welglen's nipples. She wouldn't have noticed if the chickens perched on his head. She didn't take her gaze off his chest, her jaw hanging open, uncharacteristically silent.

"This is a friend of mine—Glen. It's such a mess in here." Ellen blocked her neighbor's view of the little ones, took her arm, and led her back to the door. "I wouldn't want you to get hurt. Glen's here to help me clean up things. In fact, we're about to go out to the store for supplies. Thank you so much for stopping by. I'll let you know if I need anything."

"Come over when you're done. I could use those muscles of yours," Mrs. Delalo called over her shoulder to Welglen. An unwanted mental picture of the neighbor using her man-dragon's muscles flashed through Ellen's brain. "Your door is broken."

"Yeah, Glen's going to fix it. See you."

She pushed the door closed, then pulled the broken door trim hanging from its last nail and laid it against the baseboard. Welglen turned back to the babies. "Humans are unusual creatures."

"Thanks, I guess. Do you plan to help Mrs. Delalo while I'm at the store? Seeing as how you are genetically predisposed to helping humans, it might be out of your hands."

"I'm not obliged to clean up after humans, only protect them from danger."

She tried to squelch the pleased smile that flickered across her face. "How did you deal with the protection thing all this time? You must have run across a human or two in peril. It would be like Superman not being able to put on his tights."

"Aside from you?" Welglen reclined against the couch and stretched his long arms toward the ceiling. "I've protected a human or two throughout the centuries. The eggs were my primary duty, so I remained as a hermit to avoid the lure to protect."

"Out of sight, out of mind?"

"It helped that, for a long time, I was extremely angry."

CHAPTER 22

Welglen slid the couch at an angle to block the view of the feathery pile from the front door. The direct line of sight had nearly jeopardized their plan before it began. "I hadn't thought other humans would be appearing. Will there be others?"

"Except for a random salesperson, we're good." Ellen stacked some of the books back on the shelves. She picked up the box and placed it on a chair. "I moved here a while ago. I haven't met too many people."

"You have no mate? Do you not enjoy physical contact? I admit it was most comforting sleeping under your warmth. Reminiscent of the days I slept with my flight mates."

Ellen glanced back. Her focus dropped to his chest, a moment before she turned back to her work. "Oh, I enjoy physical all right. I just haven't made time for it in my life lately."

"I see. I have noticed most of the human females your age have partners."

Her shoulders raised a notch. She removed a wooden box from the outer cover, propped it open on the chair, and tossed the cardboard to the floor by the back door.

"I don't really have time for this, you know, since I'm kind of busy, discovering dragons are real." She rotated the Sword of Srekums. The morning light bounced on the blade.

Welglen stacked an armload of books back in the case. "I have studied humans for some time and understand there are many reasons females don't mate with a male. You love another woman?"

"I wish," she smiled. "That would take the trouble out of a man trying to understand how important my work is to me."

"Perhaps you didn't pick the right mate. Or are you barren?" Welglen rose with a fresh batch of books to face the cutting end of her sword.

"That is rude! For your information, I'm not barren. And who uses that word anyway?" The human waved the sword in a small circle near his neck. "I have, however, a condition that will likely kill me if I choose to carry a baby full term."

Welglen clutched the load to cover his heart. "This angers you?"

She shook her head, eyes downcast. The scent of sorrow leaked from her. She rested the sword in the box. Her hands shook as she tugged the lid's leather straps down. "Another of the great ironies that make up my life. We have more pressing problems. We need to fix up the old coop in the back. We'll need feed and a plan. You need some clothes. Topless isn't going to work."

"My apologies. I've listened to humans for many years, however until now, had little opportunity to converse. You have access to a vehicle and method of payment. I shall remain to guard the hatchlings while you purchase necessary supplies. Is that amenable?"

"Sure." She walked down the hallway into one of the rooms. She returned minutes later in a change of clothes, a bag over one shoulder. He expected her to walk out the door. She stopped in front of him and tapped one foot.

"Let's get one thing straight, though it's none of your business." Her voice clear, and her words direct. "I broke up with the last guy, the love of my life, because I wanted children and he wanted to be the only child. After I left, I discovered the truth about my health. Now that you know, I don't ever want to talk about this again. Understand?"

Welglen nodded. His words had caused pain. She'd drawn a boundary line around her emotions.

"I'll get to the store to buy whatever chickens need." She stared at the pile of infants. "In the meantime, will they eat regular chicken feed? I don't want to scrounge around for live meat. You've already pushed me far enough out of what's left of my comfort zone."

"That should be fine." He didn't want to say anything to fuel another outburst of human emotion.

"Good. I draw the line at lizards."

CHAPTER 23

A chainsaw buzzed in the distance. Mrs. Delalo waved her arms in an animated conversation with the couple that lived across the street. Ellen paused on the front porch, held one hand over her mouth, and shook her head. Why had she told a relative stranger her saddest story when her mother didn't even know yet?

She climbed into her car and opened the windows to clear the lingering smell of smoke from her upholstery.

At the corner stop sign she put the car in park, her hands over her face, and sobbed.

Life was so much harder than graduating college early.

A car honked behind her. She wiped her face and headed toward the market. The strange new subplot in her life would have to wait until the dragon story played out. She'd focus on the thirty creatures counting on her for survival.

The single traffic light between home and Main Street turned red. She stopped in the line of cars. Yellow caution tape blocked the entrance into the Sonoma Market parking lot. The large overhang holding the store's name in metal letters had collapsed, blocking the front door. One letter O stuck out of the windshield of a blue minivan.

She had stored enough food, between the freezer and pantry, to feed her and her man-dragon, if he wasn't picky. She didn't have a way to take care of thirty chickens. She wove her way on side streets to the outskirts of town.

One mile down the two-lane highway, the flashing lights of a police car filled her rearview mirror. Ellen pulled over into the dirt edge that separated the road from the yellow and red rows of grape vines spreading out over the low rolling hills. The patrol car passed her, followed by a fire engine, siren blaring. A plume of black smoke lifted into the sky off to her left.

She drove on until she reached the feed store's gravel parking lot. The windows were dark. The front doors hung open and two young guys restacked hay bales lying haphazardly around a tall, orderly stack. She called, "Power out here too?"

The youngest walked over, wearing jeans, a Sonoma High School T-shirt, and the casual farmer attitude of the wine country town.

"Yes ma'am. You need something? We can't open the register without power, but if you have exact change or a check, we can make it work. Come on in. Everything that could fall, already has."

Ma'am? Ellen glanced at the reflection of her puffy red eyes in the mirror. She fluffed her hair and followed him into the rustic barn-shaped store.

The plank floor creaked under her feet. She stepped through a narrow pathway of piled bags of dog food, horse bridles, and small cages. The shelves above were empty.

At the long, low counter he picked up an order pad. "What can I get you, ma'am?"

"You already ma'am'd me once. Since I bet I'm only five years older than you, we're good. I've got chickens. All of a sudden. Sort of a gift from a friend. There's an old coop at my house needing chicken wire. I could also use feed and something for water."

Ellen stepped to a rack of clothes tipped over on its long side. She dug through the pile for a shirt and pants somewhere near Welglen's size.

The clerk tugged a square green carpenter's pencil out of his tight back pocket and wrote down the order. He picked through the piles on the floor. "Some earthquakes, right? All this almost fell on my head yesterday. I thought after the big one, the others would be smaller aftershocks, not bigger. What d'ya think is going on?"

A sorcerer is looking for the last of the dragons and might bring down the town in the effort. "Nature, I guess."

He tugged a bag of feed onto the counter. He stretched a long thin leg into a spot only he could see between plastic bins and tangles of ropes, then disappeared behind a pile. "My boss thinks all the new people in town have drained the underground water making things unstable."

"I'm not sure that makes sense. I believe earthquakes start deeper in the Earth."

He reappeared with a roll of chicken wire over one shoulder. He searched the top of what might've been an orderly desk before being shaken into a pile of receipts and coffee cups. He rescued a small calculator, tallied, then turned it around to display the total. "I don't know what's up, but something freaky is happening."

As he loaded the car, Ellen tried to think of some way to reassure him the sky wasn't falling.

But reality already lay in bits at her feet.

CHAPTER 24

Welglen held the sheet of wire tight against the boards. The woman drove horseshoe-shaped nails into the wood, and cut the remaining roll free, while she recited stories of her father's attempts at teaching her carpentry.

"Hopefully, this will keep them safe." She swung the hammer against the last nail that secured the gate latch. She slid the tool into a rose-colored bucket. "My dad could have done a better job. I typically learn just enough about things to make me dangerous."

Welglen pushed against the unmoving frame. "This will do. I'll stand guard during the night when predators are harder to see."

"I can help, too. At least I'll be an alarm system. You don't have to know anything about fighting to call for help."

"We'll do what we can together. You aren't a fighter, yet the younglings hatched for you, and you have the Sword of Srekums." He motioned to the weapon which lay on the outside table.

She lifted the blade to catch the light. "I'm not convinced it didn't come to me by accident. But it sure is beautiful."

Her posture lengthened. She stretched one arm out, fingertips pointed to his chest. She raised the sword over her head, then rotated the hilt in her wrist.

The double-edged sword spiraled behind her head.

"This isn't your first time handling a weapon."

"State champion baton twirler." She rested the sword back on the wooden table. "It's in my blood. When I was little, I'd make every type of stick or pole into a baton. Of course, I usually don't have to worry about cutting my own head off."

"What's a baton?"

"Didn't you notice my living room? The metal poles you pushed the mess around with. Hang on." She ran into the house and returned with three short poles. "These are my favorites."

She tugged her shirt off to reveal a small top underneath that showed off a slighter form than her clothing would have allowed.

"Stand back." She stretched. She pulled each knee in turn to her chin before selecting the first stick. "My first competition baton. It's built for height. I'm a little rusty and there are too many trees, so I'll show you the floor movements."

The metal rod circled quickly into a shiny blur that twisted in front and behind her with a practiced ease.

She chose another and worked the pair into a rapid spin at a fervent speed that brought sweat to her skin. She dropped to one knee and stopped the batons into a cross above her head.

"It appears you are preparing for an attack. Why did you do this?"

She placed them on the table. "Competition. I won a ton of ribbons, trophies, and medals. It was fun to be on the field in the middle of football games to cheer the team on or leading the band in parades. She snorted a laugh. "We were the Dragons. Which is incredibly ironic. This next part is more impressive in the dark. I'm warning you I haven't worked in front of an audience for a while. You might want to stand back."

She ignited the ends of the last baton.

The burning ends surrounded her in a blur of light.

She switched from one hand to another, then tossed the baton into the air and knelt forward before catching the stick in her hand and jutting it forward with a chant of "Go Dragons Go!"

Sweat dripped down her face and chest. She struggled for breath, out of shape and unprepared for what would come. Yet a smile beamed across her red-splotched face.

"Most impressive."

Ellen doused the flames.

He circled her lithe figure and examined her fitness. "Whether we choose to believe in your abilities to defeat the sorcerer, a fight will soon be on our hands. You have dexterity and coordination. You lack strength, endurance, swordsmanship, and a killer's instinct. Perhaps there is a way."

"Even if we had the time to develop the first three, I'm not sure I want a killer's instinct." She rolled the dormant baton in slow circles between her fingers.

"Even to protect the hatchlings? Yourself?"

She gathered the batons. "I'd like to think I'd fight for what's right. Theoretically, if there was no other way out, I'd step up with all I had. Little as that is."

"We'll tackle one problem at a time."

A loud clatter erupted in the house.

He raced to the back door and tugged it open. Ellen pushed against him on the threshold.

Thirty dragon-chickens squawked in a cloud of multi-colored feathers.

They'd fallen asleep as dragons in their nest and awoke as chickens in the home of a human.

They were startled, scared, and hungry.

Ellen's laughter filled the room. "Sonoma, we have a problem!"

Two infants flapped against Welglen's legs.

"Calm, human." He reached down to scoop the infants in his hands. They batted against his side until he turned them. Once upside down, they calmed. "It is no time for screeching. I have seen humans handle these many times. Grab them thusly. We'll carry them to their new nest."

"What?" she called over the outbreak. She cradled one chicken in her arms.

"It's simple." He turned to carry the two toward the door.

His foot slipped on the smooth, wet surface. He fell hard on his back, the chickens freed.

Flapping wings blocked his view from his section of the floor, covered with droppings.

The human's laughter added to the cacophony. She darted outside with her single cargo while he caught two others.

Birds wouldn't best a dragon.

Hanging again from their feet, they quieted. He moved toward the door. Ellen slipped back in and cornered one of the golden birds, cradling it in her arms. He straightened his shoulders, transferred the two birds to one hand, then reached for another.

He walked carefully to the door. She opened it with her free hand. He moved to follow her through, when two broke loose.

He jumped to block their escape into the yard. His foot skidded on the slick mess, launching the chicken from his hand to the couch and landing him on the floor.

The door stopped against his shoulder. Ellen looked down, her lips quivered to hide the amusement clear in her face. "Are you all right?"

He gripped the chair arm, his bare feet sliding against the slippery muck. "Your response is entirely unproductive."

"Don't dragons have a sense of humor?"

The chicken at the edge of the couch stepped closer, cackling in a rhythm that matched the woman's laughter. "Stay on task, woman!"

"Let's team up." She squatted and spread her arms wide. "I'll grab them one at a time. You stay by the door to make sure no others get out."

Carting sleeping dragons required only minor strength and dexterity. Catching birds in partial flight around the small space required patience and luck.

He had neither. "On with it."

The woman spoke in low tones to the young ones. She moved slowly into their midst, selecting one chicken at a time. Welglen stood guard at the door, opening, and closing at her pace.

The last of the infants were secure inside the coop. They clustered around the full feed and water containers.

"At least they're safe. How long can they stay like this?" She brushed off tiny blue and red feathers from her shirt. Other than the feathers, she'd managed to stay clean.

He was a mess. "I don't know. This is the first time I've turned dragons into chickens. Alone, I possess enough power to last a dragon's lifetime. However, these thirty beings are sharing one source. Young dragons develop quickly. They'll need more energy as they grow."

"How can we keep them safe?"

"Any time spent off the surface of the Earth as dragons can skew their scent. I suspect not more than two moons will pass before they are full grown. Normally, within the week they could fly at least small distances."

"You spend so little of your lives young and yet have such a long lifespan."

"We're born to protect humans. It wouldn't do for us to require care for too long."

"At least we have time to figure this out, right?"

Welglen checked the latch for the second time. "The sorcerer will reach us long before these young ones are ready to fly."

"How soon?"

"I'd guess . . . three days."

CHAPTER 25

Ellen slipped into the low lawn chair, bent over, and hung her head below her knees. Smears of white chicken droppings covered her shoes. She breathed in for a count of five, exhaled slowly, then repeated twice before she sat up. Welglen stood close. Her eye level reached south of his waist.

She gasped and cleared her throat.

He leaned down. "Okay?"

She followed his voice up to his face and waved him back. "Trying to come to grips with the timeline. We need a plan."

Welglen moved another chair in front of her, blocking her view of the coop. He tossed his filthy shirt to the ground. "The plan to save us all was created centuries ago. We only have to follow it."

"If you mean me stabbing my sword into some dude, then no. We don't have a plan." Ellen adjusted her chair to move her sightline back to the baby chicken dragons and away from the rippling abdominal muscles.

"How can you be sure about how long it will take for the sorcerer to get here?"

"There is no way of knowing exactly. It depends on the strength of the sorcerer. The longer it takes the sorcerer to reach us, the stronger the young ones will become. Which brings a new set of problems."

"More problems?"

"The longer we remain here, the more damage will come to the town. The earthquakes will continue until they finally deliver the sorcerer."

Ellen reclined against the chair. A small crescent moon sat low on the horizon. "Sonoma is going to fall apart. Can't we just run and hide? My car is too small, but with a truck or a van we could get them out of town. That will keep them off the ground."

"It may buy us a few days, though at some point, the sorcerer will find us."

Ashamoor pecked at the grass that poked through the wire fence. Her multi-colored feathers were easy to pick out among the bright mass. "Tell me more about the sorcerers—how they change. How do they transition to being able to use lava to hunt for dragons? Give me a lesson in 'Surviving Sorcerers for Dummies.'"

"I don't understand your reference, though I do take your meaning. A blending of the forms of the Earth with those walking upon it has always been a skill of the dragons. It's not unlike the way I am able to transform between dragon and man using the energies of my soul."

"Magic?"

He shrugged.

"I have a yard full of dragons," she waved toward the coop. "Magic was bound to come up."

"Magic is merely a word humans use to encapsulate all questions of transformation into a category most don't believe. It's more a matter of what you'd call science. We are but particles and energy. We're all capable of transformation, though few take the time to master the process."

"Sorcerers have?"

"Some. When a single dragon heart is consumed, it transfers the remaining life of the dragon to the sorcerer, expanding the sorcerer's lifespan by hundreds of years, while they remain in human form. Though not immortal, their long lives ensure their ability to manipulate the people and their surroundings. A bad human can do a lot of damage in a few hundred years."

"And then?"

"Two hearts connect the sorcerer to the energies of the Earth, allowing transformation and manipulation of the core. The voice you heard must have been for a sorcerer who had eaten the hearts of two dragons."

"That voice is something I'm trying to forget." Ellen rubbed at the shiver racing through her arms. "The sorcerer is still human, right? You can't stop him? Even in your human form?"

Welglen nodded, stretching his chest upward. His back cracked in a series of pops. "Once he eats three hearts, he is immortal. There is nothing anyone can do."

"Instantly?"

"It may take moments or minutes. The light within the sorcerer expands from inside to the cells of the skin. It's in that space of time the sorcerer is no longer human, though not yet immortal."

"Can you stop him?"

"While it's technically possible, it's unlikely. The change could happen too quickly. It would have followed the death of a dragon. Which could well be my own end."

Ellen looped her fingers into the coop wire. The babies had settled against each other at the edge closest to Welglen.

"So, we have a plan B, but it sucks. Another dragon has to die, and the odds are against it succeeding."

Welglen moved behind her. The warmth of his breath spread over the back of her neck. She tightened her grip on the coop. "We have our first option. A warrior could wield the Sword of Srekums and kill the sorcerer before another dragon is harmed."

"I'm not a warrior."

"I agree. Your strength is that you care deeply about a great many things."

Ashamoor edged close to the pile and picked a spot between the solid red and green babies.

Ellen's stomach growled. "I can't think. I need food. I need rest. Let's get cleaned up and have something to eat. I want to hear more about this light. There has to be another way."

CHAPTER 26

Welglen rubbed at the drips trailing down from his wet hair and walked naked into the dim hallway from the small bathroom. He checked the coop through the back window, barely visible in the twilight. No change. He needed to eat and move out to guard the coop.

He called down the hall. "My pants are no longer where I left them."

Ellen peered out from the kitchen, scanned his body from eyes to toes before ducking out of sight.

"I threw them into the washing machine with your shirts, but we'll have to wait for the power to come back on," her voice squeaked. "By the time you finished mopping the living room, there wasn't a clean speck anywhere on them. I spot cleaned your old pants and left you a large blue beach towel. Wrap that around yourself until they're dry."

The towel lay on the hallway floor. He draped it around his waist and tucked it in. An interesting aroma drew him into the kitchen where a single candle lit the counter space. She stirred a chunky red sauce while a pot bubbled behind it over the flames of the gas stove. "What is this?"

"Spaghetti. If I jump into a quick shower, think you can handle stirring until I return?"

He took the spoon from her outstretched hand. She avoided his face and left the room. He'd allowed her quiet while they'd cleaned. He needed her to face her part in what was to come.

The sauce tasted mildly of tomatoes and garlic. He sniffed through the rack of spices on the counter before stirring a few into the mixture. He left it to simmer, moved to the sink, and washed the stack of dishes.

She returned to the kitchen, tying her wet hair at the back of her head at the same time a buzz sounded from the stove. "I'll check the dryer in a second." She gaped at him. "You're doing the dishes."

"They're done," he turned the last glass over in the drainer. "I have skills in a home."

"Uh, yeah." She slipped her hands into two oven mitts to lift the boiling water. "Stand back. Hot water coming through."

She drained the noodles into a strainer, then dumped them over the sauce. "What'd you do? It smells different."

"I merely added a few herbs. I hope you don't mind, I spiced things up."

She laughed. "I have no words."

Welglen leaned against the back of the couch, considering his warrior. He waited until they'd eaten, and he was back in his old clothes before he brought up the plan he'd been developing. It was risky and not likely to succeed. Yet she'd wanted another option. The fate of all lay in the small hands of the woman stretched out on the cushions, exhausted from tossing a stick and chasing unruly chickens. "There may be another option to avoid killing. Though it would be a long shot."

"Yes. A non-violent option." She leaned against the side of the couch and signaled for him to sit next to her. "What is it?"

"It focuses on the actual source of a sorcerer's power. The light." He moved to the opposite side of the couch. "Sorcerers are not born, they are created. Born in a human form, either male or female, with all the potential vices and virtues. During the change of life to adulthood, they are exposed to the light of the world. Beings from the outer universe created this light to ensure there would be leaders, caregivers, and suppliers of faith among all societies. What wasn't calculated, was the greed among some humans. This greed turns enlightenment to manipulation, and humans into sorcerers with a ready tongue, and an ability to persuade."

"It could be anyone? A regular person? Personally, I don't get why anyone would want immortality. They would lose the best of life—sharing it with someone else."

Welglen studied this human who lived alone and talked of sharing life. If he had more experience with her kind, perhaps he could better read her expression.

"The loss of loved ones is unbearable, I agree. Sorcerers react to the light of life differently, I fear. Having power outweighs love. Once a sorcerer has achieved this immortality, the only threat will come from another sorcerer who has the power to kill. Many sorcerers have achieved this level—"

"They ate three dragon hearts?" she interrupted. The candlelight flickered over her pained expression.

"Or met death by a rival sorcerer. Their only protection is to enslave the humans to build a wall of stone where the humans' prayers and worship create a shield from others. A sorcerer cannot create something out of nothing. He needs humans. Of course, if a more intelligent sorcerer could find a way to break the spell over the humans and convince them to fight back, not even immortality could provide protection."

"Modern people won't put up with slavery."

"They already do. Slavery starts in the mind."

"None of this is making me feel better. Give me some hope."

"My brother Roglir mentioned another path. Legends track the first sorcerer to achieve eternal life to a pharaoh who enslaved the people to build temples in his honor. His reign lasted until a small band of dragons pulled the light from the sorcerer and rendered him a mere mortal. Once the light of eternity was removed, he died within the day of both poisoning and stabbing."

"Back up! You mean those stone pyramids in Egypt were built for sorcerers? This is a whole new series I need to write."

"Not every pile of stone or fortress is the result of a sorcerer, though every sorcerer since before the time of Ramesses has created one."

She ran her fingers through her hair, tossing it in each direction. "My mind is blown. Stonehenge, Mayan ruins, the Great Wall of China." She shook her hands as if erasing her thought process. "Let's get back to us. Can you pull the light out of the sorcerer coming for us?"

Welglen shook his head. "I tried to commune with the ancestors to learn the spell, but I failed. I'll contemplate and try again to communicate with the ancient ones for the knowledge. Even if I have the spell, it may not work. It's safer to believe we won't learn the secret. We'll have to rely on your ability to eliminate the threat."

"Not safer for me." Ellen collected a notepad from the table, angling toward the light. "How would this work?"

"Assuming I'm able to develop the skill to render him helpless, I'll need a distraction. While I concentrate on the spell, I'll be unprotected. I need you to distract the sorcerer to buy me time to pull the light."

"How? Tell jokes? A few cheers? I can't fight. I don't know how."

"You have the coordination. I've seen you with those rods you throw. I'll teach you what you need to know about your sword. If I can learn the spell and you can buy time, we may save everyone."

"I'm not sure you want me to fight," her heavy breaths slowed, and she rolled to stand, "or if I'm the bait."

"You might take solace in imagining yourself more as the hook."

CHAPTER 27

Pain shook Ellen awake. She winced and massaged the arm muscles she'd managed to pin beneath her while dreaming of a sword battle where she'd showed up naked.

"Injured in my sleep. Not a good sign."

The clock next to her bed blinked in proof that the power had been restored. She turned on the lamp and grabbed her journal. She hadn't written a word since she'd been stuck in Welglen's basement.

Maybe she never did. Perhaps she'd been taking dictation from the real author of her stories. That was the book she needed to write. She clicked the pen into action and focused on the empty page. Where should she start her story? When she met Welglen, or earlier? Maybe back to her childhood when Slatetail's stories appeared in her dreams.

She was living in a contemporary fantasy. Given the choice, she'd have preferred a romantic comedy.

She left the journal on her side table and dressed in sweats to take over guard duty. She wasn't ready to start a new book when the plot was still unfolding.

The clock on the microwave blinked twelve. Finally, the coffee machine could work its magic.

She stepped out the back door with two steaming mugs. The motion-detector light turned on. Welglen lay on his side between the chair and the coop. His knees were tucked near his chest, his head resting in the crook of an arm.

He spoke, his eyes still closed. "You're awake."

"I thought you were out." Ellen sat in the chair and balanced his cup on the grass at his side. "I brought you something to drink, but it's caffeinated. You might want to sleep instead."

He arched his back, exposing a rash of grass impressions along his skin. He stretched with a ripple of popping sounds. "This human body is not comfortable. It's stiff from the cold."

She sipped the hot coffee, hoping the caffeine would enter her bloodstream quickly and do its magic. "I see you ignored the blanket I left you. I'm sure the ground didn't help. You can stretch out in my bed. I'll keep watch."

"I cannot sleep. It's too painful."

Welglen twisted his long form while Ellen rubbed her neck muscles. A good hostess might offer to work some pain ointment into his sore shoulders. But touching her attractive man-dragon might take her over the edge. "How do you feel about hot tubs?"

"I'm familiar with the concept, though I have been limited to the small tub in the nest. I couldn't venture out for prolonged periods strictly for enjoyment." He tugged his shirt over his head and raised his arms toward the stars.

"It c-can be heaven." She feared the stuttering signaled she'd been celibate far too long. "If a dragon in the body of a man has no problem with hot water and jets."

A large moan erupted from him. "Heat is what this meager shape craves. We shall see about these jets."

"One second." Ellen ran in and rummaged through the closet to find the large-sized basketball shorts she'd bought by mistake. Her swimsuit collection included a string bikini for the tanning she never got around to, and a serviceable model she used at the gym. She pictured an attempt at seducing a man-dragon, then covered the new tattoo with a waterproof bandage. She chose the one-piece.

Welglen stood in front of the coop. She tossed him the shorts. His eyes raked her body, creating a feeling of self-consciousness. Perhaps he had the instincts of a man. Maybe she should have kept on her sweats.

"You have many wounds." He pointed to the bruises along her legs and arms that she hadn't seen yet—only felt.

Weird fantasy ended. "I'm not built for battles. Yoga, baton twirling, and couch vegging—I'm ready for."

His body was just a man-costume. It wasn't real.

He slid his pants down.

A line of dark hair led downward.

She lost it and looked away. He wore one hot human suit.

He snapped the waistband against his skin. She turned around. "Must I wear this? You humans have clothes for many occasions. Isn't the skin you were born with enough?"

"Yours might be." He followed her out past the coop to the hot tub. "We need protection from the elements. We don't have scales."

"What little protection do these clothes provide?" He motioned to the nylon of the shorts stretched tightly between his hips.

Ellen set her refilled coffee cup on the edge. She flipped back the lid on the tub, turned on the jets, and climbed into the warm water before she answered. The cover had retained most of the heat. It would take a couple hours to bring it back to the level of hot she craved. "These are to protect our modesty."

"Ah yes." He touched the water with the tip of his toe. "I'd forgotten about that human emotion." He slipped into the tub without making much of a ripple and settled in to face her, the coop behind.

He didn't speak. He sank deeper into the hot water until only his face appeared.

"Do you soak regularly?" Ellen couldn't picture his long body in the small claw-foot tub she'd seen in his bathroom.

"Humans didn't invent the long hot soak. All areas of the Earth where the lava and thermal points meet have created steaming pools. Before humans existed, dragons enjoyed them to keep the chill of the air from freezing the soul. It is, however, my first time as a human." He smiled. "I must admit the brush of the bubbles against my light armor is quite pleasurable."

He moved to his side and raised an arm out of the water. The basketball shorts hung from his outstretched hand.

"Uh..." Ellen tried to focus on the shadows behind him. "You're supposed to keep those on."

He reclined against the jets. "As I suspected. Without the clothing, the water movement soothes all parts of the body. Remove your clothing and you will see."

"I'm aware that nude bathing is pleasurable, but I'm not about to sit in here naked with a man I just met."

He shook his head. "I'm not a man." He held his hands and shrugged his broad, bare shoulders. "I'm a dragon."

"That's not what you look like to me. Keep seated."

"Humans."

Ellen averted her gaze to the trees above.

A moving shadow caught her attention. Two sets of reflected light passed over a branch and down the trunk.

"Arm yourself!" Welglen rose, bare, in front of her.

Ellen stared open-mouthed at the vision of a perfect man before her. She floundered to climb over the slippery side behind him and ran toward the chickens.

Two raccoons tugged at the coop door.

She screamed. "Raccoons! They bite!" She grabbed the closest weapon and waved a rake at the animals.

They hissed and held their ground.

Fire blasted in front of Ellen. She backed away from the heat into Welglen's cool chest.

The raccoons dashed past her, leaving a trail of singed fur over the neighbor's fence.

The burst of flames had come from the chickens.

The baby dragons had found their fire.

CHAPTER 28

Welglen scanned the trees. A rustle of leaves faded into the distance. The branches above were silent and animal free.

The disguised dragons settled back into their quiet pile, oblivious to their own growth and the swift change of plans.

"I wasn't expecting that." Ellen propped the chairs against the coop gate.

"The raccoons are gone. I doubt they'll return tonight."

"Not them." Ellen studied the quiet pile of living feathers. "The babies. We have fire-breathing chickens. I don't suppose it changes anything for you, but this is right up there with discovering dragons exist."

Welglen stepped behind her. "It does change one thing. If they already have their fire, their disguise won't last as long as I thought."

"You said three days." She rubbed her hands over her eyes.

"I've never raised dragons before." He thought for a moment. "We'll have to set out tomorrow. In only a few more days, they'll be able to fly. Their energies will be too large to be transferred by one dragon. We'll need to travel far away from other humans, staying out of sight. A highly forested area would provide cover and feeding grounds."

A long sigh rumbled in her throat. "If you're talking about camping, I don't own the type of cookware, instant meals, or packs large enough to carry them. Or a vehicle big enough to carry supplies and the babies. Any ideas where we could go?"

"The sorcerers will bring the battle to us." He stepped to her side. She kept her focus on the coop. "We must buy time. We shall begin the planning and leave at the first opportunity. We'll need a secluded location, to prevent the same damage that befell Sonoma from affecting another community."

She stood close enough for the hair on their arms to touch, her skin bumpy and cold, but didn't respond. She stared ahead at the young ones.

"Are you all right? Did the battle with the racoons weaken your resolve?" Welglen turned her shoulders to force her to face him. She gazed at the dark treetops.

"You're still naked, right?" Her teeth chattered. She avoided both his eyes and every other part of his body.

"Unclothed, yes."

She spun around. "I may know of a place. Let's start our planning back in the hot tub. I'm freezing and you need to get something on, even if it's only water."

Humans focused much of their thoughts on the forms of others. He'd witnessed it for centuries. Dragons didn't share the same modesties. Males and females alike flaunt their sex in pride to secure the best match for future generations.

"I'm a dragon, not a man," he repeated. He followed, convinced he would never understand this species.

"You keep saying that." Their eyes met the instant he slipped back into the warmth of the bubbling water.

"There's a place I used to live that might work. The houses are far apart, and the land is heavily forested."

"Is it far?"

"Only about five hours if we drove straight through. We'd never make it that way with the babies though. It's a major freeway. Even without the crazy earthquakes, the traffic is usually fierce. Someone's bound to see us. We could go on the back roads and camp along the way. I've never done it, but I think we can figure it out."

"Extending whatever time we have for your training and the young ones' growth would be good. Can we count on our safety once we arrive?"

"It's my friend's house—my ex-boyfriend's house."

"You trust him with our lives?"

She nodded.

"I don't understand the human concept of former mate. Dragons join for life. We wouldn't select an incorrect mate."

"Humans are different."

CHAPTER 29

Ellen backed a large white get-away van into her driveway, filled with enough cages from the feed store to keep thirty fire-breathing dragons in chicken suits from knocking into each other.

Welglen met her outside as she opened the back double doors. "That's a large vehicle."

"We'll have to pull the cages out, get the chickens in, then restack. It should be shady enough here to keep the inside cool. If not, we can turn on the air conditioner and leave it running. We can tuck our supplies behind the front seats for easy access."

"Let's load quickly and get out of town." Welglen lowered the cages onto the garage floor.

"Without being seen." Ellen pulled two bags of supplies out to start consolidating.

She turned back, only to face Mrs. Delalo coming across the small front yard. "Oh Ellen, isn't it awful?" Mrs. Delalo's gravelly voice gushed.

Ellen moved to block Welglen. He was a head taller. Mrs. Delalo fanned her bright fuchsia shirt at her waist.

"Didn't I call this earthquake weather? You should see the mess across the street. The Lindy's pool is cracked. How is your tall drink of prosecco?" She chatted to Ellen but stared at Welglen hungrily.

"Uh, Glen is fine." Ellen tapped the side of the van. "He's moving out of town, and I'm helping out. I'll be gone for a couple of days."

Mrs. Delalo pouted. "You're leaving us, Glen? Well, that's obviously our loss. How long have you lived here?"

Welglen stretched to his full protection mode height. "Eons."

Mrs. Delalo shook her head slowly, the right corner of her mouth turning up into a bright red smile. "I know about everyone in town, and I've never seen you before. How odd."

He raised an eyebrow. "Indeed."

Ellen wanted to communicate to Welglen that agreeing with Mrs. Delalo would send her away faster.

Mrs. Delalo stared. "With all the drama that's happening across the state, it's critical to know who you are sharing your spot on the planet with. If people aren't the right sort, you need to know. Don't you agree?" She pointed at the sky. "The weather has been most unusual. First the earthquakes. Now this hot day so late in the season. I'm not quite sure what to make of it all. Something's afoot. I should be taking some sort of action, but I'm not sure what. What do you think, Glen?"

Welglen folded his arms, mimicking her stance. "Store up on food, water, and weapons."

Mrs. Delalo stared; mouth opened wide. She let out a loud snorting laugh. "You're teasing me! Imagine needing weapons!"

Ellen tried to channel thoughts to Welglen to shut up. Feeding into her neighbor's suspicions would only fuel the fire. She might hang around long enough to notice they'd acquired a load of chickens.

Ellen guided Mrs. Delalo by the elbow to a spot a few feet away from the van. "I'm sure he means to remind you to check your earthquake survival kit. Please keep an eye on my house for me. You know where the hide-a-key is."

"How long will you be gone?"

Ellen glanced back at Welglen, then shrugged. How long would it take to save the world? "I'm not sure yet."

"Good to know. I'll watch things. I'm prepared for more earthquakes."

Welglen squared his already large shoulders. "Be prepared for battle."

Ellen shot him a look to say "stop!" He didn't catch it.

Mrs. Delalo turned back to him, nodding bobblehead style. "You're so right. If we need supplies, it's war getting through the market."

Welglen nodded. "The intruders will try to take over. Barricade your fortress. Don't allow strangers through."

"Oh, I will! I've been meaning to fix that lock on my garage door. It wouldn't do to store up on supplies only to have someone steal them. I'd better run. Thank you so much for the advice, Glen. Bye, Ellen!"

The large spray of blue flowers on her hips swayed their way across the lawn as she scurried to prepare for the next earthquake.

Ellen faced him. "Are all humans that dense to you?" No matter what Welglen said, Mrs. Delalo heard what she wanted to.

"It's not their fault." He tugged two more cages out. "Their sense of reality and perhaps survival will not allow them to acknowledge the existence of anything so fearful."

Ellen closed the van door. "Why am I different?"

"Because you're the chosen one."

"I wished that sounded comforting." She walked toward the house and called back to him. "You can start loading the young ones into the cages. I'll gather what I need. Of course, if you haven't figured out how to handle chickens yet, I suppose I could do both."

A sound something close to a growl made Ellen smile.

She accepted her character role and followed the plot. They'd drive to the foothills below Mount Shasta where Josh lived. She'd no clue what he would think when she showed up, uninvited, with a van full of formerly mythical creatures. She hoped his determination to live in Neverland would help—what kid doesn't love a dragon?

They had to move fast. Welglen's transformation wouldn't last long. The babies could be forced out of their feathers at any moment. All those little dragon claws on the ground would bring on more earthquakes and nasty lava. The sorcerers wouldn't be far behind.

Ellen's thoughts split between what to take with her and her traveling partner. She much preferred dealing with Welglen the dragon to Glen the man, in his seriously muscular, ruggedly handsome, and well-endowed human shell. Camping in the wild, on the way to Josh's, would be intimate.

She'd picked up a stove, fuel, sleeping bags, canned food, water, a coffeepot, and a bag of marshmallows.

What Ellen needed couldn't be found on a store shelf.

Her story had an incomplete outline.

She prepared for a trek to a place where sorcerers fought dragons. She worried whether Josh still loved her. She wanted to take control—to plot out the parallel stories. She had let the tale unfold.

At the open closet door, she stared at her clothing options for an adventure of an indeterminate length, varying weather, and mixed odds of survival.

She tossed her warmest jacket, a lightweight jacket, and sweater onto the bed, followed by nearly everything else she owned. After some inner negotiations, she pared it down to an amount that would fit into her backpack. She added extra tennis shoes and her favorite sun hat. In the bathroom, she filled her makeup bag with aspirin, first aid supplies, soap, and a yellow pocketknife with her insurance company's logo on the side.

Unlikely her life insurance included a dragon clause.

Ellen carried her load into the kitchen, then surveyed the stack for what was missing.

She added two potholders and a pair of barbecue tongs.

No telling how hot things were going to get.

CHAPTER 30

Welglen guarded the loaded van from the kitchen window. He leaned over the sink and cleaned the sweat from the dozens of chicken scratches along his arms. If the younglings were in their original state, instinct would rule. As flight alpha, the dragons would follow his directions. In their current evolution, feathers flew, and claws marked while he coerced, pleaded, and trapped the chickens by threes into the carriers. He lacked the woman's finesse.

Ellen raced from room to room and piled odd items and stacks of clothes she wouldn't need in a heap on the kitchen floor.

The confines of clothing got in the way of close combat. Human armor provided no protection against a sorcerer.

He didn't share the fact with her yet. Her grasp of the situation was naïve.

"Hurry, human. The young ones are loaded. We must go."

"Almost ready." She studied the mass that included cans of food and bottles of water. "Do you notice if I've missed something I might need?"

"I can't be much help in this process." He picked up an oven mitt decorated with a recipe for something called clam chowder. "I'm unfamiliar with the terrain of our destination and the usefulness of specific objects. I would say this pile contains both more than you will need and yet is undoubtedly missing something essential."

She twisted her mouth in a manner he understood as frustration. "That doesn't help at all. I'm going to go with whatever fits into the van. We'll camp our way there, so we'll need bedding, food, and protection. It'll be hot during the day and cold at night. Once we get to Josh's, assuming he lets us through his gate, we'll be able to restock food and wash clothes. I have no idea what we'll do after that."

"We must leave quickly." Welglen scooped an armload of items up from the floor. "The sun is high, and the young ones are anxious."

After Ellen's items filled the last spaces between the cages, Welglen waited near the vehicle and spoke in calm tones to the squawking young. She made two last sweeps of the house before sitting behind the wheel.

"We'll need to stop at the nest first."

"Aren't you worried they'll find us there?"

"It would be worth the risk, though I don't believe our current state will attract their attention. There are items I need to collect."

She turned the key. A rough vibration shook through the vehicle.

He strained out the window. "Sorcerers!"

"Where?" She turned the key and jumped out. The vibration stopped. "I don't see anything."

"Didn't you feel that? The Earth moved."

Ellen's eyebrows twitched and her mouth curled into a smile. "You've never been in a car, have you?"

"No need until now."

"Why drive when you can fly?" She fastened a belt across her chest and slipped the key back into the slit. "When I turn this, the engine will engage. The car will vibrate. It's supposed to."

She turned the key, restarting the tremor. She adjusted a lever and the van rolled forward. An uncomfortable dizziness waved through his body. He clutched the door through the open window.

She stopped at the edge of the driveway. "Are you all right?"

"I'm surprised at my body's reaction to the movement, that is all." The lightness that had lifted his stomach passed.

He waved her forward with one hand and tightened his grip with the other.

She moved onto the roadway. The acceleration pushed him against the seat back. She stopped at the corner to allow another driver to pass. His body weight moved forward. The dizziness returned.

Bile rose in his throat as they neared the nest.

She made a sharp intake of air and stopped in front of the blackened rubble. Her eyes watered at the sight of the remains that had been his home for so many years. "How can no one see that? It radiates sadness."

"They can see nothing that does not make sense to them." He stepped back onto the earth and paused to scan the debris. "I'll return in a moment."

Welglen crossed the steps that had led to the portal into the skeleton of walls, avoiding the large crater left where the nest had been. He searched through the remains of the kitchen.

From the unscathed rock chimney, he collected the chain and harness used to carry items in flight. At the steps, he collected a filthy, but intact, deer hide. He took one last look at the past and turned toward Ellen.

He wished he had her hope. Hope would have the power to carry them forward.

In its absence, he would act.

CHAPTER 31

Ellen selected a radio station playing the softest rock she could find to create an illusion of calm. Welglen clutched the door with one hand and the dash with the other until they left the crowded roadway and reached the empty narrow lane circling the back of a lake. His grip released as he stared at the water.

Staying off the beaten path away from other humans wasn't the fastest route. It did provide the bonus time to create an opening line for her ex-boyfriend. Each mile closer wrenched her anxiety.

Josh would be home. He rooted deep, with locations and people. He'd been the one to call regularly to keep in touch after she'd left. She didn't know if they could work again but was sure she had the next move.

The radio connection faded on the curvy road and views of the lake opened and closed in small breaks between the thick trees. Small cottages with extended fishing docks dotted the shore.

Welglen's complexion turned from carsick-green back to a ruddy tan and his head bobbed softly against the headrest. Riding in a vehicle had taken a toll on this creature of the sky. Ellen adjusted the mirror to watch him.

The lines around his face softened while he slept. His bottom lip, chapped, and his lashes, long. His dark hair held golden and red highlights mimicking the colors of his natural scales. For a centuries-old dragon, his current human form was well cut.

Ellen missed sex. On the rare occasion she met a man anywhere near interesting, she froze when it came to her status. "Hello, my name is Ellen," she would murmur. "I'm an Aquarius with a fixation on dragon lore who chose life over children."

Random possibilities existed, of course. If she waited until the men her age fell in love with someone else, married, had kids, then divorced, she'd have a chance with the scarred. The fifty-fifty marriage stats were in her favor. If she waited.

If she were unusually lucky, she might find a life with the one man she'd ever loved. She rolled over a pothole. The van bumped in a sharp jerk.

Welglen groaned and stretched against the seat belt she'd forced him to wear, drawing her attention away from her whiny thoughts. Soon she'd be able to see him as a dragon again. Both of his characters intrigued her.

His voice surprised her. "Are you finished staring at me, woman?" His eyes remained closed, chin against his chest.

"Uh . . . I thought you were asleep." She straightened and pretended to check her lip gloss while she moved the mirror back to its regular position. "You are something to look at. When I think of you as a true dragon, wow. I mean, from a purely scientific angle—oh, never mind."

He lifted his arm over the back of the bench seat, his fingers brushing her shoulder as if they were two lovers on a road trip. "Is there much further to travel? My body wearies more from this sedentary position than from flight."

Focus, girl. She'd clearly been alone too long.

"We're nearly to the first campground. We can drive up the hill until the road ends. We'll have to see how far this van will take us into the wilderness." She imagined living in the forests with thirty-plus-one dragons in the small tent she'd purchased, and no bathroom in sight. She shuddered. "Tell me again what to expect with the babies."

He looked back over the seat to the noisy cargo. "We'll have maybe two days at most before the younglings outgrow their shared energies. Once they transform, they will be rowdy, craving a fight, and voracious. They'll scatter for food."

Ellen pictured herding thirty baby dragons around the wide-open backcountry. "How will we keep them contained?"

"We won't. They'll need to care for their own feeding. They'll return together for warmth. Dragons are of a flight. We are the leaders of their herd."

Partners. At least for now. "How did you make it alone for so long?"

He shook his head. "I discovered the longer I stayed in the human form, the more accustomed I grew to loneliness, to the point it no longer bothered me."

"That's sad."

"Why?"

Ellen tried to find the words to explain loneliness as a horrible norm, then shrugged. "How long before the lava stuff and the sorcerer find us?"

"It depends on many factors."

She waited for Welglen to complete the thought and give her some hope in parameters. He stared ahead, unspeaking.

"That's all you've got?"

The paved roadway veered right. Ellen took the fork to the left, onto a dirt road toward the small hills, to Josh, and her past.

CHAPTER 32

Welglen revolved slowly in front of the fire to scan the darkness for signs of trouble. He'd draped one of the heavy coverings over his stiff shoulder muscles against the cool night air. Ignoring the tent, Ellen slept tucked inside her bag, close to the fire. He wanted his body free, ready in an instant.

She'd kicked up dust pacing between the fire and the shrubby forest for hours as the young dragons had scratched at the ground. Once they'd settled into a cheeping slumber inside the low fence created from abandoned crates between four of the pine trees, he'd said she had time for rest.

He lied.

The energy flowing back into his being foretold of the younglings' growth. They could transform at any moment.

When thirty dragons touched the Earth, the battle would soon follow.

He gazed at the star-filled sky. At least he'd fly soon.

Piles of feathers dusted the surface around their makeshift nest. Through the firelight, Welglen could see the pink skin of four young ones where the squabbling had turned rough.

If they had been back on the mountain of his birth, their beginning on Earth would have been different. Dragon eggs were protected from predators and each other. A hundred or more might share the nest, though seldom did more than two or three hatch at the same time. Variables included the season of their parents and needs of the humans. For all remaining eggs to have hatched at once, the need was dire.

Ellen rolled over near his feet, groaning. The many hours of practice with the sword after the long drive surely accounted for the pain that transcended sleep. Small and untested; it remained beyond belief that she could possibly be the one to save all. Yet she was all he had.

He'd protect this human while she fought to protect life on Earth.

A loud squawk pierced the air.

Then, a roar.

A burst of flame lighted the scaled face of the green female. She spread her wings and sprinted over the barrier into the dark. The first of the younglings had shed its protection. The others followed in a succession of growls and howls.

The dragons were back.

CHAPTER 33

Ellen sprang for the hilt of her sword. The sleeping bag tangled around her legs.

She fell toward the embers of the dying fire.

Welglen lifted her into the air, the cover dangled from her feet as she squealed. "What is it?"

"Dragons."

She'd slept through another miracle. She slid down the front of the safe, strong chest and followed his gaze to the edges of the firelight. A trail of feathers led into the brush. Dozens of shadows darted around her. None identifiable.

Ellen freed her legs. "What are they doing in the dark? We have to gather them up."

"They don't require light to hunt."

A shrill filled the air. She scanned the ground, sword pointed outward. "Rattlesnake! I've never seen one, but I've heard that sound before. What do we do?"

"You're safe here." Welglen gazed out into the darkness. "The young ones aren't susceptible to the venom. The sound doesn't scare them away; it alerts them to their next meal."

The rattling increased. The circle of light was small.

"I need to see." Ellen reached toward the dark wood pile, then snatched her hand back. She stuck her sword into the wood pile and rolled a log into the light. She added it to the fire.

The rattle swelled, then stopped.

"Someone has found their supper." Welglen carried several pieces of wood over to the edge of the fireside near Ellen's feet.

"At least that sound stopped. I couldn't have listened to that much longer." The rattling restarted and escalated. "Really?"

"I believe they've located a nest." Welglen's tone carried a hint of fatherly pride.

"Oh God." She shook her boot upside down before jamming her foot in. "You need to do something."

"They must hunt separately, then they will return to the flight to sleep. Every kill is an important step in their survival training."

"I'm supposed to sit here in the middle of rattlesnakes and just wait to see if my babies make it on their own?"

"They are not your babies. Though I admit they are uncommonly attached to you. Seeing you at their first sight has created a bond. Now that you are awake, I'll leave you to care for the fire. I must soar in the hopes the normal activity will return the knowledge of how to pull the light from a sorcerer."

"You're leaving me in the middle of angry rattlesnakes to meditate?"

"I wouldn't go if I didn't feel you were safe. The young ones will return when fed."

She jabbed at the fire with her sword, creating angry bursts of sparks. "Go fly already, dragon." She refused to watch his first transformation in days. She didn't look his way until the sound of his wings patted against the ground in takeoff.

He disappeared into the dark sky.

The rattling intensified. A chill rippled down her spine. Alone felt different in the dark.

Helpless.

Ellen shook her hands out and exhaled deeply. She could do this. She stacked more wood on the fire and stirred the dry fuel into a flame. She covered her back with the sleeping bag and perched on a rock near the heat.

The nerve-wracking rattle pulsed. Each time the sound lowered. The dragons were either picking off the snakes, or the reptiles slithered away. Hopefully in the opposite direction.

She faked calm.

For about five minutes. Patience wasn't her thing—right up there on the 'don't do list' with wandering around in a dark brush filled with venomous serpents to check on her babies.

She grabbed the sword and launched into a firelight routine.

A red sliver of dawn appeared over the horizon as she re-started the old moves for a third time, eyes on the forest. Light filtered between the trees and brush falling in odd patterns on the dust where her feet had left a trail of circles.

She angled toward a sound in the distance, hoping the babies returned. A pair of birds flew over her head singing to each other, dashing her false hope.

Silence. Except a distant rattle.

Ellen picked up the water bottle and reclined against the pack.

Something wiggled at her back.

"Ahh!" She beat the bag with the sword, then hopped to the other side of the dwindling fire.

Her scream silenced nature's rattles and squawks.

One familiar sound remained.

She pulled her ringing cell phone out of the side pocket. Mrs. Delalo's number displayed. Her voice higher pitched than usual. "Ellen, dear. I've been so worried. Someone broke into your house."

"What?" An adrenaline rush pounded in Ellen's ears.

"I answered nature's call around two and noticed a light in your back window. I know you're on a trip with your handsome friend and since the earthquake around midnight, the power has been out all over town again. I called the police. The intruder ran off before they arrived. A dark figure ran out the back door in a flash of weird light. I couldn't see him anymore—you know we've been having the strangest weather."

"Did he carry anything out? My TV or laptop?" She'd backed up all her files but would still hate her stories to fall into anyone's hands.

"Nothing. Probably someone looking for a place out of the cold. We've had so many strangers coming into town with all the earthquakes. I called the governor's office and told them we need the National Guard to keep these strangers away."

"Whoa, let's not give in to paranoia." Ellen produced enough of that herself. "Thank you for keeping an eye out on my house but aren't you on the Welcome Wagon committee? Don't you usually describe strangers as friends you haven't met yet?"

"I guess so. That doesn't count people who break into houses."

"I'll give you that. Things are pretty crazy there?"

"The earthquakes have put everyone on edge. The power keeps going out while so many people are coming into town from the hills where rockslides have cut off rural roads."

The scraggly brush to her right rustled.

Ellen climbed on top of the rock she'd sat on earlier.

Three of the larger younglings raced into camp.

Ellen's tense muscles relaxed. Their safety trumped everything else. And getting off the phone.

"I have to run, but thanks again for keeping an eye out for me. I don't have much left after the quakes worth stealing. Let me know if you need help. I'll see what I can do."

Ellen perched on the rock and watched her babies return. Compared to their chicken suits, the dragons looked huge. Extended stomachs proved their hunt had been successful.

They crawled toward the embers of the fire. Huddled in a pile, they dropped into another deep, enviable sleep.

Half an hour passed before the next group filtered back. She counted down from thirty. After an hour, all but two dragons had returned. Ashamoor was one of the missing. Ellen circled and strained at the edge of the clearing where the dried grass thickened for any glimpse.

"Welglen, a little help here," she called to the empty sky, lightening with the sunrise. "These are the last of the species you have spent centuries protecting, and I'm supposed to believe you are willing to let nature take its course?"

The smallest black dragon slipped quietly into camp and crawled to the edge of the pile. Ellen's stomach turned into a pool of antacid-craving anxiety.

Everyone except Ashamoor.

For thirty additional minutes, Ellen straightened the bedding, stacked broken limbs into the burn pile, covered the pile of dragons with light brush, and perked a pot of coffee she didn't drink.

The sleeping crew didn't move. "I can't sit here and wait any longer. This is driving me insane."

Ellen grabbed the sword and raced toward the edge of camp, where the last dragon had appeared. "Can I really do this?"

She flicked the blade against a branch dropped on the trampled path, then took a step in and lifted the next.

In ten feet she was knee-high in grass, shouldered by blackberry vines, and shaded by tall trees. All or nothing.

"Ashamoor needs me," she whispered. "You can do this."

She leaped forward. Her ankle twinged when her foot rolled on an unseen object.

Hopping to her other foot, she moved through the trail indentations the dragons had left in the brush. About twenty steps in, where the path forked, she picked the widest option and hoped Ashamoor had made the same choice.

The scene screamed fall. Early turning leaves among the evergreens would have been beautiful if not camouflaging a colorful dragon and whatever snakes the dragons hadn't eaten. At least it was quiet.

Blood was smeared against the base of a wide tree. Ellen gagged at the sight of scattered mice tails.

The trail ended at a pile of rocks covered by a family of sunbathing lizards. They bobbed their heads, staring. Ahead, a wall of brambles grew to her waist. She stared into the trees ahead. Ashamoor was small enough to slip through without making much damage. Ellen examined the ground around her. The base of a grass clump had been disturbed. Something had come this way.

"Ashamoor? Where are you?" She strained for a response. A small breeze rustled the leaves.

Nothing.

A whimper, or the whine of a distant bird, drew her to the right.

She pushed the dry grasses apart and stepped into the unknown.

Ten steps in, the rattle restarted.

Ellen turned in a slow circle. The noise came from all sides.

She tried to swallow and discovered a painfully dry mouth. She could run back to the path. There was water at the camp. And other dragons that would protect her if she could wake them up.

Another sound merged with the rattle.

A soft whine.

Ellen followed the sound another twenty feet off the beaten path, then dropped to her knees. She peered into the greenery surrounding a thick-trunked tree.

Ashamoor lay on her side, one foot caught in the jaws of a metal trap.

"Ashamoor, baby." She reached out.

The smallest dragon snapped at Ellen's hand with a flare of fire.

"Ow!" She rubbed at the hot skin on her fingers and tried to calm the little one. "It's all right, girl."

Ashamoor hissed.

Ellen sprawled on her stomach and froze. Neither one of them could freak out now. There would be plenty of freaking-out time later.

"I can help." The young dragon drew back another inch, her shoulders held her wings forward in a defensive pose.

Ellen tried to process a plan.

Any plan.

Ashamoor's stomach flattened at the middle, unlike the roundness the others boasted as they'd returned to camp.

Injured animal 101. "Are you hungry?"

Ashamoor didn't move. She didn't hiss either.

Ellen hurried down the trail to a point where she'd seen the lizards.

Unsure how to catch dragon food without a net or experience, she improvised.

She took off her top.

The morning breeze discovered the trickles of nervous sweat rolling down her back. She tossed the shirt over the rock and trapped a lizard.

Ellen held its body in one hand then peeled back her shirt a bit with the other. The lizard's head appeared, mouth wide and snapping.

"Sorry, dude. My baby has to eat."

Stickers and rocks met the skin on her stomach as she crawled back to Ashamoor.

Ellen held out the fresh meat.

Ashamoor snatched half of the lizard. Ellen gagged and tossed the other half in front of the youngster. The little dragon polished it off.

The lizard gone; the shirt forever stained with Ellen's first kill.

Ashamoor settled back on the trampled green vines and stared, her breaths calmed.

Ellen scooted closer to the fluttering wings. Heart pounding, she reached out inch by inch with one hand, cooing. "It's okay, Ashamoor. I'm going to try to free you. Please try not to incinerate me."

Ashamoor allowed the touch, but strained her neck, keeping watch. Ellen stroked the young one as if she were a cat on her lap on a lazy afternoon, instead of a dragon caught in a death grip.

"Good girl. You'll be fine." She reached out with her right hand toward the sword. Ashamoor's muscles tensed. "Don't freak out. I need to use this to free you."

Ellen decided to believe the baby dragon understood her. She moved closer to the trap.

The metal jaws were intended for much larger prey. Ashamoor's back leg had been caught near the hinge.

Ignoring the fact a fire-breathing dragon hissed inches

from her face, Ellen slipped the flat tip of the sword into the gap at the other end. A small growl rolled out of Ashamoor.

"This might hurt both of us." Ellen climbed to her knees for leverage, one hand on the hilt, the other on the trap. "One, two, three."

She twisted the blade and leaned in.

Ashamoor hissed a shot of flames near her leg. The metal wrenched open.

In a flash of color and pain, Ashamoor bolted free into the brush.

Ellen gasped.

White light exploded in her brain.

Her eyes squeezed shut. The darkness made it worse. She forced them open. The outside edge of her right hand was pinched in the hinge.

Her sword had wedged between the rows of teeth and stopped the metal sides from meeting. She caught the back of the trap under the heel of her shoe and twisted the blade with her left hand.

It didn't budge.

She leaned her weight forward. The metal opened enough to pull her hand and sword free.

Ellen held her hand above her heart and released a series of obscenities. They escalated into sobs.

She forced her heartbeat to slow through several minutes of prolonged inhales and exhales.

"Please don't let it be broken," she prayed as she built up the courage to look at her wound.

A large black mark outlined the pinch on each side of her hand between pinky finger and wrist. It had already swollen to twice its normal size.

Ellen wrapped her hand with the bloody shirt. She needed to get back to camp.

"Ashamoor, where are you?"

A small rustle sound proved either the young dragon remained close, or snakes surrounded her.

"Come on, baby." She tried to coo, but it sounded more like painful whining. "I don't know if there are any other traps. We have to get out of here. We both need help."

Ellen's hand pulsed in pain. She had to hurry. Either the hunter or what he hunted could come along at any time.

She crawled on her elbows. Stickers from the grass caught in her hair.

A tiny snout appeared.

Ashamoor licked at her injured leg, a small drizzle of blood seeping from under the scales.

"Please come with me." Ellen winced at the throbbing, worsened by lying on her stomach. "If your leg hurts anything close to what my hand does, you must sense we need help. Come with me."

Ashamoor stared, then lifted her head and opened her mouth. Ellen braced for the fire.

A tiny mew sound trickled out. Ashamoor sounded like a sad cat.

"Come, baby." She stretched out her uninjured hand. Ashamoor limped over and flicked out a long thin tongue, a sandpaper lick. She allowed Ellen to lift her from under her belly.

Ellen rolled over on her back, cuddling Ashamoor to her chest. She slid out of the brush and trekked back on the path.

Welglen's human eyes were on Ellen when she walked back into camp.

She laid the injured dragon at his feet. "Leave no dragon behind."

Ashamoor crawled toward the sleeping pile. Welglen blocked her path, running his thick calloused hand down the shining scales of the haunch. He paused at a smear of blood.

He slipped out of his clothes.

Welglen's chiseled back tucked in at his waist. His skin darkened and morphed into scales. It had been three days since she'd first seen his dragon self. She'd begun to think of him as human and intensely male. He doubled in size and glory to his full stature.

With a long tongue, he cleaned away the blood from the scales.

He waved at Ellen to stand back with a brisk nod of his massive head. He sprayed a thin stream of fire at the infant's wounds.

"Stop!" She stepped between them, covering Ashamoor with her body.

Welglen gently swatted her away with one wing. *Be still.*

Ashamoor whimpered, her breathing shallow.

"What have you done to her?"

I've only healed her. You saved her.

CHAPTER 34

Welglen rested the agitated young one among her nest mates. The other dragons circled her. She calmed and closed her eyes. The smallest dragon would survive the day, though due to her size, may not escape the next attack. He'd healed the infant in tribute to Ellen's courage. She was right. While unnatural to interfere, they must continue to evolve. There were far too few left to let the old ways eliminate even one more dragon.

He transformed back into human form, then covered them with thick pine branches.

Ellen tossed the blood-stained shirt into the fire as he dressed. Smoke billowed until the flames caught the fabric. She hadn't let fear keep her away from an injured dragon capable of ripping her skin to threads. She'd carried her charge back to safety. And the little one had let her.

Perhaps Slatetail had chosen wisely.

He sat at the fire's edge. Smoke blocked her face, though the bruises from the battle preparation were slashed with scratches from the undergrowth across her ribs.

She cradled her sword hand in the other and winced.

He moved to her side. A swollen black mark spread along the side of her palm. "What is it?"

"Hopefully only a mean blood blister." Her voice caught when she attempted to fold her hand into a fist. The thumb and first finger complied. The others remained still. She shivered and sat on a rock.

"What can I do?"

"I'm pretty sure your fire tricks aren't going to work on my skin." She squinted. "If you're offering, I could use an ice pack, a cold beer, and a clean shirt, in that order. I'm exhausted."

Welglen dug through her pack and located a folded shirt. She tenderly slipped her right hand in first, then stretched it over her head, unable to pull it down at her waist. She looked up at him and sighed.

He knelt and covered her skin. "I'll check the ice chest to see if there is anything that hasn't melted. I won't be able to provide you with ale."

"Toss me the first aid kit. I'll take an aspirin cocktail."

Welglen soaked a small towel in the cold water. She wrapped it around her hand, expressing some relief after she swallowed the tablets. "What caused your injury?"

"I caught it in the hinge of the trap when I freed Ashamoor. Luckily, I think it only hurt the fatty part of my hand. I don't think I broke anything."

"Do you anticipate this type of wound would take long to heal?"

Her voice rose. "Are you worried I won't be able to do my job?"

Yes, would answer her question. He sensed that her pain levels had combined with human emotions in a manner that would make her unresponsive to this line of conversation.

"I'm concerned with the amount of time you'll be in pain."

She adjusted the injured hand to a position above her heart. "Sorry I snapped. Now that Ashamoor's safe, the adrenaline's gone; all that's left is a throb like a son of a gun."

"Shh," Welglen hissed.

"I said sorry—"

He held out a palm to silence her and gazed out into the trees behind her.

Steps approached from the trail she'd returned on with the young dragon.

"Someone comes."

"What do we do?" she whispered.

"We don't have time to load the younglings into the vehicle. We will have to hope they stay quiet and hidden under the branches."

"And that no one has a baby dragon nightmare." She glanced around the camp. "What's our plan?"

"Keep your injury covered. We'll keep his attention at the fire." Welglen sat opposite from her, stretched out his long legs, and listened to the soft quick steps.

The man entered at the edge of the camp wearing the traditional colors of a human on a hunt trying to blend into the woods. He carried a large bag, bearing a small blood stain in one hand and a rifle in the other. The muzzle angled slightly down to appear not to be pointed at them, though close enough he could take a quick shot.

Welglen had seen the faces of human hunters. They either needed the food or sought the kill.

This one craved the kill.

"What do we have here?" The man's voice echoed in the quiet of the forest. He gazed over their camp from the pile of branches to the fire. "Are you some of those radicals from the valley trying to stir something up with us mountain folk?"

Welglen waved a hand. "Certainly not. We're camping

out." He reached behind him and picked up a large branch for the fire.

Ellen stared at the rifle.

The stranger moved closer to the heat, only feet from the pile. "My apologies."

Welglen pushed the branch into the fire. Tiny sparks snapped as the branch caught. "Can we offer you some food? We're about to start pulling it together, though it's unlikely it will be ready soon."

"I'm good." The hunter drew a small package out of his pocket. "A protein bar will get me back down to my Jeep. How long are you guys out here?"

Ellen smiled. "Two or three more days, right Glen?"

"About that. We wanted to leave the city for some peace." Welglen stirred the fire into a healthy blaze with a long stick. "I'm sure you understand."

The man smiled, opened the package, and took half the bar in one bite. Crumbs dropped on the shelf his stomach created when he sat. "It's a mess down there. People are going crazy thinking that our local industries have had anything to do with the mountain coming back to life." He stuffed the remainder in his mouth, then tossed the package into the fire and warmed his hands over the flames. "I've been tracking for hours. It's starting to get cold. I'm Rob."

He held his hand out and shook Welglen's.

"Glen and Ellen here," Welglen said. "You're a hunter. What are you tracking around here?"

The man's chest puffed out. "I've had some traps out in this brush to capture a mountain lion that's been eating the local chickens. You should be safe if you don't step too deep into the brush." He leaned his gun against the log. He appeared to try to look friendly, though the weapon stayed close. "Of course, why would you be crawling around in the brush?"

Ellen made a small laughing sound. "I hope you catch him soon. I'd hate to run into a mountain lion."

"I might have wounded him." The hunter scanned the pile on his left. "A trap snapped about a mile away. If I didn't know better, I'd swear someone let him go."

Ellen shrugged. "That's weird. How could anyone let a wild animal go without getting hurt?"

A gust of wind sent a cloud of dust across the camp. A bright red feather caught in the branch to the hunter's left. "I have no idea." He picked the feather out and examined it before stuffing it into his pocket. "Of course, I don't know for sure what I caught."

A gold feather flitted past his foot. It stuck in one of the branches covering the young ones.

The hunter pointed the rifle at the nest. "What've you got here?"

Welglen tucked one leg under the other, ready to lunge.

"Nothing," Ellen said loudly, then softened her voice, "just brush."

Welglen leaned back with arms behind his head in a non-aggressive stance. "What she means is my wife hates to go camping. She wouldn't agree to stay here unless I swept all the loose branches into a pile so she wouldn't have to worry about any little critters."

The hunter laughed and turned his back on the young ones. "I hear you, brother. I couldn't get my old lady out here without a generator for her hair dryer. Not that I mind. The mountains are for men."

Ellen opened her mouth. Welglen expected her to defend her outdoor skills. Instead, she said, "It's the little spiders I hate!" She held the towel over her hand. "And now you come to tell us there's a mountain lion on the loose. Honey, we need to find a nice hotel."

The hunter chuckled and stepped back toward the path.

The pile of brush rustled.

Welglen crouched, ready to spring, torn between transforming into his full force and battering the hunter with his bare human hands.

The hunter pointed his rifle at the nest. "There may be a little varmint in there after all, little lady. I'll take care of it."

Ellen jumped in front of the sleeping dragons. "Don't shoot." She grabbed at the gun, the towel falling off the injury on her other hand.

The hunter twisted her arm off the gun and aimed the weapon at her feet.

"Never step in front of a weapon." He looked at the swollen blackness on her palm. "If I didn't know better, I'd say you had your hand pinched in the hinge of a trap. It's happened to me often enough. What I want to know is what you released. Seeing as how it's rightly mine."

"Let her go."

The man released his grasp, then turned slowly, the end of the rifle still too close to Ellen. "No harm done here, mister. Let me have the critter she stole. We'll call it even."

Ellen stared at the barrel. "We have nothing of yours. Just leave… please."

Welglen sensed the tingle of vibration from the Earth. The abrupt jolt knocked the man to the left. A car alarm sounded in the distance.

Welglen tugged the gun out of his hands. He disarmed the hunter and pushed him to the ground in one movement. "As my wife said, we have nothing of yours."

"My mistake," the man scooted back in the dirt before standing. The blaring horn continued. "That's my Jeep alarm. If you'd kindly return my rifle, I'll be outta here."

Welglen didn't move. "I have a small problem with your request. I don't trust that you won't turn this on my woman again."

"You have my word. I have to go or that alarm will kill my battery. It's an old system."

"You can do better than that, can't you? What do you think, wife?"

Ellen moved to his side. "He did accuse me of stealing, twisted my arm, and threatened us with a gun. I'm not inclined to go back to victim. What do you think, Rob? What would you do in our place?"

"That rifle is worth a lot of money," he huffed. "You can't keep it."

She shook her head. "Rob, Rob, Rob. On the one hand, we're just a couple of lovebirds having a quiet camping trip and along comes a hunter with accusations and threats. On the other, keeping your gun doesn't feel right. How about this? You can have your gun back, but we get to keep your bullets."

"What do you want those for?"

"So you don't use them on us, duh!"

Ellen opened the backpack and set it on the ground. She reached for the rifle and fumbled through unloading it with her only usable hand. She collected the bullets lining the hunter's vest and bag. "Good thing I took a hunter's safety course when I was sixteen. See you."

The man jogged down through the brush swearing.

She steadied herself against Welglen. "Next time, you can play the dumb blonde and I'll be your protector."

He moved to the edge of the camp, listening to the hunter's steps.

Ellen stood beside him. "Think he'll be back?"

"Yes."

"We have to get out of here. It's all my fault. If I'd stayed in camp, this wouldn't have happened."

"You had no choice but to save a dragon." It had been the only human option.

"But my sword hand is worthless."

True. To save one, she may have risked the survival of all.

CHAPTER 35

Ellen squeezed the steering wheel with her left hand and trapped her right hand above her heart in pledge mode. Her eyes stung against the dashboard lights. The road had disintegrated into parallel ruts. They needed a place remote enough where she could heal, and the babies could fly.

Welglen flew above on the pretense of searching for a campground. He didn't want to be trapped in the van during this rough ride. By his flight, they could've been at Josh's in less than an hour. If they were driving on the highway, it would take about three.

She'd been on this rough trail for hours. At this point she suspected she was getting further away.

Welglen disappeared for moments at a time as he circled in a series of rolls. Moonlight reflected against the glorious white skin of his under-wings. Easy to imagine the first dragons being mistaken for guardian angels—protecting humans and ferrying them to heaven.

The angelic vision didn't completely fit Ellen's vision of Welglen. She'd love to wrap her arms around that hot rascal. Of course, she'd never have a future with him, being a dragon and all. But he did have some nice man parts. And they all appeared to be working.

The van drifted off center, spinning in the deeper gravel at the edge of the narrow road.

"Whoa, girl!" Ellen jerked the wheel back toward center. "Wake up—you're dreaming." She had enough to worry about without going gaga over a dragon. She should be thinking of Josh.

She could count on her ex. Josh accepted things. Even strange things . . . and sad things. After she'd left, he'd kept in touch, checking in.

She'd avoided his calls after a routine visit to her gynecologist changed Ellen's life plans. She'd needed time to absorb the devastating news and the irony of why she'd left him.

He took the hint. His calls relaxed to once a month. The last message said he wouldn't bother her again unless she called him.

Rattling metal cages announced the dragons were awake. They sounded hungry, and by the intensity of the growls, they were frustrated being back in the cages.

"It's okay, babies." She turned up the radio, hoping they were fans of country music—the only station that came through clearly. "I'm sure we'll be stopping soon."

They're awake? Welglen's voice penetrated her brain. Ellen jerked the steering wheel.

"I forgot you could do that." She tried to clear her head of earlier thoughts. "How long have you been listening?"

I have kept watch to see that my flight is safe. There is no option for a secure camp in this area. Can you continue driving?

"I guess I have to," relieved he hadn't mentioned her other thoughts. "I'm tired and getting pretty punchy."

I'll fly a greater distance ahead to find a spot and circle back.

He dipped in front, then soared out of sight.

"I'll have to watch my fantasies," she told the rumbling dragons. "Perhaps I should be clear, I'm only imagining what a character in my place might be thinking."

She needed to focus on a possible fight. It wasn't like she was headed for the state sword competition. On that trip, she'd be thinking of placing—taking away a ribbon or a medal.

In this challenge, winner would literally take all.

An evil sorcerer's impending world domination and her potential death was another daydreaming option.

In her sleep-deprived state, it was easier to dwell on whether she and Josh had a chance together. "How self-absorbed would I be to believe that maybe this entire bizarre reality is fate's way to bring us back together?"

Ellen imagined a romantic reunion that for some reason played in slow motion. Josh running toward her, his long brown hair blowing in the breeze.

The cages rattled against each other.

Hungry dragons weren't happy dragons. Music or promises of being almost there wouldn't pacify them. They'd passed the tree line and the headlights outlined the large boulders along the road.

Welglen soared past and guided her to the left.

Five minutes off the road, he signaled for her to stop in a clearing. He swooped gracefully to the ground. He transformed to naked male in the beams of her headlights. She shut off the engine and with it the artificial energy that had kept her awake.

He opened the back of the van and in moments freed the babies. She leaned her head back and closed her eyes.

She jerked awake when he opened the driver's side door and lifted her out.

Comforted by his touch, she allowed him to place her on one of the cool boulders. Stone had never felt so comfortable.

Ellen slipped out of the sleeping bag Welglen must have provided. She'd dozed a couple of times, but real sleep wasn't going to happen when her mind was so busy. Her hand throbbed each time it dropped below her heart. She stirred the low fire. Welglen clearly had no trouble starting a campfire. The babies were out of sight feeding, and her dragon kept watch above her in the crisp night air.

She scrawled a few lines into her journal with her non-dominant hand, then squinted at the page in the dim firelight. Completely illegible. She stuffed it back into her pack, placed a small log on the fire, and stared at the brilliant stars.

Key figures in history who started out with nothing and ended up either world leaders, entertainers, or literary phenoms, all had that "certain indescribable something." How often had the answer been the powers of the light?

And aliens gave the light to humans?

The flames grew taller. "I'm going to pretend aliens aren't real for now. This is a completely different story line. There aren't enough compartments in my brain to deal with both dragons and aliens at the same time. My mind's already blown."

Sorcerers, on the other hand, were the topic of the day. Ellen paced across the circle of light, thinking through the story lines to nail down focus.

Not everyone who accepted the powers went on to become a sorcerer bent on world domination—Martin Luther King, Moses, and Gandhi would probably make the good guys' list. Each had an ability to convince others of the goodness in man.

Dictators who used genocide probably topped the list of those who might have used the light against the world.

She paced outside of the fire's warmth. Cold air cut through her sweatshirt, bumping her back to reality. She dug out the metal pot, adding water and coffee. It fit on a small rock she pushed into the edge of the flames to heat.

Welglen flew low over the camp.

You must sleep. Your human body cannot respond to what is ahead if you don't store your energy.

"Tell that to my mind." She willed the pot to perk. "I can't stop thinking about all my little-girl dreams. I don't remember you appearing, but the young ones were there, particularly Ashamoor. I saw their colors, their shapes, the turns of their eyes, and every time, they needed me. I'm not sure if I helped them or if I imagined it in my writer's mind. Right now, I can't tell the difference between my dreams, and my stories. What if Slatetail left me the solution to help the dragons, and I mixed it up in my fiction? Maybe the secret to removing the light is in my head."

As the humans say, you are a hot mess.

"Thanks a lot, Yoda." She positioned the coffee pot closer to the heat. "Later I'd love to hear more about the old sorcerers building their stone fortresses. Tell me what you know about this Nilrem dude. Why you think he's the sorcerer after us."

Welglen glided above her, then narrowed his circle to stay within the range of their camp.

I saved the life of the son he wanted dead.

"You're telling me this now? A sorcerer with a dragon-vendetta is kind of a big deal. Explain!"

When I first saw Nilrem's son, Trigore, he hung from a peg nailed into a tree. His bindings dripped with excrement; his face chapped from the summer winds. I watched from a tree. Each night a woman would take him into the house. Each morning, she would refasten him to the peg and offer a small amount of goat's milk before going about her work, out of sight of the young one. I chased away predators and kept him safe, speaking softly and soothing his mind. He understood I existed to protect him. He had screamed his last sounds days before, leaving him with only whimpers.

"That's horrific! Child endangerment."

Merely the way. Children required hands. When caretakers were busy, the children needed to be kept out of reach of some dangers. When Nilrem and an old woman walked to the tree where the boy hung, he'd asked 'He's still alive so many days after his birth killed his mother? I don't need another son. Particularly this one. I have seven others.'

'You want me to snap his neck?' the woman had offered. 'Nay,' he'd said. 'I'll not bring the wrath of the great one down on my prosperity for this one. His survival will be his own.'

I provided shade, water, and sprigs of herbs for days until his body cooled enough to cry. Nilrem caught me at the child's side. 'Usurper! Pagan! You have interfered with the fates. Be gone!'

He threw rocks at me that bounced back on the babe, then carried Trigore into the castle. I didn't see him for years until the familiar pull led me to his side where he nearly drowned in the stream trying to keep up with his older brothers. Young Trigore craved the love of his father, though I believe he understood his father wanted him dead. Nilrem exploded when he caught me protecting his son again. I learned to keep out of sight during the years as I watched over and protected him from his older brothers' rough antics.

Nilrem has never forgiven me for protecting the son that killed his wife.

"What happened to Trigore?"

Trigore's desire to please his father never diminished. Though we were bound by the connection of the Earth, he chose to fight alongside his father in the last great war. I don't know how it ended for him. I was already gone.

"That adds another layer of crap. Not only does he want eternity . . . he can't stand you."

CHAPTER 36

Welglen patrolled the cold night sky above their small camp where only a few shrubs managed to scratch out life against the bald landscape. The tree line to the south wrapped the nape of the mountain in a fringe of forest where the young ones hunted.

The first ones returned and circled into a pile at a distance from Ellen's low fire, where she reclined in her sleeping bag against a boulder, sipping hot coffee. She lifted her head in their direction, ensuring all were accounted for. Since her thoughts often drifted to the odd, and blurred the lines between realities, he avoided listening without her awareness—less unsettling for them both.

The remaining dragons arrived moments later and moved to the others.

Except for the smallest. She settled alone, in the rocks nearest Ellen.

A yellow female lifted her head and stared at the odd pair. She pulled out of the group, causing a ripple of snarls. She resettled against the tiny female near Ellen.

One by one, the entire flight moved to form a protective crescent between Ellen and the darkness beyond the firelight.

A most unusual bond.

Welglen admitted to a similar pull. Last night he'd cradled her in his arms briefly for comfort—the first intimate human touch. It consoled her, and his human shell found it pleasant. But this preoccupation his flight mates shared for this human's safety, and her focus scattered between her mate, her ability to have children, and a preoccupation with his maleness, drew them away from their true purpose.

Though she was temporarily a member of the flight, there could be no confusion in his identity—no more a man than she a dragon.

Only the flight's survival mattered.

Welglen soared away from the group. He focused on the piece of time remaining before he would face the sorcerer.

He needed the spell.

Welglen rose higher and let the life energies of the ancestors envelop him in warmth. He would need to feel their presence to take his mind back to the stories of his youth.

He forced his thoughts back further, to his earliest years. A distant vision of flights with his nest mates and the constant training from the elders. It had been too long since he had been part of a family, flying together. Always, with the teaching chants of the elders.

Snow dusted the distant mountaintop. Years since he'd seen snow fall. A vision of the cooling flakes remained etched in his youngest memories of fire and ice. Roglir had knocked him into the snowbank. Welglen had blasted his way out with his new flames and tackled his older brother, rolling together down the slope. His brother always a little quicker, a little stronger. Always there for him.

Welglen spread his wings parallel to the world below. He drifted in slow circles chanting the old rhythms and searching for a time when the elder dragons reared the young on secrets. He had the knowledge of pulling the light from a sorcerer in his mind; he only had to find it beneath the stories of a dragon's half lifetime.

Soaring into a cover of clouds, he sent his mind back to the past.

Pain registered first.

Tacoma's last moments jolted into his mind and transferred him back in time.

They swirled side by side trying to frighten the humans back down the path with great waves of wings and flames igniting the few remaining pieces of brush. The burning glow below shown against her bright scales. Her eyes reflected the fierce joy she took in battle.

In the flat near the forest's edge, sorcerers gathered behind their human shields. Together their strength commanded the entire village. They chanted spells bending the humans that surrounded them to fear dragons. Once the sorcerers consumed the dragon hearts, their partnership with humans would end in a bloody siege.

Tacoma released a fearful cry and rushed to separate the sorcerers by fire.

Wait for the others. Welglen cried.

There's no time. It's our chance to drive them away from the humans.

The villagers lobbed burning masses from slingshots, filling the air with sulfuric smoke and debris.

Tacoma darted around the obstacles. Welglen flew cover, as she widened the gap between the humans and the sorcerers. Burning tar singed her wings, the trail of smoke filled his nostrils.

She wound between the sorcerers, igniting anything flammable with precise threads of flame. She'd created a break in their spell.

The sorcerers scattered. The air volleys halted. The humans looked to each other for purpose.

Tacoma swooped to torch an escape route of two fleeing sorcerers.

A lone human drew back his bow.

Tacoma! On your left! Go!

I do what I must.

Tacoma drove the sorcerers back into the open.

The arrow split her breast before Welglen could reach her.

The present returned to Welglen in a chill of icy winds.

He had no answers, no spell. From his memory, Tacoma had seen only one way through. Like her, without the powers to pull the light from the sorcerer, only one option remained.

Sacrifice.

He would need to separate the young dragons and offer himself to the sorcerer. If he didn't, they would all die. They couldn't count on one injured human to save all dragons.

He hadn't been able to save a warrior like Tacoma. He prayed he'd be enough to save a human.

CHAPTER 37

The deep-green female climbed onto a boulder. She stretched and flapped her glorious wings in a slow-motion dragon Tai Chi. Ellen mimicked the movements with her left arm. Swollen to the size of a mitt, her right hand didn't cooperate.

She sat next to the edge of the dwindling campfire, prepared to brave a peek at her injury. She needed to know if her future included a two-handed plan.

Welglen transformed behind her.

She raised her arm. "I guess it's time to see how bad this is." He dressed quickly and sat next to her, pulling on his boots.

Each length of wrap left tiny indentations against her puffed skin. The tips of her smallest two fingers had turned a deep red shade, which darkened to purple in a path along her fingers to the palm. A black stripe highlighted both sides of her hand.

She tried to make a fist. Only three fingers complied, sending a sharp pain along her forearm.

Ellen squeezed her eyes closed and focused on deep breaths.

"Whew," she whispered when the pain cleared enough to see again. "I guess it could be worse. The nasty teeth of that hunter's trap missed breaking my skin. I'm not sure if the little bones in my hand are broken or not, but the color is gruesome. On the plus side, no apparent gangrene, blood poisoning, or amputation necessary."

"I worry about your ability to hold the Sword of Srekums." Welglen studied her hand.

"And there's that." She leaned back and elevated her hand back across her chest. "I have to believe it's going to get better. I can't bear the thought of everything that failure stands for. Help me get this wrapped. It felt a little better with soft pressure. What I really need is an ice pack."

Welglen rewrapped her hand, following her directions for tightness.

She cradled the redressed hand against her chest. "Let's talk about success. What's going to happen after the sorcerer? I mean, let's say we win. What will we do?"

Welglen sat across from her. "I'll disappear with the flight until they are safe to live alone."

"And me? What will I do?"

He poked at the coals in the fire, stirring a flash of sparks. "You're human and thus must remain with your own kind. There's no choice."

Welglen's comment made sense—practical and realistic.

It also sucked. "I hear what you believe. What do you want?"

Welglen's head cocked slightly to one side, like he tried to understand her question.

"I mean, if you had a choice for how you would spend the rest of your life? What would you pick?"

"The past I grew up in is gone. It can't be resurrected.

I'll move forward and complete whatever is required, until I'm not needed anymore."

"That's it? Throw me a bone here. You've lived as a human for centuries. Is there anything you hope will be different from today on?"

Welglen turned away. "I would prefer in whatever future fate brings me, I'm not alone."

Loneliness she understood. Any vision of a future without dragons was Ellen's worst nightmare. She followed his gaze across the fire. The aqua-blue male stretched at the edge of camp, then crouched, his focus on the deep-green female, her wings extended to the sun.

The male bounced behind her and nipped at her back leg. They swung into a squawking blur, tussling, and rolling in the loose dirt. The female hissed and raised her wings back to the sky.

Ellen punched her good hand into the air. "You go, girl! Did you see that? She doesn't take crap from the boys."

"It's a good sign. They'll need leaders."

Ellen reclined against her backpack. "They have you."

"That will not always be so. I'm much older. The battle ahead may not go well."

"Okay!" Ellen waved her good hand in front of her. "That's it. We need to go back over our plan. We need a plan B, C, D, and however many others ensure we survive."

"We're getting closer to your Josh. If we're truly safe there, we might have enough time for the young ones to start to fly. They're safe in the air. Flight is their only hope."

"What do we do if the sorcerer arrives, and the babies can't fly?"

Welglen dug into the food box. He opened a protein bar and handed it to Ellen.

"First, I'll have to split them. Together, they're a large target. Their number is greater than needed, which increases the chances the sorcerer will achieve immortality and slaughter the rest. I can't divide them if they can't fly."

A chill rushed over Ellen—a vision of young dragons in danger.

Scared she could manage. Scared to death, not so much. "Then what?"

"I'll use all my strength to keep the sorcerer engaged. While I can't attack, I'll be able to use my flames as a protective wall. If we can keep the sorcerer away from hearts long enough, and if I'm able to learn the spell, I may be able to pull the light from his being."

The morning sun sliced behind the trees, sending the colors of the mountain into an orange haze. "A con job." Ellen eyed the babies, their roughhousing growing louder. "Only, in this con, if we don't win, someone dies?"

Welglen tore into another piece of beef jerky. He washed it down with water before he answered.

"When you meet him, he'll be human. You can stop a human. If not, with each dragon heart the sorcerer consumes, he'll change and strengthen. Once he bites into the third, I'll have my chance."

"That isn't a plan. I haven't come all this way to sacrifice them." Her voice squeaked. She shook her head trying to dislodge the picture of losing even one. "You have to remove his power before that happens."

"I'll try. If it works, there'll be a moment where the sorcerer will no longer have the protection of his humanity and isn't yet immortal. If I'm alive, I can kill him."

"If?" She hadn't considered Welglen's death.

He leaned against the boulder near her legs. "As a dragon, I'll be, at some point, at his mercy. I'll have to trust you'll be there for the others."

"I'll do whatever I can." She rubbed at her tender fingers. "I hope it'll be enough."

"There is one more service I ask of you. Once a sorcerer has killed me and is about to eat my heart, you must stop him. Destroy the heart so he must start the hunt again."

Watch him die, then destroy his heart?

"Don't you mean if? You said when." The crap piled to a new high.

A pair of wrestling dragons stirred a cloud of dust at Welglen's feet.

Ellen flattened the sleeping bag and propped it up against the boulder for a view of the dragon show. Hope lived with them.

They woke one or two at a time. Instead of rushing back out to hunt, most joined the largest two in a game of king of the hill. By the time the rest of the flight was awake, only Ashamoor and four other small dragons had chosen to stay at Ellen's side over the mosh pit.

Ellen stroked Ashamoor's head. The little dragon leaned into her touch. "The babies are jacked up."

"That's the way. They'll fight each other as training. As it was with you, before your injury. Your powers with the sword were much improved after only a few days. Perhaps in another day or two you'll be able to train again." Welglen patted Ellen's good hand, which struck her as only slightly awkward. His attempts at human comfort improved daily.

Four of the dragons circled the green female, teasing her with a nip at her wing or a step on her tail. She kept her hold on the top of the pecking order. Her reflexes were fast, snapping back and chasing the others away. Ellen envied her obvious enjoyment. "I need to know if there's another option that doesn't involve me sticking my sword through someone. Any hope all this will turn out well?"

"It's possible. We'll continue to draw the battle away from other humans and their cities. The distance may help."

"My life isn't special in the grand scheme of world events, but it's mine. I don't like it being reduced to days." Ellen sipped at the last of the cold coffee and focused on the babies, tired of hearing about time running out.

The blue male pushed the green female onto her back and nipped her neck—she pushed him off. Flapping her wings to force him back, she rose a foot off the ground.

She screeched and dropped to the dirt; eyes wide.

Ellen clutched Welglen's arm.

The young dragon spread her wings again, posed. She slowly raised them to the sky and in a single fluid movement, hovered.

She leaned forward and flew across the camp, tumbling in a rough landing against the brush.

Rolling back to her feet, she screeched a flame of fire to the sky.

"Oh my." Ellen clapped at the lump in her throat, unaware Welglen had transformed until the breeze from his takeoff blew hair into her face.

He dropped low over the ground, nuzzling the new flyer, encouraging her to try again. She followed him across, landing with a stumble. The other dragons flapped and jumped in a frenzy of wings and tails. The large blue male took flight, then crash-landed into four others, knocking them over like bowling pins.

Welglen called to them from the sky above. The group of dragons lifted off the ground, hovering or taking their first short flights, zigzagging into each other.

The green female soared highest, following Welglen's calls, while the blue male screeched from below as he tried to catch her. He collapsed near the fire, panting.

Ellen rose, clapping her hands high. "That was beautiful."

A soft shake pulled her attention back to the Earth. She steadied against the large rock, her focus darting between the babies around her and Welglen above until the ground stilled. She let out a long breath.

A jolt knocked her back to the ground.

Her knees smacked the rough surface with enough force to reopen the scabs. Blood stuck to her jeans.

The young dragons surrounded her.

"It's okay," Ellen cooed. "It'll stop soon."

It grew sharper.

She pressed her bandaged hand to her chest and bounced helplessly on top of the rocks on her knees. "What do we do?" A crack in the ground opened at the edge of the fire, molten steam escaping over a red hue.

Go! Take the smallest that haven't attempted flight. Find shelter with your human. I'll lead the remaining further into the mountain. You'll not see me, yet I'll be close.

CHAPTER 38

Fly or die.

Welglen commanded the straggly group north, flying a wing's breath above the ground to ensure all could follow. The small dragons bounced across the warming earth, taking their first flights in short spurts past steaming cracks.

In the mad dash to distance themselves from camp, they'd stretched into a long line. Strongest of the flight, the green female and blue male flew beside him. Others sunk lower, until they dropped to the ground, exhausted. The last ran over the surface with mad flaps generating occasional short bursts of flight. It would only buy time if they kept off the ground.

Welglen picked up the two slowest in his claws. He tore past the bedraggled line of flyers, rising high into the winds. He dropped them on a current above the green and blue flyers. The flow should allow them to glide for several miles in the correct direction.

He dove back, counting down dragons to the slowest pair, waddling across the ground, far from the others. He swooped down and grabbed them.

An explosion of steam erupted into the air and pelted his underwings with debris. The young dragons squirmed in his grasp. Welglen spiraled, his back taking blows. The hot, stinging rocks forced the memories of his last flight with Tacoma into his skull. She'd been more on his thoughts in the last days than the last decades. She'd been skilled and strong. The strength of her courage led to her death.

He spiraled clear of the threats. The young ones shook, shocked by their injuries.

Welglen flew past the others for a safe spot to put them down. They didn't have the strength to hold their wings open to the currents.

Clusters of short-needled pine trees spread across the rugged mountains scattered with human homes on the south and west sides. At the tip of a desolate hill, he spotted the dark opening of a cave. The stillness of the area proved the location was, at least for now, outside the sorcerer's reach.

He flew ahead and settled the two smallest in their temporary nest. The flying rocks had drawn blood, but the cuts weren't severe. He used a low healing flame to seal their wounds.

The green female circled over the cave. She'd displayed remarkable skill in flight. The blue male had done well in his attempt to keep up with her, though from his slumped posture, was at the end of his energy. Ten young dragons staggered to the cave on their own power.

Welglen directed his thoughts to the young female. He had to rely on her. *I'll return for the weakest, then tend to the wounds. Watch over the smallest.*

Only when Welglen carried the last two dragons to the small spring near the opening, did the young female move her guard duty from the air to the ground. She looked to Welglen for direction.

He nosed further into the cave, using low flames to light the deep interior.

A large den of mice scattered between the legs of the young ones for hiding holes. The exhausted dragons pounced on their first meal of the day.

One mouse neared freedom at the entrance. The lead female scooped it up and swallowed.

Rest little one. You have done well today. She joined the flight, still jostling into a sleeping pile. She chose a spot at the edge, nearest the opening.

He squatted outside the mouth of the low sanctuary. The cool air flowing over his back smelled of years of rodent habitation, coupled with a fresh kill, and mixed with the smoke creeping in from outside.

A low rolling sound vibrated from the lowlands. The sorcerers hunted. The knowledge that the lava preceded the sorcerer's arrival, coming in jolts, provided the only solace on this still spot.

Would he know the face of the sorcerer coming for them? The line of sorcerers Tacoma had died trying to separate from the humans etched in his brain. Some had likely been killed by the others. He couldn't be certain after so many years, though he suspected if Nilrem had survived, he'd be the first to find them. He was the sorcerer with the greatest hate for dragons, and for Welglen.

He relaxed the first covers of his eyes, blocking the dust churning from the earth by the winds. He'd fly into the skies after the green female had time to rest. He'd fly high enough to join close to his ancestors to learn how to pull the light from a sorcerer.

He gazed upward, slipping into a conscious point, neither dragon nor human; simply being.

The creators of the light bestowed the privileges Nilrem and other sorcerers had used for evil. He needed to learn how to reverse the process.

Welglen had been weaned on stories of the past—battles, spells, bravery. The spell of how to pull the light would've been part of his flight's history, along with so many others. He needed help to pull the single story out of lessons that covered centuries. If the last battle hadn't ended abruptly, he'd have witnessed the spell in action.

The young dragons quieted. They could use days to recover and strengthen. Though the longer they stayed, the closer the sorcerer would creep.

What of the others? Had Ellen made it to safety with the smallest? Would she recover in time to fight?

Before her injury her sword skills had increased. Her belief in the lives of dragons also strengthened her cause. Yet she had no knowledge of offense. She'd need to know how to attack.

If she were with him, they would talk it through to find a solution together.

Welglen opened his eyes to the stars above him.

How odd.

In a few short days Ellen had become part of his dangerous journey. Part of him. He wished her here to help.

Perhaps living two lives for so long had created two souls.

One dragon. One man.

Niks Kukar. Niks Kukar. He chanted and matched a breath with each repetition, praying the ancestors would hear his call. If he were able to calm his thoughts in this hazardous environment, he might see what was already inside him.

Niks Kukar. Niks Kukar.

CHAPTER 39

The front right tire bumped over a large rock and jerked the steering wheel out of Ellen's one-handed grasp. She forced the van back into the rough parallel ruts disguised as a road.

Crap. It was like the earthquakes, all over again. She didn't have a choice. She couldn't slow down. Five baby dragons needed her.

She needed Welglen.

The babies growled over the squeaking shocks, and the scratching of branches against the sides of the van. Unable to pile together without sliding between metal walls, they'd dug their claws into the seat backs for support during the kidney-busting drive.

Dragon drool dripped down her side of the seat, sticking her back against the vinyl.

She shouted over the rumble. "Sorry guys. I have to get us out of here."

And, of course, we need gas.

It had taken the last two bags of beef jerky to lure Ashamoor and the other four small dragons back into the van. The earthquakes slowed from constant to random, the further away she drove from their camp.

A dual anxiety brewed. She was closing in on the time she'd need to face her ex-boyfriend.

With a cargo of baby dragons.

The road forked. Ellen took the arm leading away from the setting sun. If correct, she'd link to the county highway.

Short brown grass blurred the edges of the fire road.

The road dipped downhill. She slowed into a grove of trees.

A yellow metal gate crossed her path. It wasn't attached to a fence at either end. Ellen got out and walked around the front of the van. Past the gate, the already worthless road narrowed even more. To the right, a thick batch of trees completely blocked off the route. On the left, there were no trees, but a litter of large rocks.

She might be able to drive over them.

Going back wasn't an option. She couldn't turn around. She couldn't drive the hill in reverse.

"Hold on, kids." Ellen buckled, angled left, and pulled out of the ruts. She gave it a spurt of gas. The van tilted, right side high, as the front tire rolled onto a boulder.

She tapped, then released the brake. They rolled down, the underside scraping against the rough surface. Ellen winced through the sound of metal on rock. "If that broke through the oil pan, we've had it."

They jerked to the right. The front left tire climbed.

The van rocked and knocked her head against the window.

"Ah!" She gritted her teeth, plowing through the uneven hillside.

The back wheels reached the same rocks and nosed the van down, then forward.

Ellen lined up on the road and rolled down the path a few feet before stopping to check for damage.

The bump on her head above her left ear was smaller than the one at the back of her head, from her living-in-a-basement-during-earthquakes fiasco.

She cracked open the driver's side door. The dragons pushed against her side to get out.

"Hang on, guys. We're almost there. I have to check things." She pushed an elbow out against the largest dragon and slipped out the door. All five pressed steaming faces against the glass.

She circled the van. The fender area on the left side sported a crumple not there during the ten-point inspection when she'd rented the van. Explaining that would be interesting. She didn't have any mechanical experience, but nothing visibly leaked onto the grass. That had to be good news.

She pushed her way back in.

Fifty or sixty feet through the trees, the view opened to the familiar country road below.

Ellen stopped at a lookout point and exhaled. Civilization.

The sun had just set. The small town ahead should have glowed on the horizon. The only light came from scattered fires.

A few cars passed her, heading south. She took the first exit through the tree-lined road, her headlights illuminating broken branches and two downed power lines. One power pole lay across the top of a garage.

At the bottom of the incline, the first signs of life appeared.

Ellen slowed near a home and cracked the window open. The air was acrid with smoke. The hum of a generator slowed as the lights of a barn turned on.

She rolled the window up and drove the narrow valley into the darkened main street of Dunsmuir. Toward the south end, regular service continued. A gas station sign blinked ahead. A few people gathered in the parking lot of an adjoining mini mart.

"At least I'm not the only human left on the planet."

Two cars were parked at the pumps, filling up. Ellen rated her options. She could circle town a couple of times in the hopes of an empty station. She'd look conspicuous cruising the narrow, empty main street. And the fuel light had been blinking for the past ten miles.

The back windows were heavily tinted. No one could see in that direction. If anyone glanced through the front, they'd receive an eyeful.

The fuel light won. She turned into the gas station next to an open Jeep.

A large black dog began a rhythmic deep bark that sounded like canine for 'look boss, there's dragons.' A series of snarls answered from behind her.

Ellen held her hands at the seat belt buckle and watched, engine running. A stocky bearded guy came out of the store with a brown paper sack wrapped tightly in the shape of a bottle, and a lottery ticket. He yelled a single word that quieted the dog, then stopped briefly to meet her gaze before starting the Jeep.

She expected the look any character would give to a stranger in their town. He grinned in recognition.

Hard to miss Josh's crazy neighbor Dirk in his loud shirts. She waved with her good hand and waited for him to pull out.

She pleaded with the dragons.

"If you can understand me, staying out of sight would be good. I can have us out of here in a couple of minutes." They grunted in response to her woman-to-dragon talk and huddled together, apparently satisfied by the stillness of the van.

Ellen slipped out, closed the door, and started the pump. It would take time to fill the large double tanks.

The station attendant restacked boxes of air filters scattered in front of the register. He glanced out the station window at her, then returned to work.

A thick layer of dead bugs curtained part of the front window. The hose clicked off and Ellen started the second tank. Halfway to free.

"Hello."

"Uh!" Ellen swung to face a sheriff. The plump, dark-haired officer had an arresting set of clear blue eyes. She took in the clean lines of his jaw, muscular chest, and stress level. "You startled me."

"Sorry miss. Can I ask where you're coming from? Our communication systems are down. We're trying to figure out how widespread the extent of the earthquake damage is."

Ellen moved toward the bucket with the windshield cleaner, so his back would be to the van.

"I've been camping a little south of here. The earthquakes freaked me out. I decided to come down to a friend's house."

"You were in the mountains alone? Those are some serious scratches you've got there."

"Yeah, one of the shakes knocked me to the ground. I managed to trip into a berry bush. I think I might have sprained something in my hand." Ellen tugged her sleeve down to her wrist. One of the dragons leaned across the steering wheel and gazed out. *Stay put!* "I'm a writer, so alone time works. It was great until the ground moved under me."

He nodded, accepting the oddness of writers. "Any sign of volcanic activity?"

"Not that I could tell. I camped deep in tall trees. I probably wouldn't know volcano action if I saw it." She shook the excess water off the scrubber. "I don't know anything about volcanoes. I do know an earthquake when I feel one. I'd say at least a five-point-five."

Behind the officer's head, Ashamoor and the blue-green female peered out between the gaps in the seats. No amount of insect splatters could hide their toothy faces. The pump clicked off and Ellen's heartbeat pounded at her neck. Ashamoor climbed over the seat and sat behind the wheel.

"So, officer..." she leaned against the trash can, "I don't know about you, but I'm so nervous about all of this."

"Are you going far?"

"Not at all; my friend lives nearby."

"Drive safely."

"Thank you." Ellen waited until he walked back to his patrol car before she squeezed into the van, pushing Ashamoor aside. She started the engine with a sigh of relief.

The attendant stared open-mouthed at the dragon riding shotgun.

Holding her breath wouldn't make her invisible. She exhaled and shifted into gear. She rolled past the young man with a forced smile and wave designed to illustrate normalcy.

He lifted his hand halfway up. In the mirror, Ellen watched him shake his head and return to work. He couldn't understand what he had seen, so he decided he hadn't seen it.

Had she ever been that human?

Ellen drove the few blocks through the end of town, then turned to climb the hill. She passed Dirk's Jeep at a turnout, empty of dog and the bearded one.

Months had passed since she'd driven the opposite way on this road, fueled by early success and a desire for a family.

High beams lighted the darkness. She slipped into low gear to maneuver around a downed water tank and counted the driveways. She reached the wrought iron gate Josh had created during his metal phase. That was followed by his wood-carving phase, then ceramics.

His new phase could be anything since the time she'd turned down his offer to live with him, grow pot without a license, make goat cheese, and never grow up.

The last day she'd spent with him, they'd celebrated her first substantial royalty check. He'd wanted to spend it on new pot plants they'd grow next to the house they rented from his uncle. She'd wanted to save it for their own place, and invest in her writing and his art.

That's when she learned he didn't want to turn his art into a business. And he never wanted children. She'd made her plans to leave that night. She wouldn't be a permanent part of his ongoing childhood.

She slid out of the van, pushing a dragon head back inside. They wanted out. They were hungry.

She walked over to the latch. A purple bike lock held the gate closed.

The van rocked behind her as the dragons fought to get outside. The hinged end of the gate looked low enough to climb over. She'd never get the dragons to follow her. Once she opened the van, they'd be gone for hours. Josh needed to see them, to believe them.

The numerical lock had four digits. Josh wasn't a complicated guy. She entered his birthday 1208. Then 0420 for his favorite marijuana holiday. His address. None worked.

She entered her birthdate and the lock opened.

Good sign.

Ellen pushed the gate wide, blocking it open with a large round rock. After driving through, she fought her way in and out of the van again to close the gate.

"I hope he's home."

In daytime, the view from the hill showed off the tree-covered canyon.

In the dark, only thick branches were visible from the narrow dirt drive. The three-room log cabin sat at the top of the property. In front, there were openings cut within the forest for his gardens.

They passed the large barn. The dragons fell into hissy fits as the scents of goats, ducks, and chickens blended with the wild animals that likely included mountain lions, raccoons, and black bear.

Her cargo was ready to hunt.

Light poured from the front door. The tall thin figure of her ex-boyfriend appeared on the wide porch. A rifle slung over one arm signified it must be near harvest. She slipped out of the van and into the light so he could see her. His first words would mean so much.

"Hello, Josh."

He squinted into the headlights with eyes she knew were the lightest of browns. Then he smiled.

"Sugar, you're back!" He leaned the rifle against the house and rushed toward her. He gathered her up and spun her, feet off the ground, creating a comfortable sensation of coming home. His scruffy beard rubbed against her cheek. She clung to his tightly muscled shoulders.

Ellen laughed and wiggled her way back to the ground, struggling with where to start. The shocks screeched. The dragons threatened to rock the van over.

"I have to make this fast, so prepare yourself. In that car, I have five young dragons who I have been trying to save from a sorcerer I'm prophesized to kill, to save the entire species of dragons. And they're hungry."

She had left the dome light on so that Josh could see through the windshield where five dragon heads bounced. He glanced at her, back at the van, and laughed. "What do we do with them?"

Living in a fantasy world comes in handy sometimes. "We have to let them out so they can feed. They'll eat rodents, snakes. I'm not sure what else. Are your animals locked up?"

He nodded. She moved to the back door of the van and grabbed the handle.

"Stand still. They'll come out and probably run off to hunt. They always return to where they've started, once they've fed."

Ellen opened the door to a reptilian blur. Josh gasped.

Ashamoor ran back to stand between them, stared at her, and spit a small flare at Josh's feet. He jumped back.

"It's okay, Ashamoor." Ellen reached out to touch the snout of the smallest dragon. "He's a friend."

Ellen's dragon glanced between her and Josh. Apparently satisfied; she raced out into the forest.

"There's nothing to do but wait for their return. I might need a little sleep." She yawned. The stress of the day crashed in.

Josh let out a slow whistle. "I might need a little more of your incredible story first. That, and a smoke."

CHAPTER 40

Sprinkles of starlight fought through the haze above Welglen's perch. He stretched his neck, stiff from staring into the skies for answers that hadn't come. He needed to be in the sky.

He hovered at the mouth of the cave. The young ones lay in a dark, unmoving mound. The green female slept closest to the opening. He nuzzled her side to wake her.

She sprang, searching for danger.

We are safe here, little one. I'll fly to secure our path. We'll also need more game than this barren hillside will provide. They won't have energy for their journey if they spend it scratching out a meal.

She moved forward.

Welglen shook his head. *Stay. Watch over the others. I'll return at dawn.*

He stepped out of the cave and snapped his wings open to the air in a single move. He rose and circled low. No humans were in range. The Earth held steady.

He rose into the safety of the night.

Ellen's instructions pointed him toward the far-off lights of the highway. Tomorrow, he'd lead the flight north to the home of her former mate.

He flew high toward the roadway. Thick traffic flowed at a steady pace, outlined by the lights of surrounding homes, ranches, and clusters of businesses. The flight wouldn't make it very far in the daylight unseen if they followed this direct route. Even at night, the glow from the headlights of the cars zigzagged brightly across the main road to other smaller arteries. He angled toward the dark ridge to the west.

The steep, rocky terrain didn't allow for roads or homes. The clusters of trees could provide shelter. He glided through openings between the trees up the steep hillside. It would be possible to stay unseen, though the thick undergrowth would prove a rough trip for those without the strength to stay aloft.

He broke through the trees, letting the freedom of the air under his wings ripple over his scales. He turned east across the highway. Strings of housing developments and sprawling farms bordered the open farmland. They could reach Ellen quickly this way, but not without being seen.

The pull toward his human competed with the desire to soar into the heavens and try again for the spell. He lifted high above the roadway, allowing a brief flight north. Ellen and the smallest dragons were only a few hours away. Separating the flight had split his attention.

Red glow cracked a bold crimson over the horizon and blocked his options. He returned to the western ridge and calculated a route on his way back to the young ones.

For the weak flyers spending more time on the Earth, the trip over the forested terrain would be difficult to impossible. He'd need to ferry the slowest into the currents to glide. He could rotate back and forth to help move them along, two at a time.

If the wind blew in their favor.

CHAPTER 41

Josh leaned forward at the edge of his seat. His back never touched the edges of the chair he'd built from the slats of an oak wine barrel. He didn't drink from the zinfandel-filled jelly jar he'd poured or light the pipe ready on the side table. Ellen's story had his full attention.

She stared at the face she knew so well. She fantasized ripping his clothes off and pushing him to the floor. But that required courage and energy. She slumped deeper into the scratchy, overstuffed, cow-printed couch. She'd drained the contents of her jar twice. The combination of wine, lack of sleep, and the soft light from the propane wall sconce tugged at her consciousness.

She couldn't sleep until the babies returned. "We needed a safe place." She struggled with where to start the personal part of the story. "I thought of you. I knew as fantastic as this all seemed, you'd be able to help us out."

In two steps he gathered her close in a familiar caress, her head against his chest. He smelled like fabric softener, marijuana, and reality. "I'm stoked you're back. This dragon thing is beyond cool."

"I know, right? I haven't been able to talk about it with anyone yet. It's been busting out of me. All these years writing about mythical creatures only to find out they're real. And they're so much more beautiful than I'd imagined."

"You've been writing. What else have you been doing? Seeing anyone?"

A perfect opportunity. "I focused on my work."

"And us?"

"Uh..." She opened her mouth to express fear, loss, and hope. Nothing came out. *Damn writer's block*. "What time is it? They'll crash for hours when they get back. We should plan a spot for them."

"They can sleep here in front of the fire." He pushed the coffee table in front of them to the side with his shoe.

"You don't want them in your house. I love them, but you'd never get the smell out of your wood floors. I'm pretty sure I've bought that rental van."

"How about the barn?"

"What other animals are in there? They do a good job clearing out any rodents or snakes. I don't think a chicken, goat, or duck would be safe either."

He collapsed back against the cushion and tugged at the long hair behind one ear. "I have the perfect place if they don't mind the late morning heat."

"They're dragons. Heat's their thing."

"Awesome."

Ellen met the first to return at the screen door and pushed through. The blue dragon sniffed Ellen's leg.

"I'm okay, baby." Ellen offered her hand. The little one touched it quickly with the side of his head, glared at Josh, then ran into the dirt driveway. Two other dragons scurried into sight and wrestled with the blue.

Ashamoor squawked through the brush. The others beat the ground with their wings, creating a dust cloud.

Each flap lifted them slightly off the ground, almost floating. Close, but not quite safe yet. Ellen rubbed Ashamoor's slick scales.

Josh brushed his hand across her arm. "Let's see if they like the greenhouse."

He walked toward the brush. The dragons stared at Ellen.

She followed Josh. They followed her single file through the dense brush in the cool early morning air into a clearing.

Nestled in the tall brown grass, dozens of windows scrounged from different colored projects were nailed to a greenhouse frame. Inside, stacks of black plastic pots waited for their starts for the next season.

They moved under the glass top. Without their usual bicker and tussle, the dragons piled quickly.

Josh sat on the wooden counter. "I'll watch them while you get some sleep. Anything special I should be on the lookout for?"

"Besides earthquakes, lava, and evil sorcerers? Not a thing."

CHAPTER 42

The dusty morning light revealed lush green fields to the north of the cave. Ripe with small prey, they were also full of humans, arriving by the truckloads for the day's work. Welglen skirted the tree-lined edges. He climbed back into the ridge and circled, expanding with each revolution.

To the south of the cave, a small crescent-shaped lake tucked into the crevice of two pine-covered hills, bordered by rocky crags. Birds sounded from below and the smell of fish rippled upward.

Welglen flew to the cave where the lead female remained alert. Cool spring water revived his lagging energy.

He settled next to her at the opening. Heavy breaths whistled out, signaling the flight's deep sleep. *Our path will be difficult, but we aren't far from the smallest of our flight. I've seen a lake to the south. I'll bring all the fish I can carry. Wake them so they're ready to eat and fly.*

She hurried into the cave, her sounds soft and constant.

The air cooled as Welglen soared closer to the water level. A soft breeze ruffled the surface in tiny waves. Multiple tents dotted the distant shore. At the near side, a lone canoe floated at the edge, tied with a long rope to a tree. Blackened logs in a ring of rocks were cold. One fishing pole leaned against a table. The occupant's snores scratched out of a tent.

Welglen glided over the lake until the early morning sunlight caught the shimmered reflections of the plentiful silver and pink scales below. He blew a slim flame. Tiny embers dropped like small insects on the surface of the water. Lured by the promise of breakfast, a large fish swam up to feed, its mouth opened full.

Welglen clutched the thick meat in one claw and carried it into the tree cover. He laid the flopping trout on a tuft of grass, returning for more. He widened the droplets of fire, drawing several fish to the surface at once. He captured all he could carry and added them to the growing pile on the bank.

A large shadow passed him on the ground.

Welglen slipped under the cover of the branches and scanned the air.

A full-grown eagle circled, her wingspan matching the height of a human, screeched out anger at the poacher in her hunting grounds.

Welglen rose through the trees to face the bird. The startled eagle raced to the opposite shore and took refuge in a flat nest at the top of a branchless tree, still blackened from a long-ago fire.

The eagle didn't stop squawking.

An easy prey, Welglen could add the meat to the food pile.

A man's gruff voice sounded from the tent. "Shut up, bird!" The animal had caught the human's attention. Welglen swooped away to the water.

With one eye on the small camp and under the bird's watchful squawks, he fished until he had enough for his flight.

Using mouth and claws, he carried a load to his flight, waiting on the ledge in front of the cave. He rained the trout over them, then returned for another load.

The eagle's cries could be heard before the lake came into view. Welglen dropped into the trees away from his catch, the sounds of cracking branches covered by the eagle's squawking.

A tall bare-chested man stood near the canoe and stared at the nest, hands on hips.

"What are you freaking out about?" he waved his arms. "You're going to scare the fish."

The man bent over the fire circle, piling small pieces of wood.

Welglen stayed under cover until the man started a flame and rifled through a large ice chest.

Welglen crept toward his catch. The eagle swooped down from his perch, talons forward, and stole a fish. Welglen charged, snapping his wings open triple the width of the bird.

The eagle spun away with the prize.

Welglen was on the bird as it reached the clearing near the camper but ducked under cover before reaching the open.

The eagle screeched, claws tight on the fish. He sailed over the man to the opposite bank then faced Welglen. The fisherman watched the eagle eat the stolen fish, oblivious to the dragon behind him.

Welglen sunk back into the trees, gathered the last of the fish, and returned to the others. The green female soared close enough for Welglen to pass her news.

Rest and eat. I'll stand watch. We must leave as soon as they've fed. We have a long way to go.

Too soon for her thoughts to transfer to him, but not too soon for her to understand his mind. In the old days, the stories would have already been passed on to her—those same stories he searched for.

In the bright light of day, Welglen led the young dragons along a looping route through the treetops. They stopped in the branches when they needed rest, keeping their traces off the Earth. The flight instinctively understood the need to move—an instinct that might keep them alive until they were old enough to communicate.

Half a day into their flight, instincts sharpened. The green female, the most advanced flyer, circled in the opposite direction, keeping a watchful eye on any dragons out of his sight. The blue male joined her and together they worked as a pair.

When the last of the young ones dropped into the cover of the forest to feed and re-energize, Welglen directed the young leader to eat. She flew down to join the others without a sound.

Odd how quickly he had become used to human conversation. He missed his chatty human. She added strength of belief to their team. She made him believe they had a chance.

Are you there? he called, though certain the distance blocked their ability to exchange thoughts. *Are you safe?*

Welglen flew guard long enough to ensure all had time for food and some rest, then led them back into the sky.

CHAPTER 43

Ellen stretched under the tattered blue quilt, listening to the ridiculously loud tick of the old clock on the mantle. It was already after noon. Only days ago, she'd counted time by watches, calendars, and deadlines. The most important marker was the height the babies could hover above the ground.

She untangled her legs from the blanket, propping against the back of the lumpy couch. She could've slept in Josh's bed since he was watching the babies. He'd offered. She'd chosen the couch.

They hadn't had the talk yet.

The bandage around her hand hung loose. The ice pack she'd pilfered from Josh's freezer had reduced the swelling. She removed the wrap and studied the purple bruise. It wasn't pretty but looked less serious than the day before. She tested a fist.

"Ow," she winced and smiled at the same time. All her fingers followed her mental command and rolled down to her palm together. Starting at the thumb, she massaged her hand to gently stretch the undamaged tissue, avoiding the dark mark.

The sun angled into the porch and hit the window. Time to see what she could do.

Dressed and with the coffee percolating, Ellen stepped into the driveway. She twirled the sword in her left hand, baton-style—the double edge humming.

Chanting to increase the workout, she repeated her old high school fight song, alternating the lunge at the end with each leg. She stepped deeper each time to lengthen the stretch until sweat beaded on her body.

It was time. The babies depended on her. She slipped her bruised right hand into the hilt and twirled. The razor-sharp weapon spun easily, following her backhand.

Her pinky finger cramped. The sword flew out of her grasp. "Ahh!"

The Sword of Srekums bounced on the ground, just missing Josh's feet.

He skidded to a stop in the gravel. "Whoa!"

Ellen's heart thumped in her chest. "I'm so sorry. Are you okay?"

"I'll live, I guess. What are you doing? I thought you were still asleep."

"Training." She stretched the cramp out of her finger.

He raised an eyebrow. "Do I want to know what for?"

"I told you about the prophecy. Someone must use this sword and kill the sorcerer. Apparently, that's me."

He walked over to the porch and turned on the radio. "You're not a killer. This may be unreal, but it's not like a video game. If you are sent to kill someone, you'll be a murderer."

"It won't come to that. I'm only the backup, just in case." Ellen restarted the routine in slow motion to the beat of the soft music, focusing her grip on the thumb and forefinger. "Welglen has a plan he hopes will pull the powers from the sorcerer and reduce him to a human. He'll be protecting me at the same time. I'm there to distract the bad guy long enough with the sword for the spell to work."

He rubbed his eyes with the back of his hands. "If it doesn't work? You could be killed, or you could be forced to kill."

"I'd only really fight in self-defense."

"It's not self-defense if you go into a situation armed. Killing changes people. You should run… now!"

She'd thought that too, before she fell in love with baby dragons. "I agree this is crazy dangerous. But you've seen these beautiful dragons. And there's so much more at stake than their existence. If the sorcerer wins, all of mankind will become his slaves."

"Come on, you don't believe that do you? That's preposterous."

"Exactly more or less preposterous than living, breathing dragons in your greenhouse?" She tossed the sword, completed a turn, but let it drop to the ground when she realized she'd be too slow to catch the hilt. "It's already happening all over the world. People just don't know it."

"Would you stop throwing that around for a second?" He leaned in. With a light touch, he moved a strand of sweaty hair back from her face. "I haven't seen you in so long. But you're back looking toned and sexy under the most incredible circumstances."

He followed a drop of sweat from her cheek, down her chest. His eye color deepened. She'd stepped back into her old life: the same tender connection mixed with a new appreciation of his ability to accept. Exactly what she'd wanted. She choked on the appropriate dialog. "I don't know what to say."

He held a hand up. "The world has changed. We're in danger and the one person you come to for the end-of-the-world experience is me. We're matched."

A shiver ran through her. Welglen described his mate Tacoma the same way.

"There's so much to talk about, but I can't get into that. My brain can't absorb anything past preparing for a battle I'm pretty sure I'll lose."

"You don't have to." He lifted her chin. His familiar scent filled her nostrils. "How about you protect these dragons, and I'll protect you."

He leaned closer. The radio played a soft love song—a soundtrack to a "happily ever after."

A loud obnoxious buzz squelched from the radio.

Traffic on Interstate 5 has slowed in both directions as scores of residents near Mount Shasta are voluntarily evacuating after recent earthquakes. A team of geologists are currently researching small clouds of what appears to be smoke, or steam spotted along the tree line. Officials tracking seismic activity around the area confirm that the volcano is not generating the earthquakes. No volcanic activity is expected.

Northbound traffic is also thick with the anti-fracking protest drawing thousands for the debate that blames the recent seismic activity on the fracking industry.

Officials are announcing the area is safe and asking residents to stay in their homes and away from the demonstrations at the base of the mountain.

Branches snapped behind them in a rhythmic, crunching pattern.

Ellen held the sword up. "Turn off the radio. They're coming."

"Who?" Josh scanned the woods beyond the driveway.

The trees rustled at their left.

Twenty-four dragons trailed out of the cover. Welglen glided down from the sky and transformed with the first touch to the Earth. Wearing only his man suit. Ellen's dragon walked directly toward them. She ran into his arms.

"Are you well, Ellen?" Welglen allowed her to nestle into his bare shoulder. She looked into his face. His focus was on Josh.

Josh's mouth hung open.

"I'm okay. Glad you're safe. It's been awful being apart." She stepped back from Welglen's smooth skin and pointed to Josh. "This is Josh. He's helping us. Josh, this is Welglen, or just Glen. He's the leader of this flight."

Welglen raised his hands to his hips.

Josh found his voice. "Holy shit."

CHAPTER 44

The shorter male crossed and uncrossed his arms twice. His focus shifted between Ellen and Welglen's face.

Welglen placed a hand on Ellen's shoulder.

The other male settled strong hands at his waist. He puffed out a meager chest.

Welglen tightened his muscles, commanding a ripple from his shoulders down his abdomen.

Ellen giggled. "Seriously guys, you look like a remake of an old-West shootout. Of course, if you had guns, and if both of you were dressed. Get acquainted. We have a lot to figure out. We need to be on the same page."

One of Josh's eyebrows raised into his forehead.

Ellen squeezed Welglen's arm. "I'm so glad the family is back together. I'll take the young ones to the others. They're sleeping in a secluded clearing." A flock of waist-high babies surrounded her, sniffing at her legs. She touched the top of a red head where two small bumps rose slightly off the skull. "Telling boys from girls just got easier. What do they need? Hungry or sleepy?"

"Both. Rest is critical."

She disappeared into the brush with the flight.

Josh scanned Welglen's body, shaking his head slightly. "I guess we'd better find you something to wear."

"A hasty retreat didn't leave time to search for non-essentials."

Josh blew a large breath out his mouth. He motioned for Welglen to follow him into the small house.

A pile of blankets at the couch smelled of Ellen. In the back bedroom, Josh tossed a couple of clothing items out onto the made bed. "Wear whatever fits. I'll start breakfast. I'm assuming you eat like a real man?"

"In this human form, I am a man, with all the same hungers."

Josh chewed on the side of his bottom lip. He shook his head, then closed the door behind him.

Welglen smiled. It would be easy to set the male's jealousies at rest. But this male had disappointed Ellen in the past. It wouldn't hurt him to have to re-earn her attentions.

Threads popped against the stretch of the garment over his chest. The pants slid up with more ease, resting without a tie at his hips. In truth, the sport of sparring with another male satisfied both of Welglen's incarnations.

He followed the smell of ham into the kitchen. Josh spread additional slices of meat into the hot skillet.

"These pants are a practical style for my use," Welglen ducked into a series of squats that illustrated the stretch fabric against the strength of his thighs. "I believe they'd come on and off with ease."

Josh turned for a quick gaze, then back to the skillet. Ellen entered and motioned to a chair for Welglen to sit. "Tell me what's been happening. We have to piece together a plan."

Welglen polished off the large drink before speaking. "Most of the young ones took to flight immediately.

Others I had to ferry through the mountains in pairs. The winds were strong in our direction this morning, so we were able to complete the trek."

"Did you figure out how to pull the light from the sorcerer?"

Josh flipped the meat over in the pan, his attention on Ellen.

"I have remembered a few of the stories, though not the spells, or if any succeeded."

Josh cracked eggs loudly against the counter and dumped them into the pan. His shoulders raised; lips pursed as he worked. He placed three filled plates on the table, then wedged a chair next to Ellen. "There is one other thing." He faced Welglen and shook pepper over his eggs in hard shakes. "How can you sit here calmly, knowing you're placing Ellen in mortal danger? I'd never let anything happen to her."

Ellen waved at him. "Hey. I'm not helpless."

Josh's voice had been strong, though his hands shook in small tremors. His protective instincts were admirable.

Welglen met his gaze. "I understand your desire to keep her safe. I also wouldn't want harm to befall my human."

Josh spun to face Ellen. "My human?"

Ellen patted her chest with her good hand. "I can take care of myself."

Welglen met Josh's gaze. He didn't believe her either.

The chair squealed against the floor as she stood. "Look. I plan on surviving this chapter in my life. This helpless character role I've been dealt is making me reactionary. I, we, need to control the action. We have to come up with a new plot." She walked out into the living room.

Josh polished off his eggs in a few bites. He grabbed a hunk of ham and set his plate in the sink. "Eat up. I've seen that look before. She's going to need room."

Ellen placed her bulging backpack onto the table as Welglen finished his meal.

She rifled through the contents and found a notebook. "We want to beat the sorcerer at the end, making sure he either returns to helpless human or dies, right?" She tore out several pages and laid them end to end across the tabletop. She wrote "location" on the first sheet. "We can only run so far with the young ones and time is running short. Instead of running away, let's race to set a scene where we might have some advantage. Is there any situation that might give you the advantage while trying to pull the light out of this guy? Like high ground, or a heavy forest?"

Welglen would be highly vulnerable during the fight. It would be difficult to protect others. "I see where you're going. The sorcerer will follow us. We could lead him to an end that will benefit us. A remote area where the dragons could scatter if our plans don't work might ensure more survive. Otherwise, they may be shot by hunters trying to escape."

Ellen added a few notes. "Thanks for yet another creepy option. We're getting somewhere here. We should be far from town, and close to tree cover. What else?"

"You are small, so high ground could help. If we keep the sorcerer between us and I stay below, you'd have leverage during swordplay."

Josh cleared his throat in a low growl.

Ellen scrawled a note. "So, hills or mountains. Do you have a paper map Josh?" He glanced at Welglen. When he left the room she asked, "What's with you two?"

"He wants only to protect you. He's coming to grips with the fact that you want to protect everyone."

"What do you want?" Ellen placed a hand over his.

"I want to save everyone too. I'm with you. Remember, he doesn't see me as a dragon. To him, I am another male challenging his relationship with a mate."

Josh stepped into the kitchen, wedged between them, and unfolded a map of Northern California over the top of the table, forcing their hands apart.

Ellen leaned over the map and drew a small circle. "What do we know so far? Sonoma is here. We camped somewhere around here on our round-about trip to get to Dunsmuir. I don't think any of those areas will work. There's either no mountains, or too many houses."

Welglen traced a line on the map he'd followed days ago to his brother. "On my flight north there were inactive mountain ranges that might work, but there was plenty of sorcerer activity, and way too many humans."

"That's a good point. Since the earthquakes signal sorcerers are close, let's track them. Can you check the emergency site on your computer Josh? The one that maps local quakes?"

He left the room, returning with a laptop.

They studied the screen. Ellen marked the map with an X anywhere there had been recent activity. The series of marks turned into one path flowing from Sonoma to Dunsmuir and another near his brother's nest in Oregon.

Josh pointed to the map. "The magnitudes of the quakes have been lower here than in Sonoma. Could elevation play any part? What is the elevation in Sonoma?"

Ellen shrugged. "About thirty feet. We're close to the bay."

Josh traced a finger over the mountain. "We're twenty-five hundred here at the base of Mount Shasta."

Ellen sat back against her chair and rubbed absently at her bandaged hand. "I talked to my neighbor yesterday. She confirmed the earthquakes stopped almost the moment we drove out of Sonoma. Those were a lot stronger than the ones we've been having in the mountains."

Welglen tried to pace in the too-small room. "We must stay away from other humans. We must also climb. These points you've noted, Josh, show the higher we are, the less damage. The thickness of the Earth must slow the sorcerer. What is the highest peak around?"

Josh stabbed the map with his finger. "Mount Shasta's in our back yard. It's an old volcano, so lots of rock. It's not far from here as the crow flies." He shook his head. "Sorry, dude, not sure on flying metaphors etiquette."

Welglen nodded. "The old lava scars would succumb more slowly to the sorcerer's heat than the ground at lower levels. If I fly with the others and Ellen climbs from a different angle, it might throw the sorcerer off the track for perhaps another day. Is there a spot on this mountain you think more advantageous?"

"Misery Mountain might work. It wouldn't be far to the tree line for the dragons. It's a rough climb. I guess you all don't have to worry about that, but Ellen does."

Welglen met Josh's gaze. "I understand your fear. I'll protect her with all I have."

"It might not be enough, right?" Josh stood. His knuckles gripped the edge of the table and whitened.

Ellen started to repack her bag. "Let's not start that again. We need to worry about the babies first. We still have five that can't fly. We have our location. What's the best way to start?"

Welglen looked out the window for the sun. "After the flyers have slept a bit, I'll take them toward this Mount Shasta. We'll wait for you there. The height might slow the ferocity of the earthquakes. The distance to other humans will limit damages. You must stay and buy time for the final five."

Ellen grasped Welglen's hand. "Don't leave again." Josh's deep grunt sounded close to a bark.

"We shall reunite soon, I fear." He sandwiched her hand between both of his. "We cannot run from this fight much longer. Our best hope is to draw him away from other humans. If we're lucky, we'll be able to pull his powers or scatter the flight, making his quest more difficult. A strong dragon can stay in the winds for days. It would be difficult to find them."

Josh grunted. "Uh . . . hmm." His gaze on her hand, still held in Welglen's. "I think I'll check on the animals."

The door slammed.

Ellen touched his arm. "Sorry about that. This is new for him."

The corners of his mouth turned up. A rusty laugh burst through.

She shook her head. "Seriously, now you found your sense of humor?"

"He is the mate you lost that you want back?"

"Yeah. Maybe. Other than the babies' safety, I don't know what I'd even wish for."

"Know this. I have never known a human I could place trust in, until now. I believe in you. No matter what happens, remember you have the strength and the heart needed to help others. With you, anything is possible."

CHAPTER 45

Grunts and snorts forced Ellen from the private pity party she'd been holding since Welglen and the flyers had flown away. She tugged on the clothes she'd left by the couch and walked to the barn. These animals didn't know they had a plan to fight a sorcerer. They wanted to be fed on time, every time. It was up to her to handle the chores.

Last night, as she'd paced and twirled the sword until the dragons returned from hunting, she and Josh had talked about everything.

Everything except dragons, love stories, or the future.

Ellen grunted against the pain in her stiff shoulders as she lifted the barn door. She stepped into the dark, pungent interior. The shadows cleared to rows of goats and pigs. The animals were safely tucked away from the dragons.

At the end of the barn, a roost opened to an outside coop. She filled the water troughs first. She fed each stall in order, enjoying the feeling of normal action. She could imagine staying here with Josh once the dragons were safe.

By the time she'd reached the end, the anxious noise had changed to a quiet munch. She opened the back of the roost to allow the plain white chickens some outside coop time, then shooed the pigs to the pen.

The last little goat wasn't interested in food. He wanted to know why a stranger was in his pen. He butted his horns against her thigh.

"It's okay. Josh is busy." She poured the feed out. The goat backed up, intent on ramming her again.

Ellen dashed for the gate.

The goat charged.

Ellen swung through the gate and hit the latch into place, safe.

The ground jarred. She lost her footing and slipped to her butt.

The goat poked his head into the fence and brayed.

An earthquake rolled under her.

A huge crash echoed through the barn.

A vision of her loved ones sleeping under a canopy of the glass greenhouse flashed through her brain. She ran.

Panic blinded her view of the path ahead when the sound of a second crash sliced through her heart.

Ellen cut through the brambles, not waiting for the path. Thorns ripped at her skin. She broke free of the thicket and ground to a halt in front of a large pile of glass.

The remains of the greenhouse.

She willed her feet to step toward the mutilated shed, trying to both close and open her eyes at the same time.

"Babies?" she panted. She stepped to the shattered frames. "Josh?"

A branch snapped behind her.

"Uh!" Ellen spun toward five dragons and one bearded, dirty pot grower running from the brush.

Josh lifted her so only her toes touched the ground.

Held up by his squeeze, she trailed her arms at her sides to touch the young ones. They grunted and rubbed their noses against her legs, confirming the smell of life. She sniffed against a runny nose. Tears spilled down her cheeks.

Josh lowered her back to her own power. A shaking vibrated from deep inside her. The aftereffects of fear vibrated from her legs, into her hips, then crawled over her stomach to her breasts.

His arms tightened. He leaned down, rubbed his soft beard against her face. "It's okay, babe. I'm all right. I'm okay." He kissed one cheek and the other before moving both hands to her face and making direct eye contact. "I'm still here."

Ellen threw her arms around his neck. She kissed him hard on the mouth. He responded instantly.

She craved him—craved life.

She wanted to crawl back in time to before she'd left, lost her chance for a baby, and her innocence. She dragged him to the ground and rolled Josh on his back. She tugged her shirt over her head. He ran his hand over her stomach to the button of her pants while the backs of five baby dragons circled her, each guarding from a different direction.

Her thoughts went to the other babies she couldn't protect.

And Welglen.

Josh slid her pants down her legs. He drew her thoughts back to the moment with a carefully placed finger. Ellen arched and closed her eyes to a vision of Welglen naked in the hot tub.

"No!" She forced her eyes open and tugged Josh's shirt off. Except for a few new hairs between his dark brown nipples, his chest took her back in time. A mental picture of Welglen's rippling abs sent a flood of heat down to her lady parts.

The lyrics to "Love the One You're With" pulsed through

her brain. Thankful for the IUD, she climbed on top of Josh and took control for the first time in a week.

When she lay on his shoulder later, covered loosely by his shirt, the scratches from the brush stung and the stickers dug into her hip.

"Scared . . . so scared." She wiped at her wet face with the sleeve of his jacket. "I heard the glass crash. I pictured you cut all to pieces."

He rubbed her back and spoke in a low tone. "I had the same picture at the sound of the first crack. But these little reptilian guardian angels had already pushed me out to safety."

Ellen wiped her running nose as she dressed. "That's their way. Dragons are the sworn protectors of humans. That's why they can't kill a sorcerer—because sorcerers start out human."

"Well, I'll be." He surveyed the pile of glass. "What now?"

"We need to find out more about that earthquake. The closer the epicenter, the closer the sorcerer. It won't do us any good though if we are not ready because they can't fly."

"I mean us." He picked up the shirt she'd tossed his way. "I haven't seen you in months. Suddenly you're back. It's like you never left."

"It feels like one hundred years to me. I'm sorry for this," she waved at the pile of wreckage. "I'm putting you at risk simply by being here."

"Don't say you're sorry." He slid his pants up over his thighs, strong from gardening squats, but still thinner than Welglen's. "We've always been able to count on each other. I'm here for you."

Probably not fair to compare a dragon-man to anyone. Ellen kissed his cheek but didn't offer any decisions. Trying to have it all could be frightening. The last time she'd tried, she'd ended up with less than half.

"Although you haven't said anything, I wanted to let you know I've thought a lot about the fact that you want children, and I could get used to it." Josh beamed, totally unaware of his non-ridiculous evolution.

The perfect moment to tell him the truth.

The words caught in her throat. She walked back to the house. The young ones flanking her like tiny protectors, hopping, levitating, and flapping. Even as they passed the barn where the animals were penned in the open, the baby dragons gave the fresh meat only a couple of glances.

She sat on the steps and five restless dragons circled her.

Imminent crap waited. They knew it.

"The power's out," Josh called from inside. "It's a mess in here."

In no mood to view the wreckage, she stroked the back of Ashamoor's scales with one hand and the tale of the red with the other. The screen door screeched. The winding of the emergency radio filled the air. When the dragons stared at Josh but didn't make a move to give him space to sit, he dragged a chair over.

The dragons hissed at the initial squelch of the radio, calming when he found a clear signal. "Armageddon," sounded through the static. He scrolled between evangelist and talk radio to local news.

This is the emergency notification system. There has been confirmed volcanic activity in the Mount Shasta area. All residents are encouraged to monitor the situation. No mandatory evacuations are in effect. Authorities will update the situation in two hours.

Spirals of smoke from the base of the volcano can be seen miles away. We have Professor Sangretti from the University of Oregon Geology Department with us at the base of the mountain. Professor Sangretti, is there any real fear that this volcano is again becoming active?

A gravelly voice replied. *It is always a possibility, though unlikely. Surveyors are being airlifted to the reported sites. The answer could be anything from brush fires resulting from a careless camper, or a rare chance the earthquakes have opened some thermal pools with high water temperatures. The steam from one of these pools would look like smoke from a distance. None of the activity is coming from the mouth of the volcano.*

What do you recommend for the residents of the area? the news reporter asked.

I recommend they stay put but remain alert. There are always more casualties caused by those running in fear than any natural disaster.

A louder and younger male voice broke through. *No accident! The over-drilling and recent fracking by oil companies has caused a chain of disturbances in the Earth's crust that's going to kill us all! March on Washington!*

We're breaking for station identification, the announcer spurted.

Ellen sighed loudly. "It's begun, exactly as Welglen predicted. Sorcerer's feed on distrust. They play humans against each other in times of crisis to take control." She rubbed the muzzle of her tiny dragon who calmed at the touch. The other four wouldn't be consoled. They paced and flapped across the porch in noisy scratches as their claws dug into the old wood with each attempt to lift off. The longer they could stay off the ground, the harder it would be for the sorcerer to find them. All options required strong flyers. "The smoke they are seeing is probably from the lava. It's like steam, then it glows hot. The first time I saw it, it petrified me. I won't be able to stay here much longer."

"I have an idea," Josh called on his way toward the barn. "We might make a flyer out of one of them yet."

She inhaled deeply, trying to erase the images of the nest in Sonoma melting into flames. "We need the rest of our family, Ashamoor. I won't feel safe until we're back together."

She rubbed Ashamoor's nubby head. Josh returned from the barn with a basket of eggs. "Hungry?"

"Yes, but we have work to do. Come on, boys." He held an egg out to the dragons. They stared down at him from the porch. "There isn't an animal I know that wouldn't do anything for an organic, still-warm-from-the-hen egg."

Josh rolled the egg across the soft, dusty ground toward the steps. The dragons huddled around her, staring at Josh and the egg.

"It's okay, babies, you must be hungry. If this doesn't work, Josh, you might have to offer up a few whole chickens."

The red dragon stepped toward the egg and hovered over it. He looked at the egg, to Josh, then back at the egg. In one quick movement, he sucked it in. He flapped his wings and squawked.

The others quickly rushed at the red. Together they circled Josh, pushing against the basket.

"You have to earn it." Josh held the basket and his fingers above the hungry dragons. He held one egg above his head. "Fly up and reach it."

The dragons danced below the egg then flapped enough dust into the air that Ellen almost missed the red rise two feet off the ground and snag the egg in a gulp.

"Ahh!" Josh shook his hand above his head.

"Did they get you?" She laughed, half worried.

"A love bite." He held the next egg and the same dragon flew to grab it and swallowed it whole. "They probably learn to fly from their mothers, like birds."

Josh tossed another egg high into the air. The red dragon swooped about fifteen feet to catch it before tumbling in the long dry grass.

"He's doing it." Ellen moved to Josh's side while the red flew from one side of the house to the other, more interested in his newfound abilities than the egg basket. The other dragons were hungry and nipped at Josh's legs to get to the eggs. "Do it again."

Josh launched an egg high. The two young ones jumped. The winner swallowed and stayed close for another chance.

Covered in small scratches, Josh switched to a safer alternative, and threw the eggs at a distance.

Near the end of the basket only the red had taken to the sky—swooping, turning, and repeatedly falling back to the grass. All her baby dragons hovered above the ground a few feet at a time.

Ellen pictured Welglen leading the green female into the sky and hoped the dark blue male would be able to guide the others.

Half to encourage the other dragons, and half survival inspired, Josh ran with the basket and tossed the last eggs high into the air.

Each dragon fought with the others to catch the egg before it hit the ground.

"That's all I've got until this afternoon." He made a show of the empty basket. The dragons sniffed the wicker, then ignored Josh and nipped at each other. Not safe yet, but they had a chance to live.

Thanks to Josh. Had she left the right guy for the wrong reason?

Ellen joined the others on the open porch at sundown, not ready to sleep under a roof.

The babies were becoming flyers.

Perhaps too little, too late.

CHAPTER 46

Welglen perched on the hillside, resting his aching muscles in the sporadic flashes of sunlight. The air hazy but calm. The ground dropped sharply before him, leveling for a small pond. To the south, small spirals of smoke highlighted where Ellen and the others remained.

Days might pass before the remaining flight reunited. The smallest would need to fly. Ellen would need to find him.

Josh's accusation rolled through Welglen's thoughts. He couldn't deny Ellen was in danger. He couldn't keep her safe without increasing the risk to the young ones. He needed the entire team.

He must focus on the sleeping dragons huddled behind him.

Footsteps crunched through the undergrowth below.

A thin figure appeared through the trees.

Welglen hunched against the rocks. Had he conjured Ellen to his side?

A young woman headed up the hill below the pond.

Not his human.

She veered toward the water and the path leading to his sleeping dragons.

No time to scatter the others.

He dropped to the pool, transformed, and slipped waist deep into the icy clear water.

The woman climbed to the pond's edge. "Oh!" She raised a hand that held a walking stick up to shield her eyes. "Sorry, I hadn't expected anyone here."

Slight, she wore short pants that revealed most of her muscular legs. Her olive top matched her shorts, and the hat she wore bore a symbol he'd seen elsewhere. "It's of no consequence. I've stopped to cool off. Though my clothing is up there." Welglen pointed to the site where the dragons slept. "What are you doing around here? It is unusual to see a female hiking on her own."

She reached to a toolbelt at her waistband. He smiled. She dropped her hand.

"I'm conducting a geologic study to help determine the cause of the activity in this mountain after the last two days of earthquakes. Have you seen anything unusual?"

"Down near the bottom of the mountain." He pointed away from camp, "there's a small crag shielding a narrow cave. A great deal of steam rose in that location."

"Steam?" She pulled a notebook out of her backpack. "That might be Lunar Cave. I'll check the bluff ahead, then head back down." She stepped in the direction of the young dragons. "You don't mind, do you?"

"Of course not," Welglen climbed out of the water, exposing his human self to her. "Pardon my lack of attire. I'll accompany you."

She rested her hand at a spray can buckled into her belt. Her gaze lingered on his abdomen, then dropped for a brief glance before clearing her throat and blurting, "I'm on duty. Guess it would make more sense to check out the cave first."

She hurried back to the path, disappearing down a short drop on the hill.

It wouldn't take long for other humans to find them.

The Earth shook. He dropped a hand to the ground to steady his fragile body, then climbed to the young ones. Alert in their resting pile, they looked to him for direction. He motioned for them to stay in place.

A second sharp jolt loosened the hillside at their left. A landslide rolled in the direction of the human.

Welglen launched forward, skimming the wave of rocks.

The woman's body tumbled in the dusty gray slide below.

He dove and grabbed her flailing arms.

Cuts covered her skin. She coughed out dirt and fluttered her eyes open. She stared up at her savior—into the face of a full-size dragon.

Twenty feet off the ground, she struggled against his grip.

So human.

Don't panic. You're safe.

Her gaze moved across his chest to his wings. Her body went limp. She whispered. "An angel. I'm dead."

You're alive. Though you need to leave. It's not safe for you here.

Welglen lowered her to the ground. He sat on haunches a few feet away while she took stock and tended to her many injuries.

"Th-thank you," she stuttered. "What are you?"

What do you think?

She touched a hand to a growing knot on her temple. "You must have been sent from heaven. Or I'm having a hallucination."

Perhaps both are true.

CHAPTER 47

All five babies squawked for Ellen's attention in the driveway and played the dragon version of 'Look what I can do, Mom.'

The red dragon could fly from the house to the barn. Three could flap the length of the porch. Even Ashamoor fluttered inches above the ground.

Energy pulsed through her muscles, along with something that felt slightly like hope. She wanted a full dragon reunion, a little control in an incredible situation, and the time Ashamoor needed to survive.

Josh walked out of the house reading his cell phone. "People are crazy. There's a rally at the bottom of Mount Shasta with the anti-fracking campaign and there's a huge evacuation in effect. Seven people have been sent to the hospital, two critical. They estimated one hundred thousand people are at the base of the mountain."

"Crap." Ellen needed the flight. She ran toward the van and swung open the back doors.

A huge gust of dragon smell smacked against her senses—a combination of a sweaty locker room and toasted marshmallows. "If there's that much activity, Welglen must have reached the mountain. He'll need me."

The gear she'd managed to save when they bugged out of the last camp lay scattered over the van bed.

The growing dragons needed more space. She climbed in and tossed loose items out.

Ashamoor squawked when the coffee pot landed near her feet.

"Oh, baby." Ellen dropped to her knees and softly stroked her head. "I'm sorry. I didn't mean to scare you."

Ashamoor nuzzled Ellen's neck. This little dragon wasn't a strong enough flyer to be safe, yet.

"Josh, I'll need Ashamoor to stay with you. She needs more time. The other four are large enough they may be able to scatter and increase their odds." She turned around as the front door swung shut.

Ellen brushed the floor of the van out with one of her last clean T-shirts. She glanced back at the pile for what could be carried.

The sword would go in the front seat.

She'd need water and the small backpack she'd brought from home. The remaining camping gear would be too heavy to carry on any mountain hike.

Ellen refilled the water jug and a few empty water bottles at the hose near the porch.

All five dragons climbed inside without a fight.

"Not you, Ashamoor. I need you to stay with Uncle Josh. I don't know what's going to happen, but Welglen said you need to be strong flyers to survive."

Ellen reached out. Ashamoor hissed and snapped.

"Really? After all we've been through?" She walked around the van, hoping Ashamoor would follow out of curiosity.

She collected the sword and her backpack from the porch.

Josh stepped out. She'd completely forgotten he existed. That couldn't be good.

He'd changed into his favorite brown plaid shirt—his hot look. He had a backpack slipped over one shoulder. "I've packed some energy bars and a canteen. We'll have to stop for more supplies to climb Mount Shasta. That's all new for me."

She reached out for the backpack strap. "Thank you for your help, Josh, but I got this. Know this—you probably saved my life." Not that she knew how much longer her life would last.

He drew back. "You don't think for one minute I'm going to let you go alone? I already called my uncle to watch the animals. He'll be here in a little bit. I don't know what's going on, but I'm in it for the long haul. I might even fight a sorcerer."

"You're a pacifist!" She waved her hands to erase her comment. "Okay, that sounded silly. This will be dangerous. I need you to keep Ashamoor safe until she's stronger. If I don't come back, let her go once she can fly. Hopefully instinct will lead her back to the others."

Josh circled the van. Ashamoor huddled near the driver's seat. The other four dragons stood between the smallest baby and the door. "I don't think Ashamoor likes your plan either."

"I need to do this on my own."

"Why?"

Ellen shrugged. "I don't know."

"Then get over yourself." He closed the back doors and moved into the driver's seat. "I'll take the first shift. I can get us to the other side of town on the back roads. No way people are on those yet. The local growers have set too many traps."

Ellen tossed him the keys and climbed into the passenger seat.

She couldn't turn down volunteers when her team had been split up.

CHAPTER 48

The fir tree swayed under Welglen's weight. He clung to the branches until the dust from the woman's truck trailed far down the hill. He dropped into the air and scanned the surroundings. No other humans in sight. The flight would be safe for a time.

He flew between the treetops to confirm their route. The steep terrain on the ridgeline remained the only option free of humans. He drifted over the flight and took guard at the edge above the spring.

A few dragons jockeyed into position in the sleeping crush of tails and snouts. The green female lingered outside the moving mound. Already showing signs of leadership, she could be a great asset, if Welglen didn't survive the upcoming battle.

The flight relied on him for everything. They need to find their strength. He wouldn't be able to save them all.

The green female rested next to him. He reached out to her mind. *We have a little time and there's much for you to know. I don't know how much you understand my words yet, but I must try.*

She turned to face him, as if in conversation.

A great battle will begin soon. I'll need you. A sorcerer comes for the hearts of dragons. I'll face him, though I cannot fight. I'll use the little bits of resistance allowed to us against humans to buy time. You must scatter the flight.

She cocked her head to one side, looking into Welglen's face.

We cannot separate too early, or the sorcerer will easily track and prey upon the weakest. We need to wait until he is focused, certain he has the desired heart. That will give us the head start needed. He won't care initially that others flee. But he will after he's reached immortality. He'll hunt every dragon down, one by one. I'll act as decoy and distract the sorcerer to ensure you've saved all you can. I'll likely not survive this battle. Even if I manage to find the spell to remove the light, I'll be vulnerable to one who wants me dead. If Ellen arrives in time, she'll challenge the sorcerer with the Sword of Srekums. If you can help her, do so. But first, protect the flight. Scatter.

The young female hissed and blew a shot of flame against the ground, blackening a small weed.

Fair is different than necessary. Small groups are best, mixed male and female. The flight won't be able to reconnect while dragons. Once you've matured, transform into human forms. Then you'll be able to live in larger groups.

Flapping her wings against the dusty rocks, she screeched into the sky.

One day, you'll likely be drawn to protect humans. Take care not to trust all. Our Ellen is different.

A small sound, more rhythm than audible, softly vibrated at the base of Welglen's brain as she spoke. *I understand.*

Welglen flung out his wings, flooded with relief. *You've found your voice. What is the name you give yourself?*

Samote.

I'm pleased to have you at my side, Samote.

I'm honored to be with you.

The young ones are safe for a time. Let's fly together. We need to prepare for loss. Dragons were created to protect humans and to ferry the lost to the afterlife. We'll start there.

May we also search for the answer of the light? Together we may find it.

You're right. Welglen hovered over the ground. *We must prepare for success. Come. There's a great deal to share.*

He lifted to the sky. He flew slowly at first, ensuring her speed, then angled sharply upward and soared.

CHAPTER 49

Ellen clutched at the back of the seat and twisted around to calm the frustrated dragons rocking against the metal sides of the van. They'd tripled in size since traveling in cages. She unrolled the sleeping bags and they clawed into them.

Twenty minutes on the bumpy trail designed for off-road vehicles and donkeys, they'd covered less than a mile.

Josh stopped the van.

"What is it?" Ellen stared through the dusty glare of the windshield.

The slight indentations in the grass ahead identifying a road disappeared at a right turn into a forest of shrubby manzanita.

"I think there may be a booby trap here."

He scrounged the ground and picked up a long stick.

From ten feet in front of the van, he tossed the branch forward.

A bang echoed through the trees.

Josh dropped to his knees.

Frantic dragons pushed against the sides, sending the van into a rocking crescendo of squawks and squeaking shocks.

"Josh!" Ellen grabbed her sword. She winced at the pain in her wounded hand. She slid through the door and ran to his side. She pointed the blade toward the trees.

"Are you okay? What happened?"

He rubbed at his ears. "I'm all right. Or I will be once the ringing stops."

Ellen held her good arm down to help pull him up.

"This is the edge of Dirk's property. He expanded onto Ramsey's old place after you left. I don't think Ramsey got the straight end of the deal because he's been coming around a lot, trying to get his place back. I figured Dirk would take trespassing seriously. He has a lot of plants. Plus, he's crazy paranoid."

Josh lifted a small wire from the grass under the branch he'd thrown.

"I wouldn't have seen that even if I was looking for it. I remember Dirk. He's the first one I saw when I got to town."

"He's not someone we want to tangle with. He's purely into the business for the money, not personal rights or freedom."

"Will there be more traps? More guns?"

"Probably, though I hope that's the worst. Most of his crop should be well off the road."

The noise from the van grew louder. The dragons wanted out.

"Do you think we'll be able to check it out on foot before we bring the dragons through?"

"Maybe. I know this area pretty well. In the old days, I'd drive through here with my uncle. He was friends with Ramsey. There's a path through the trees to the right, then it opens through a meadow. Let's look through this part of the trees. Only step where I do."

Ellen scanned the knee-deep grass for wires and the trees for guns. She couldn't see where the shot had come from.

Twenty feet into the dark brush, a nervous laugh escaped her throat. "Do you see anything? I could be looking right at something and have no clue."

Josh stopped and scanned the area. "I think we're good. I don't see any of the typical traps. We should be safe in the van at least this far."

On cue, a squeaking sound radiated through the trees.

"That's the babies. We'd better get going. They don't like the driving and hate waiting. I think they know a battle's coming."

Josh placed a soothing hand on her shoulder. "This is a man-made threat. I can deal with that. I can't wrap my brain around the supernatural. Are you sure you want to go through with this? I admit I want you to stop this crazy journey."

"I don't have a choice." She waved the sword across the top of the grass. "Running away won't stop the sorcerer."

"It might stop you from being killed. Do you know what you're doing with that thing?"

Ellen looked down at the sword she clutched—tight enough for white knuckles to show above the curve of the steel dragon hilt. She loosened her grip and stretched her sore fingers.

"I'm learning."

A quiet settled over the brush.

The van door closed.

"What?" Ellen ran toward the roar of the van engine. She turned in time to see Dirk pulling away with her babies.

"Stop!"

Ellen tripped through the underbrush as the futility of chasing a car already shielded by trees hit her. The sound of the engine drifted away.

Tears blinded her vision and her lungs burned for air. She lost the tracks but could hear the engine in the distance. The sound dropped to an idle.

Josh panted beside her. "There," he whispered and pointed.

The top of the van was peeking over the edge of a tall mass of brush.

Josh motioned her to move. They crept closer.

The driver's side door hung open—no dragons. The motor still ran.

A tiny sound came out of the grove on their left.

She twirled around, blade ready, and pushed through the plants. Dirk huddled at the base of a tree.

Five small dragons surrounded him—a ring of burn spots in the shrubby grass at his feet.

The stocky man topped off at about five foot ten, with large bulky muscles on his arms that kept his elbows from touching his sides. A shocking amount of black hair surrounded his head and jaw, every hair sticking out straight as if electrically charged. He wore heavy black boots, camouflage pants, and a Jimmy Buffett T-shirt with a large cigar-smoking pirate face.

Relief flickered over his scruffy face.

"Uh . . ." Dirk spoke without moving from his spot, "no hard feelings, right?"

The rapid pulse in Ellen's throat matched the painful throb in her hand, but she raised the Sword of Srekums at Dirk. No one threatened her babies.

Josh rested a hand on her shoulder. "I think the dragons have guard duty under control."

"He could have killed them! Stealing the van and driving like a madman through these trees."

Dirk called out, "Stealing's a harsh word. I commandeered an abandoned vehicle on my property."

Ellen glared.

The dragons took turns igniting the small weeds burning into the rocks at Dirk's feet. His voice rose a couple octaves. "I had no idea you had dragons in the van. I mean, how would anyone believe that? There isn't anything like this. Were they genetically engineered, Jurassic Park style? They can fly and spit fire! They must be worth a fortune."

Josh held Ellen's arm. "I'd quit running off at the mouth if I were you, Dirk."

Ellen whispered to Josh. "I'm beginning to believe that one day I might meet someone I'd love to kill. What do we do with him? He's seen them."

"I don't think we have a lot of choice. It's your call. He could come in handy. We still need to get through his property. After we make it to Mount Shasta, it's a tough climb. Dirk's old-military and still in shape. If nothing else, we could use him as a pack animal. We still have to get to a store of some kind for boots, gloves, and supplies."

"Add him to the team? I don't trust him."

"Neither do I. I do trust his greed. If he thinks there's something in it for him, he'll be all over it. Plus, if we leave him alone, he's likely to call one of those magazines that print Bigfoot stories. It's up to you."

Ellen focused on Dirk, encircled by five dragons hovering inches above the ground. "I'm in no position to refuse help. But I sincerely doubt he'd be interested."

Josh walked toward Dirk. "I respect you've got some private activities going on in this area that you'd rather not advertise. We need to cut through your property to get to the mountain. As you can probably guess, we'd prefer anonymity."

"It's a little hard to negotiate with fire-breathing dragons in your face. Can you get them to stand down?"

"Ashamoor, babies, it's okay." Ellen used a soft voice. They quieted and moved to her side. The moment they backed off, Dirk ran. He made it ten feet before the dragons had him pinned at another tree. He climbed to the lowest branch, about four feet off the ground.

Ellen laughed. "Are you done running? They won't hurt you, unless I ask them to, of course."

Josh stepped up to Dirk. "We have a proposition."

Dirk whispered to Josh, "Is she crazy?"

"She's got shit going on you could never dream of."

Dirk fixated on the dragons flapping at his level. He slowly slid back to the ground before he spoke, not taking his gaze from the babies. "So, what's your tale?"

"I need to get on Mount Shasta without being seen." Ellen decided not to mention anything about sorcerers, fights to the death, or endless enslavement. "Get us through your booby traps safely, and I'll call off the dragons."

Dirk shook his head. "There's more to it than that. If you're in trouble and need my help, then I want more. What else have you got?"

"Besides not letting these young ones dissolve you into dust?" She raised her chin in a way she hoped vibrated tough character. "I'll make it worth your while. I'd like to think that helping to save the world from evil would be enough for you. I'm willing to bet you'll be wanting something more tangible. I have the last of my advance in my savings account. We'll need safe passage, and some supplies. What you don't have, we'll need you to get."

He snorted. "What kind of booty are we talking about?"

Ellen sighed. "What an idiot."

Josh stepped back to a fallen tree and sat. "We're going to have to trust that idiot," he whispered. "But there's no reason why we have to let him know that yet."

Ellen turned her back on Dirk to hide a smile, then pasted a stern look before sitting next to Josh. "What do you think we'll need? Maybe he has them at his house."

"Not likely he'll have hiking boots or gloves your size. He'll probably have some survival rations. If we're lucky, some venison jerky. It's great protein for hiking."

Great. Another couple of days on jerky and water.

Dirk called out. "Hey guys, do you think you could call them off anytime soon?" He took a step forward. All five dragons squawked. He retreated.

Ellen softly elbowed Josh's ribs. "How long do you think we can keep him there? This is the funniest thing I've seen in a long time."

"Let's give him another five."

Ten minutes later, Ellen faced Dirk. "One thousand dollars." Her savings account didn't offer the same sense of security it had a week ago.

Dirk squinted and wrapped his arms in front of his chest. "I'm of the notion that if you can say one thousand, you could also say two."

She could wring this guy's neck. "I'm not giving you the money that pays for the roof over my head. I'll go up enough to pay for the supplies, so the thousand would be all yours. My partner is waiting for us on the mountain. He has special skills that might also benefit you." *I hope Welglen kicks your ass.*

"How do I know he has anything of value to make it worth the risk?" Dirk's eyes narrowed.

"Besides the fact I have five fire-breathing dragons flying in front of you?" She shook her head. "No reason. There's also no reason to believe you won't be part of something so big it'll blow your mind."

He spat on the ground. "Everyone thinks they can blow my mind. I've seen things that would make you want to crawl into a hole and die."

"Where we are going, five small dragons are petty change. We'll need a ride through to the mountain and directions to the top of Mount Shasta. We may also need a diversion. Someone who can divert the attention of others when needed and be there when we need supplies. We're here to save the world. Are you ready to do your part?"

Dirk shook his head, a grin smeared across his face. "I'll be damned. If nothing else, it'll be an adventure. Count me in for Dragon Ops."

They loaded into the van. Dirk jumped on the side step next to Ellen's open window, one hand on the side mirror, one on top of the van, and one pungent armpit at Ellen's face.

She leaned toward Josh as he zigzagged across the wild acres while a pot-growing, ex-military zealot guided them past unhooked triggers. She gave Dirk the short answers to his questions, filling him in on the links between earthquakes, lava, and sorcerers. She didn't mention how many dragons there were altogether, or anything about Welglen. Between the dragons' grunting, the stuffy van's worsening shocks, and Dirk's smell, Ellen's stomach lurched. She wanted out as bad as the dragons.

"Stop here a minute." Dirk motioned to a dilapidated shack in a small clearing. A Jolly Roger flag waved from a pole at the porch. That had to be his home.

Dirk hopped off and ran into a smaller shed at the right.

Josh pointed the vehicle toward the exit road and kept it in drive, ready to roll. "I don't trust that guy. We have no way of knowing if he plans to grab a rocket launcher and take the van out. He's been on his own for a long time. I'm not sure everything is working in the brain department."

"He got us this far." Ellen kept her focus on the shed door. "We're in too deep to be particular. We wouldn't have made it down the hill without him."

"Let's see if we can use him as backup. If he follows through, we'll be better off. If he doesn't, it won't matter anyway. I'll handle him."

Ellen tried not to laugh at Josh's macho display. They climbed out of the van. Dirk returned with a barking, squatty, muscled bulldog. A black bandanna tied around its neck made it look like Dirk's younger brother. "Quiet, Cay." Dirk untied the dog's chain and harnessed him to a leash, the other end he tied to the van mirror. "He'll watch the dragons while I pack. We can make some plans."

The van rocked. Ellen suspected the dragons would be watching the dog.

The steps of the old wooden porch screeched against Dirk's weight as he bounded up to open the two padlocks on the front door. He waved them forward, then disappeared inside.

Ellen stared at the door. "This is exactly the type of place my mother warned me never to enter. I'm picturing plants drying from the ceiling. Weapons and taxidermy displayed over the walls."

"I don't think your writer's imagination is too far off. I'll bring the rifle."

"I won't mention you don't have any bullets."

Weapon in hand, Josh stepped into the dark shuttered room ahead of her. Before Ellen's eyes could adjust to the lack of light, the door shut with a soft click behind her. She grabbed the shirt at Josh's back. He shuddered in laughter. Her pupils returned to regular size to see the single-room cabin decked floor-to-ceiling in Jimmy Buffett paraphernalia. To the left, a dozen different bottles of rum topped a bamboo bar with a single stool. A mural above depicted a sandy beach on a blue ocean. A toy red-feathered parrot hung from a small ceiling swing.

To her right sat an enormous sound system straight out of the seventies with a turntable and speakers doubling as end tables. Albums covered the shelves. Posters of Jimmy Buffett in concert lined the remaining walls. The bedroom area consisted of a woven hammock hung from the palm-tree painted rafters.

This was one strange character. Story lines erupted in her brain. Ellen clamped her lips together and squeezed Josh's hand. He squeezed back.

Dirk packed a vintage military duffel bag with a few clothing items and some food from behind the bar that apparently served as the kitchen. "Park yer bones," he motioned to the Adirondack chairs in the living room area.

He selected another key from his bulky ring and unlocked a chest. He fished out a small Tupperware container that looked full of weed, a Sony Walkman out of the Stone Age, and a pack of batteries. Ellen tensed when he pulled out a small, holstered pistol. He tucked it into the bag along with a small box of ammo.

The quest had been unreal and at times frightening. Here, in Dirk's house watching him pack his necessities, a real gun terrified her.

Dirk leaned the full bag against the wall next to the door. He poured three short glasses of rum from one of the many bottles and handed them out before sitting on a beer keg to face them.

Dirk took a slug of the strong buttery smelling liquid from his glass as if it were iced tea. "There's no battle plan against a river of lava. You and your friends are the bait that must pull your enemy out into the open. What are the sorcerer's strengths and weaknesses?"

Ellen sipped and her throat ignited. "I have no idea," she choked. "I understand while the dragons are still on my side, and I have my sword, the sorcerer cannot use any spells against me. He would have to kill me human-to-human."

Up to her eyeballs in the reality of this fantasy, the thought of fighting to the death still sent chills through her overheated body.

"I'd bet dollars to donuts he's arrogant. If you have

any skills with that sword of yours, hold off showing him. He'll be sloppier if he believes you aren't worthy of his talents." Dirk swallowed the last of his glass. "Let's be off. First, we'll get online and secure yer treasure."

"Half. The other half when we see you come through for us. And you have to stop talking like a Disney pirate."

He smiled. "Agreed."

She tried to connect to the bank by phone. Her cell service was strong, but a message repeated that the system was currently overloaded. She tucked the phone back into her pocket. "The emergencies and the high influx of people must be screwing with the system."

"No problemo," Dirk pointed to Josh. "Follow me in my Jeep to the crossroads. The little lady will go with me to the bank. We don't have a bank in town, so we'll have to head to Mt. Shasta city. After I have the funds, I'll drop her off, buy the climbing and food supplies, then meet up with you. We'll need to hurry before they close."

Dirk rifled through a stack of papers near the front door. He collected a map and a marker. He spread it over a coffee table covered with hundreds of beer bottle labels and drew a curving line.

"We're at the edge here. I'll open the last gate. You drive north and the road will drop you above where the protesters are holing up. Wait for us there with the beasts. Depending on how messed up town is, we should be less than an hour behind you."

"Great plan. Just one change." Josh shook his head. "I'm not leaving Ellen."

Ellen squeezed his arm. "It's okay. You watch over the babies. If anyone saw them in town, we'd never get out. I'll be all right."

Ellen's confidence waned when Josh drove the van out of sight. It disappeared completely in the front seat of a

Jeep that had no doors, no top, a slobbering black dog, and a stranger who had stolen her babies two hours ago.

The only wisp of courage came from the sword on her lap, wrapped in a jacket and pointed straight at Dirk's kidney.

CHAPTER 50

Welglen leveled off in the wispy clouds scratched across the thin air above Samote. His muscles replenished in the sky, fed on the possibilities of the flight's survival, and the joy of conversing with another dragon.

The lift of hope had drawbacks. The higher up, the further the fall.

You are doing well, Welglen said. *Rest for a bit on the current.*

I can keep climbing.

The determination in her jaw contrasted with the slowed arch of her wings. *There's much to learn about these heights. We climb not only to avoid detection. A great height is needed to commune with the elders. We rise to distance ourselves from the world below and pull our thoughts to those that have gone before us. The stories and spells of the past are part of your birthright. I'm not an elder or a teacher. But I'll tell you what I know. Together we may learn more.*

Welglen aligned with Samote, wings nearly touching. Of all the things she needed to know, the most important would be how to deal with death.

You come from a long line of dragons, born of the northern volcanoes. You were ferried with the others after the great war. Only three from my brother's flight survived. There's at least one other clutch of eggs that may still live. I suspect they are in the East. One day you may find them. But the goal is to keep as many of those we have, alive.

Shouldn't the goal be to keep them all alive?

Lives will end in the battle we're about to face. Honoring the lost ensures the circle of life and helps heal the living.

Welglen tumbled to his right and glided apart on the high winds, to allow her to focus on his words. Settling on the current with the young female enveloped him in a comfort he hadn't experienced in centuries. The cool air chilled his wings as the warmth of his fire spread through his chest.

What happened to your brother?

Welglen repositioned at Samote's side. *He fought bravely. He saved those he could. The sorcerer's fires destroyed his ability to transform back to dragon. He let go of the pain he suffered after he knew the last of his flight were in my care.*

Samote groaned deep; wisps of smoke trailed out her nostrils. Her pain, palpable.

I spoke with him before he left us. I was honored to be able to ferry him to the heavens. This is why we're here, away from the flight. We'll lose brothers and sisters, but if we follow the traditions of the past, they won't be gone. They will move on. Welglen soared higher. Samote followed. *Feel the coolness of the air. Sense the warmth grow inside you as you climb. Roglir was the first I've carried to the heavens. The presence of the ancestors surrounded me, and my load lightened, though I still held him in my claws. The soul in his heart had passed through the others, joining in their afterlife. I released his body and with the prayer of the departed, sent him back as ashes to the Earth to be reborn.*

Samote's breathing calmed. *Life is a circle?*

We play our part. He rotated in a slow spiral and repeated the prayer for the dead. *Goloo Glem Niks Kukar. Goloo Glem Niks Kukar.*

She wove beside him. *Can we commune directly with the ancestors?*

I have tried. I believe it's only in the heights we may hear their response. Even then, it's not guaranteed. I'm seeking the spell to remove the light from the sorcerer, without success. We'll need to rely on your scattering of the flight while I distract the sorcerer with my heart.

We can't quit. We can find it. Ancestors, give us the spell to save our flight. Samote struggled for altitude. She slipped lower in the winds.

Let's return to the others. You have accomplished much this night. It's time for you to rest.

I can keep going. Samote struggled to climb above him.

Save your passion as a strength to be used when it is needed most. I fear that will be soon.

Samote panted with each upward stroke. *We can't let you sacrifice your life. Ancestors, help us.*

Come, Samote. A rumbling rippled through Welglen's brain. He spiraled, searching for the source. The words penetrated his inner ears.

Oomm Rash O Woo. Oomm Rash O Woo.

Samote dropped onto the current below him. *What is that?*

The rhythmic pattern repeated.

Oomm Rash O Woo. Oomm Rash O Woo.

Welglen threw back his head and roared a blast of flames toward the heavens. Together, they were stronger. *Our salvation. The spell to pull the light. I'll need your help. As it didn't come to me alone, it won't work alone.*

I'll stay by your side.

You'll stay until I see that we're about to lose all. Then you'll scatter the flight. We cannot trust we have all we need to make this spell work.

Samote twisted as she floated down, repeating the chant. *Oomm Rash O Woo. Oomm Rash O Woo.*

CHAPTER 51

Big-city traffic jams clogged the single small-town road and trapped Ellen in the slow-moving parade for nearly an hour, listening to Dirk sing along with an ancient Jimmy Buffett cassette. He flipped it over in his player a third time when she broke her silence.

"Who are you? What brought you to the hills of Dunsmuir?" He would absolutely be a weird character in a bizarre story she'd write someday.

He snorted. "That's a long tale. I'm Douglas Randall Killigrew." He lifted his hand off the dice-shaped gearshift knob and held it out. She took the calloused mitt in her hand for a quick shake. "I joined the Marines after my big brother died in a training exercise in Afghanistan. I became known as the go-to guy for impossible missions. I ended up in the brig more often than on duty, so I accepted the graciously offered discharge. I don't have any family left. I rambled around for a while until I won the ranch in a poker game. It's as good a way to live as any."

Cheeseburgers in Paradise played through the scratchy speakers again. "And Jimmy Buffett? How does he play in your life? His usual demographic is a lot older than you."

He tapped the steering wheel to the beat of the song. "What do you mean? He's ageless. That's the soundtrack of my life. Jimmy feeds my soul. He is who I want to be when I grow up."

"A music star?"

He shook his head. "A way of life."

Ellen let that sink in during both songs "Margaritaville" and "Why Don't We Just Get Drunk and Screw." She'd no idea what Dirk brought to the party other than a ride and his personal shopper expertise. She might as well be open about it. "I don't know what I'm doing with you. Once we're in town, I could get the supplies myself."

"I come in handy when times get crazy—and baby, crazy is here." He smiled. "What about you and Josh? Is it serious? You're quite a looker for the serious type."

He's hitting on me? "Why would I want to open up to a guy who stole my dragons and is only helping me because I'm paying him?"

"You make it sound awful. It's just business. You and Josh are a thing, right? I remember you living with him. What happened?"

"That's a long story that I don't want to tell you. Don't you want to know how I ended up with dragons or what we're likely to find when we reach the top of the mountain? That's the real story here."

They turned a sharp right. The main road came into view ahead.

"I figure I'll find out soon enough. What I don't know yet is if I have a shot." He smiled without looking at her, then slowed in the traffic to a crawl.

"Your ego is incredible."

"You should see the rest of me."

"Ugh!" Ellen looked out to the right at the crowded roadway to make sure she didn't accidentally appear like she wanted to see anything of him. He had agreed to help, for a price. Spending time with him represented an added tax.

Dirk squeezed into the line of cars. They only needed the main roadway for a mile until the first town exit. Humid dog breath blew on her back. The rest of her skin tightened as the sun cracked through the dust. She'd been more worried about packing something to save her from a fatal wound than worrying about sunburn. She might end up with both.

Traffic inched ahead, then stopped. Dirk whipped the Jeep onto the side shoulder. They leaned into a ditch.

Ellen grabbed the bar above her right arm as they bounced forward. "What are you doing?"

"Jeep shortcut."

Dirk skirted through the narrow path bordered by power lines on one side and a line of car horns blasting in protest.

He swerved around an exit sign close enough to snap the side mirror in next to Ellen. He turned to the right across a landscape barrier. The road dipped ahead.

She clutched the dash with both hands. Her head bobbed and her feet bounced against the floorboards. Dirk crossed the railroad tracks, then rode along the graveled side to the back of a row of buildings. He stopped in a line of traffic.

Ellen gasped. "You're insane."

"Just getting us where we need to go." He turned into a small alley, darted around trash dumpsters, and stopped at a dead end. "Stay!"

"I don't take orders from you." Ellen stepped out onto a pile of fast-food containers that had tumbled out of the overflowing containers.

"I meant, Cay. You and your bank card, I need."

She moved the sword to the back seat and covered it with an old green wool blanket. "Do you think Cay will protect my sword? It's a little bizarre to walk down the street with it."

"No one gets past Cay without my say-so."

Ellen didn't have much of a choice. She left the sword under the enormous dog with long teeth and even longer strands of drool.

They walked the remaining blocks, crowded with people who stared at the top of Mount Shasta. The volcano was viewable from almost any position in the old town dotted with single and small two-story structures.

A security guard opened the door two minutes before closing after Ellen pressed her driver's license and ATM card to the glass door. In the bank, she withdrew five hundred for Dirk and some more cash to split with him for supplies. He stuffed both into his jean's pocket. The same guard locked the door behind them and flipped the sign over to closed.

If they were lucky, Dirk's help would ensure she reached Welglen in time to save everyone. She doubted she'd have much use for the money in the future unless her luck changed. A thousand dollars wasn't going to keep her in her house forever.

The crowd expanded off the sidewalk and filled the street, blocking any other car's passage. The Main Street Mountain Store selling the supplies they needed had closed early in defense of unruly crowds. Two men worked out front to border its broken windows with plywood.

Dirk tugged her through the crowd by the hand. She wanted to pull free, but his frame cut a smoother path. "I know another store out of town. It's past our meeting place with Josh. Should we go together, or do I drop you off and go alone?"

"Take me back to my dragons." The world was crazy. She needed her team.

A young man in a yellow zip-up hoodie and jeans climbed to the top of one of the stopped cars. An older man inside, got out of the driver's seat and released a string of swear words. The younger man clicked on the small bull horn on his hand.

"We have to unite," he bellowed. Ellen cupped one ear with her free hand. "The Earth is crying out for our help. We can't deny it. Join us and march against fracking!"

A green shiny object sailed through the air and hit the speaker in the leg, shattering into dozens of glassy pieces and knocking the speaker to his knees, atop the car. "You can't stop us. The Earth won't be denied. Watch your town crumble or join us to stop the madness."

The mob pushed Ellen side to side. The maddening frenzy was about to break into a full riot. Dirk tugged at her arm.

"This way, mate." He dragged her free of the crowd into the alley where he'd parked.

Three men surrounded the Jeep, balancing their desire to see what was in Dirk's large bag with their fear of Cay, who growled low; teeth exposed.

Ellen stopped in her tracks. Dirk signaled her to stay back. *Why is he telling me what to do*? She followed.

"Hey, dudes," Dirk smiled, his voice friendly. "What's up, man? I see you like my ride. Pretty sweet, right?"

The men turned to face Dirk. Ellen flashed on the Three Stooges—one tall shaggy blond about her age wearing jeans that hadn't been washed in forever, one older stocky guy whose only hair ran in a single eyebrow from his left ear to his right, and a guy with a frizz halo flaring out in every direction.

Eyebrow Guy looked like the leader. "We were just saying how much we want to take this Jeep for a little ride," he drawled in an accent Ellen couldn't place. "You see, our cars are stuck along with all those out-of-towners. We need to get out of here in sort of a hurry."

He drew his right hand out of his pocket, flashing open a small knife. "I'm sure you won't mind calling the dog off. Toss the keys. Of course, we'll return it as soon as we can."

Dirk raised his hands. "Whooooa. Glad you like my ride, but it won't start. That's why we left it here. I wanted to get it to the service station, but everything's closed up. Came back for the dog and my bag."

The man raised the right side of his eyebrow, creating a long hairy slant across his forehead. He turned slightly to make eye contact with the other two. They fanned out, circling them.

"You won't mind letting me check for myself, would you? My buddy here is kind of a magician when it comes to making cars move." He pointed at Frizzy-Hair Man.

Dirk laughed in a slow chuckle.

"Heck no! I've needed a ride before. I get it."

Dirk reached both hands into his pockets. He drew out the keys and threw them a couple feet above the head of Eyebrow Man, who reached to grab them. Dirk darted in and slugged him in the jaw, knocking him to the ground. The knife skidded to a stop at Ellen's feet.

She kicked it under the Jeep.

The eyes on the guy on the ground were closed.

She decided to believe he was unconscious, versus dead.

The other two raced at Dirk from either side. Dirk ducked, then grabbed Shaggy Man by the neck and used the force of a turn to knock him into Hair Man. Hair Man hit the brick wall. He slid motionless to the ground; one side of his halo flattened.

Shaggy Man scrambled up and limped out of the alley and into the crowd.

Dirk picked up the keys and gave his dog an affectionate scratch behind the ears before he jumped in to start the Jeep.

"Glad to see you don't run from a fight." He glanced over his shoulder at Ellen. "Coming?"

She checked out the two men, both moaning, and raced around to the passenger's seat. "Okay—you have skills."

Dirk performed a twelve-point turn out of the alley. He used a bike path to escape a town in chaos. The van would never have made it through. Neither would her driving techniques. This called for maneuvering skills, knowledge of the area, and a higher level of crazy than she possessed.

Forty-five minutes of driving on dirt fire roads and around locked gates that he somehow knew how to drive around, brought them to a secluded fork, where Josh waited next to the van. The dragons scavenged around the rocks.

Josh stared at her. She checked her face in the mirror. Dust stuck to the sweat, matching her skin with her hair color. She wiped her face with the jacket. "It's crazy down there. People are crazy scared."

Dirk rubbed the back of his neck. "We couldn't get the supplies we needed. The store was closed due to the rioting. I'll travel north to the next town, and you meet me in about four hours. I'll show you where."

Dirk laid his map out on the hood of the van.

The dragons circled Dirk, tossing an occasional ball of fire toward his feet.

"What's with them?" Dirk stepped on tip toe. "Don't they remember me?"

Ellen smiled. "Oh, they remember you." They didn't trust him any more than she did. And they had tremendous senses of humor.

Dirk's deep voice lightened to a falsetto as he tried to give Josh instructions, all the while snapping his head left to right to match the distance of the nearest dragon.

"Take a look." Dirk pointed at the map with the marker. "Normally, I'd start at Bunny Flats and hike to Lake Helen to set up camp, then ascend in the early hours of the morning while it's still cool past Red Banks to Misery Hill. You're going to want to avoid the regular trails. There may be crazy folks hiking when the world is falling apart.

For sure there will be some geologists or rangers or something. Start the regular ascent to the ski property. I'll meet you at the lift building here with rations as soon as I can. It'll provide temporary shelter. From there, it's a tough climb over loose rock and sand until you get high enough to add some ice. I'll bring climbing shoes and gloves." He noted their sizes.

Josh paced in front of the van door. "These are wild times. If something happens and we have to go off course, will you be able to find us?"

"Give me a break." Dirk climbed back behind the wheel, never turning his back on the dragons. "My Aunt Harriett could track a couple of city folks like you."

Dirk headed down the road in a trail of dust. Ellen stepped next to Josh. "Does anything about having Dirk on our side feel reassuring to you?"

"Not a thing. But if we make it to the other dragons and the sorcerer, we can use all the help we can get. We'll need more supplies and the element of surprise against the sorcerer. Sounds like he won't be expecting humans to fight. That should help."

"I don't think he's expecting humans at all. From what Welglen said, the last time dragons and humans were together, they were fighting against each other."

"Maybe there's hope."

Ellen propped Dirk's map on the van dash.

The Earth shook.

CHAPTER 52

The blue male led the long trail of tiny dragons climbing and flying in spurts over the rocky surface past Welglen. Samote drove the last into view, then stopped at his side in the late afternoon light.

A rock kicked loose from the dragons ahead and tumbled at her. She jumped neatly over it and hissed. *We have learned to fly, only to be forced to crawl.*

Welglen scanned the valley below. *Even with the smoke,* we *are too exposed above the tree line to risk flight. Our destination is near. It won't be long.*

What can we expect?

Anything. The sorcerers' will stop at nothing.

We have strength together. We can stop this.

Welglen climbed toward the others. *You have the confidence of the young. I was born with that too. That was before I watched humans slaughter my flight at the direction of a sorcerer.*

We have the spell. I heard it.

We have the words. I don't know if they'll be enough.

We have our human. Ellen. She'll fight at our side.

Welglen searched the hillside below him, searching for Ellen.

It's right that you believe in her. What I fear is she lacks the belief in herself. Stay on plan. I shall attempt to pull the light from the sorcerer and offer my heart to buy you time.

Should we not fight to stay together?

A low rumble of heat poured out of Welglen's mouth in a sigh. *We must separate. If some survive, there will be hope for a future.*

The mountainside leveled slightly, allowing a better view of the remaining climb ahead. He turned back to the others. *We are close. Hurry ahead to the blue male. Ensure he understands our plan. He'll lead a group of the weakest when they scatter. You'll take another. We'll have to hope the remaining are strong enough to survive in their own tiny herds. Stay low. Follow my lead.*

CHAPTER 53

Dust poured through the open van windows and masked the smell of dragon drool as Ellen navigated Josh over the bumpy fire trail that cut through the pine forest. The heavy metal bars that periodically blocked access were often unattached to fencing; the ditches on each side of the gates were enough of a threat for most drivers.

Most drivers weren't running dragons toward an epic sorcerer showdown.

Ellen massaged her green and black bruised palm, now able to move the last two fingers with only slight twinges. She twisted back to check on the dragons. "They look carsick. I know I am."

"Dirk has us zigzagging all over this mountain. He'd better be there." Josh struggled with the steering wheel. The van dipped into a rut, throwing Ellen to the right side of the vehicle.

"Ow." She rubbed the spot on her head that smacked against the door frame. It matched the bump on the other side. She readjusted away from the door and reread the directions for the fifth time in thirty minutes. From their forested vantage point, they couldn't see Mt. Shasta, the base only a couple miles away. "There's a steep climb coming on the right, then cross a two-lane highway to get to the mountainside. That'll be fun. It's bound to be packed."

"Check the news before we lose service. It's the top of the hour."

Ellen tuned in the local station. The familiar news announcer had already started. *Temperatures between the fracking and anti-fracking groups are steaming hot. Multiple sources claim the volcanic action is the result of unusual animal activity. Lennie Green, gas station attendant in nearby Dunsmuir, claims he saw strange animals the night of the first quakes. Can you tell us in your own words?*

The young man's voice sounded like he was chewing gum. *They were wicked cool dragon things. This blonde lady drove them around in a large white van. They had long snouts and looked right at me.*

Ellen slapped a hand over her mouth. "Crap. I hoped he thought he'd imagined us."

The announcer took over. *Thank you, Lennie. While the existence of dragons in the Mount Shasta area seems unlikely, a geologist checking mountain activity said a flying dragon saved her from a landslide on the mountain. She's under observation at the county hospital.*

A helicopter roared above. Ellen switched off the radio. She stuck her head out the window to follow its path but could only catch glimpses in the treetops. "We have to ditch the van fast."

Twenty jerky minutes later, Josh rolled the van over a landscaped curb behind a ski rental shop. The empty parking lot gave a view of the sea of cars blocking their path to the road up the mountain and their meeting place with Dirk.

They needed to stay out of sight.

First, they needed to stop traffic.

Ellen drummed her hand against the door and exhaled in a long push. "Let's do it."

She scrounged down in the seat, covering the side of her face with one hand. Josh rolled to the graveled edge then nosed the van toward the bumper-to-bumper stream.

Dirty looks started first as drivers refused to give up their spot in the long line of vehicles. Angry hand gestures followed, before one car waved them in.

They blocked all eastbound traffic and the honking started.

Every westbound driver stared directly into the van's windshield. Ellen crouched murmuring to the dragons to stay low.

Semitruck brakes hissed and mercifully stopped to let them through to the other side where the road turned up into a thick forested hillside.

Ellen sat up and checked the map. "Follow the ski park signs. I'll tell you when to turn. Hopefully the van will make it off-road for a bit so we'll have less to climb to Dirk."

"If he's there."

"I don't trust him either. But we don't have a choice. We couldn't have gotten the supplies with this van and the dragons. Dirk and I barely made it out." She skipped the story of the three stooges ready to fight. Josh probably didn't want to know everything.

They broke through the trees and Mt. Shasta rose ahead to a cloud-covered tip. She'd seen the beautiful volcano at a distance many times. Never this close.

Massive.

Slices of ice cascaded in ribbons from the peak. She may never find Welglen on it. Hopefully, he could find her.

"I'm just realizing I have to go mountain climbing before my first and perhaps last sword battle. The strangest part is, I'm not worried about heights, rocks, or falling. Anything sounds easier than a sorcerer."

Josh's mouth squeezed tight. He switched the radio back on and searched for a non-news station. A scratchy country music station filled the silence as he turned to climb the narrow, paved road.

The ski park was closed for the season, but Dirk's directions led them past the locked gate with fortified fencing, to a back entrance. A dark gray cloud of smoke ribboned in the westward wind from somewhere near the top of the mountain.

At a clearing in the trees, Josh stopped to let the dragons out for a nature break. "Let's get out too. It's the last spot on Dirk's map where we have any real cover."

In a game of tag, the dragons left one at a time to kick over the rocks and catch lizards. The others circled Ellen.

When they'd all fed, they leaped back into the van without prodding. Ellen sighed. "That's unnerving. Even they want to move on."

She walked to the edge of the trees to check out the ski lodge above. Two benches dangled above on the chairlift cables. "It doesn't look like anyone's here. Maybe we could drive the van up that road by the snow equipment. It's closest to the trees for cover."

The wind changed, driving the smoke closer to the ground.

"I'm on it." Josh forced the whining engine to climb the hillside through a break in the trees between boulders and large evergreens.

At the peak, a bike path allowed barely enough width to skirt down the back side, then back up the next hill to another set of chairlifts.

The wheels spun against the dry dirt of the summer hillside. They stalled out at an incline somewhere between the ski lodge and the top of the run near the edge of the tree line. The clouds and smoke blew horizontally, exposing a quick view of Mt. Shasta ahead.

Josh backed the van into the cover of the trees.

Ellen let the dragons out. They hovered close, protective dragon instincts engaged. "Try to stay out of sight, babies."

She tightened the heavy pack to her shoulders and carried the sword in front of her.

Josh left the van keys behind the front tire.

They climbed the steep incline diagonally, crisscrossing under the cables that held the chairs. The little ones flew ahead and to the right.

The air cooled as the afternoon dwindled. At the top of the crest, haze covered the view of the mountain above. The small shed used in season as a coffeehouse lay directly ahead. They'd wait for Dirk there.

Josh touched her hand and whispered, "We have company."

A thin stream of smoke curled from the metal chimney pipe on the roof of the small building.

A dark-haired man about her age appeared from the doorway, rifle butt first.

Ellen froze.

The young man swung the bullet end over toward them and slid on the dry grass until he stopped about thirty feet away. "Hey, you. You don't work here. This is private property."

He didn't have on a uniform either. He wore a Hayfork Timberjacks sweatshirt. A woman emerged from the doorway wearing a matching hat.

Josh waved. "We're geologists. You probably heard about our mission on the news. We're here to take a ground check and temperature reading. Some of our remote equipment stopped working."

"That's a funny looking thermometer you have there, lady." He pointed with the end of the gun to her sword.

Ellen stabbed the Sword of Srekums into the dirt. "It's my lucky walking stick."

The guy laughed and lowered the gun. "Thought you might be the wrong kind. There's a lot of them down there." He pointed at the valley. "They're fighting over whose fault it is. We're gonna stay here until things settle down."

Ellen searched the area around the small building for any signs of Dirk. "Sure you want to stay here? You're not afraid of the volcano?"

"Nah. I've lived here all my life. It's people that scare me."

Josh gave him a thumbs-up. "I can't argue with that. We're supposed to meet another team member around here. Have you seen anyone else?"

The man shook his head. "Just you two."

Branches cracked.

The man swung his gun in the direction of the trees. And the dragons. "What was that?"

Ellen stepped in front of the gun. "What?"

He nodded forward. "There's something in those trees."

Josh laughed. "That's probably Dirk, our seismic specialist. He's pretty clumsy. Let's walk up with him. Good luck, dude."

They moved into the trees. Ellen shushed the dragons.

At the opposite edge of the small cluster, they followed a secondary chair lift uphill for ten minutes, positioning with a view of the building where they were supposed to meet Dirk.

The dragons stayed at her side. "What are we going to do now? Dirk's not going to know where we are."

Josh rubbed the back of his neck. "Let's see how far we can get and still see the area. Hopefully we'll be able to signal him."

A gust of wind swirled sandy dirt in their faces. The sun dipped to the horizon and the temperature dropped.

Ellen wiped her eyes with the edge of her shirt. "That was ominous."

"It's a big sign telling us to get the hell off this mountain. You've done all you could. Time to quit."

"I can't leave the babies. I don't want to look back and realize I had a chance to make things better, but I didn't take it. We have to wait here for Dirk. We need the supplies."

She spread out the meager provisions.

Josh stood over the pile. "The first aid kit and the two granola bars could be useful. What's with the four changes of socks and the barbecue tools?"

"Give me a break. It's my first quest."

Josh unfolded one of the thin foil-like survival blankets and reached an arm out for Ellen.

She tucked into his warmth at sunset. Smoke and clouds blocked the moon and pitch dark took on a new level.

Josh kissed her temple. "This is a crazy mess. But even if we quit, imagine the stories we'll have for our grandchildren."

The ground rolled in a soft tremor.

Ellen shivered.

The smell of sulfur laced the growing winds.

CHAPTER 54

Fierce headwinds forced the flight to scratch for connection in the loose rock. Welglen flapped against a strong gust and rose above the smoke for bearings. Only minutes away from the meeting spot in the air, hours on the ground.

Moonlight reflected on an oval-shaped cloud that circled the mountain below, covering the others. The harsh temperature shift between the cool air and warm surface created weather limited to the area. The little bit of smoke that curled through near their destination spiraled high. The turn in the mountain ahead might offer enough protection from the wind for the little ones to fly.

But first, they had to get there.

Welglen tumbled in the twisting current, forced into the ring of smoke and clouds. He angled directly into the wind, then slipped down toward the dragons. Flying would not be an option here. None of the young ones held the strength to match the wind's fury.

Instinct led him back to Samote. A small group wedged against her. The blue male followed her lead, holding their clusters together.

Easy to see who stood a chance. The flight's trail separated the dragons by lack of strength. If Welglen could push them to the clearing at the crest, there might be time for the others to rest before they'd have to fly again.

He couldn't take some and leave others. If he separated them before he knew where the sorcerer would appear, they had no chance.

He raced to the center of the stretch of dragons and touched his claws to the Earth. The ground shook, rupturing into a split.

The flight divided.

Welglen hovered against the wind.

He leaped over the chasm to the slowest flyers. A crack in the rock sprayed out smoke. An orange glow highlighted the thick air. A burst of steaming heat blasted at his back and scorched the tip of one wing.

He rolled to his side and called to Samote. *Move ahead! Take any who are able.*

Welglen crawled to a group of the smallest, hunkered down against the wind.

Another chasm opened behind them with a loud crack, spewing out hot rocks. Blocked in.

He covered ten dragons under his outstretched wings. *Hover!*

They rose at his command, only to be smacked back to the Earth with sharp gusts.

He grasped one of the poor flyers in his teeth, and two more in his claws. He lifted over the crushing heat, then flew past Samote to a small outcrop and dropped the trio.

He dipped back into the inferno.

Three had managed to fly over the rift to the edge of the chasm, their eyes oozing to a point of blindness—agitated and afraid.

Welglen darted toward them. Winds blew the smoke into a swirl of ash. He cut through and captured their dark silhouettes. A sharp downwind slammed him to the ground, hitting his charges hard with his body weight.

He lifted into the onslaught again, hauling them to the outcrop. Unable to check on their wounds, he dropped them with the others.

He raced toward the shadows of the last four dragons. Red flames pierced the blackness. The fire's heat pierced his skin where several of his scales had been injured in the fall.

The young ones clung to a tiny island of rock surrounded by torrential blasts of steam. A lick of orange outlined the edges of the rock. The sorcerer closed in.

Welglen snatched two in his claws.

The Earth shuddered and tossed the last pair onto their sides. The sorcerer's lava splashed over the rock, driving the heat through their feet and soft underwings.

The little dragons growled out in agony.

Welglen captured two sets of wings in his mouth, the smell of scorched flesh filled his nostrils. The smallest slipped back into the heat.

He dashed ahead and dropped the bundle with the others in a quick heap, rushing back for the last.

The small female clung to the rock; claws spread.

Welglen slowed his descent into hell to capture her.

I'm here, young one.

He reached out his claws.

A flick of orange waved over her.

She vanished into the crevice.

The land jolted. The two sides bolted tight.

Flames stung the scales along his sides. Sadness pierced his soul—life lost between the crushing movements of the Earth.

Agony pierced his soul, threatening to pull him down in anguish.

He returned to the flight.
The sorcerer would arrive soon.
Not all the dragons would die by fire.

CHAPTER 55

Hours since the last quake, the dusty early morning sky proved the mountain was still there. They'd survived.

Ellen and Josh climbed and slid on the volcanic mountainside in a life-and-death version of Chutes and Ladders. Every time they made a little headway, the rocks under their feet would loosen and they'd slip back.

She sat to shake the gravel out of her tennis shoes. "Damn Dirk. If he'd actually delivered the boots we need, I wouldn't have to do this every ten feet."

Josh passed her an energy bar. "As long as you're down again, eat this. Chew slowly. There's not much left."

"Dirk abandoned us. Why should we follow his route? There's probably an actual trail nearby."

"With real geologists or rangers."

Gray gusts slapped Ellen's damp shirt against her back. She rubbed her arms. Cold and sweat were a bad combination. She bit into the bar, then stuffed the uneaten portion into her pocket. Her little babies stayed at her side, offering a little hope. Her team would have her back while she saved the world. "It's hard for me to believe anyone else would be stupid enough to climb a volcano after an earthquake."

The wind shifted, driving the choking smoke over them.

The ground rumbled in a short, rolling quake.

Silence.

A rumbling noise from high above grew louder.

The mountain moved.

"Landslide!" Ellen called. Josh pushed her against a semicircle of boulders.

A thunderous wave of gravel slid to their left, blacking out any light.

Ellen pressed her face into his chest, her nose buried in his shirt in shallow breaths.

The roar slipped away, leaving silence and a cloud of dust that sent them both into coughing frenzies.

The wind shifted, blowing the smoke to the left.

She leaned against the stone to catch her breath. She wiped the dust away from her eyes and looked to Josh.

The air had left a gray mask on his face. He opened one of the last water bottles. He passed it to her to refill the canteen. She rubbed a sleeve over her face and tried to find a clean spot on her shirt to wipe the scratchy tears. "Thanks." The warm water rehydrated her tongue, rough against the dry roof of her mouth. "Glad you're here."

Josh hugged her to his side. She lingered in his arms long enough to get her bearings. She tied one of her shirts around her neck, pulled above her nose and mouth to create an illusion of blocking smoke. She faced the last leg of the trek—straight up.

At least Dirk's instructions led them toward the top.

She tightened the straps until the backpack snugged against her body. The ground moved under her feet. She wobbled and grabbed at the boulder for support.

"Another one?" Ellen asked the sky. "Can I catch a break?"

The rolling stopped, then jolted. The dragons squawked at her side as they bobbed in the changing winds.

She heard a distressed voice.

Ellen. Ellen.

"Welglen! I hear you! What do I do?"

"What?" Josh asked. She raised a finger to her lips.

Nothing.

Josh whispered, "What's going on?"

"Welglen's calling." She waved at the dragons. "Fly!"

The dragons lifted above them, except Ashamoor, who managed to hover close enough for her to touch.

"Hurry! The other dragons are in danger."

Gravel bounced from side to side under her feet. A tumble of sharp-edged rocks poured down the mountain, pelting them with instant bruises.

She covered her head with her arms, and they ducked back under the partial cover of the boulders.

A cloud of rocks and dirt refilled the air.

The shaking stopped. Ellen forced her breaths through the thick fabric until the dust cleared.

When her heart quieted, she found her voice.

"Josh?" She cracked open her eyes.

A stream of blood ran from the top of his head down his dusty face and into his beard.

"Oh God, you're hurt!"

He tried to manage a small grin, then coughed. "That stung."

The dragons hovered unharmed while Ellen dug for the first aid kit.

She gagged. The gash stretched about an inch long. From the white and pink flesh showing beneath his hair, it needed stitches.

She washed the area with some of the meager water supply and pressed a cleanish sock over to stop the bleeding. Josh groaned. Some color had returned to his dusty gray complexion.

"You need a doctor." She pressed against his long, scruffy hair to stem the flow and block the growing panic. "I have butterfly bandages, but there's too much hair for them to stick."

"Stitches would suck," Josh's expression twisted. "The little I know about them is the time it would take us to hike back to the car and drive to a hospital would be too late anyway. Is there anything you could do to get me through?"

"I don't know. It's been a long time since my first aid course. Let's check the bleeding, okay?" A blood stain had soaked a small circle on the side of the white cotton sock. She folded it in half and pressed back down, then lifted to reveal only smudges of red on the clean side of the sock.

"How's it look?"

Ellen forced her gaze to the gash. Blood seeped near the center. It needed a couple of stitches. "How's it feel?"

"Like I got hit with a rock." He reached a hand to his forehead. "The spot hurts, but I don't have any overall headache or anything and my vision isn't blurry. That's good, right?"

"Generally, yeah." Ellen added lack of emergency medical skills to her list of warrior incompetencies. She lifted a clump of hair away from the wound and the skin moved with it. "This is going to sound weird. I'm thinking I might be able to braid the cut shut."

"You're kidding."

"Maybe." She lifted a thin wet cluster of hair from one side at the small end, tugged it over and twisted it with a similar sized piece at the other. Josh winced. "I'm sorry!"

"It feels like you're performing brain surgery. But keep going. We're out of options."

And out of time.

Adrenaline took over during the longest three minutes of her life. She braided the strands across the cut while continually providing the pressure to hold the skin together. Blood helped hold the finished braid in place.

She rinsed it off, then pressed the last clean sock on for several minutes before rechecking.

The area around the wound swelled, the skin red. But the bleeding stopped.

"I think this is going to work. Just in case, remember you gave me permission." She attempted a chuckle that died in her throat. She squeezed the sample-sized antiseptic ointment over the clean side of the sock in hopes it would kill some of the germs. She pressed it to Josh's head. "Hold this while I find your hat."

She searched the area that surrounded the backpack contents she'd torn through. His hat lay about ten feet down the slide.

She scooted down on her butt and snatched it.

The gray haze of the valley below nearly matched the color of the rocks under her. Past where Josh sat, the mountain angled up, only traces of white ice cutting through the gray.

She couldn't see Welglen, but her gut said he needed her.

The baseball cap fit tightly over Josh's head, holding down the sock bandage. He flinched, exhaled, and leaned back against the boulder, closing his eyes. "Give me a minute then we can get going."

She repacked the paltry supplies and tightened the backpack straps against her shoulders. She reached down to Josh.

He grabbed her hand, using the other to help push him off the mountainside. His knees buckled and he slid back to the ground. "I might need a few more minutes."

"We need help. We've stopped the bleeding, but I have no way of knowing if you have a concussion or something."

Ellen dug through the backpack for her phone, circling for a signal.

"911?" he asked.

"Not with this one. Let me check yours." After failing to gain any service, she dropped to his side.

"I need a little rest. I'll try again."

"I'm pretty sure there's a thing about not falling asleep if you have a concussion. Rest means not moving but staying awake."

"Gotcha, doc." He took a sip from the canteen she offered. "I couldn't imagine being comfortable enough on these sharp rocks for sleep. What now?"

Ellen dug through the pack. She unfolded the emergency blanket next to Josh. "Sit on this so it doesn't blow away before you need it. It's going to get pretty cold and there's nothing here to start a fire."

"What about you, or do I want to know?"

She placed all the contents of the pack within his reach, including the canteen. She repacked the half-full water bottle and an emergency blanket.

"I've got to go for help. We're about halfway. If I went back to the van, I might be able to call for help, assuming I'm not stopped by any crazies. Then they'd have to get here to you. It's a long way on foot." She strapped the sword on the outside of the bag. "But it's not so far as the dragon flies."

"You're leaving me injured on a mountainside for a dragon?"

"I'm thinking of you, too." She wished she could take back the word 'too.' "He could be your savior. If the sorcerer hasn't reached him yet, he could carry you down to safety in minutes, faster than any helicopter rescue team."

"What if the sorcerer has found him?"

Ellen shook the idea out of her head. "Then I'll be there to help. You could still end up riding a dragon today."

"I'm thinking my chances are better if you head downhill. At the top of this mountain is a bad guy apparently intent on killing either you, Welglen, or both of you. Downhill, you're safe and I have better odds."

She couldn't argue with that. Josh would be better off if she went down the mountain for help. "I have to believe we're going to be okay."

"Who's we?"

Ellen looked past Josh at the dragons perched on the boulders. They stared back at her. They wouldn't leave her, no matter which direction she chose.

"I have to keep going."

"What am I supposed to do while you risk your life for a bunch of animals over me? Slide down the rocks and hope I don't pass out?"

"Seriously, Josh?" She was hot, tired, and scared to death. "I didn't ask for this, but the truth is I couldn't stop even if I wanted to. You need medical help. I have thirty dragons to save. I'm thinking of everyone."

Josh stared at her, shook his head slightly, then winced. "Stay."

A reasonable request. Ellen's mother and everyone else she knew would've said the same thing.

Everyone, except Welglen.

"I know this is insane, but I have to do it," she pleaded. "You can't move. I can't stay."

"Who's going to save you?" His whisper layered guilt on top of the fear and anxiety she already carried.

"I'll have to do that too. Before I go, there's something you should know. I found out I can't have children."

Josh shrugged. "Who cares? I never wanted kids anyway. I only want you."

"I care. I want children. I want to be a mother. For reasons I can't explain, these dragons have become mine. A mother never leaves her babies."

"You're mixed up. Sit for a while. We'll talk. You'll feel better."

"Stay here in the shadow of the boulder in case more slides come down. Between our two phones, you should have enough battery to signal with the flashlight app if I'm not back by dark. I'll climb to the top with the dragons and ensure the others are safe. As soon as I can, I'll come back for you."

"And if you don't?"

She put on the Route 66 potholders. "Tell my folks I followed my heart."

She hoped his anger signified he'd be all right.

"Don't go. It's not safe. You could be killed."

No denying that. Ellen kissed him. "You mean a lot to me. I don't want to leave you, but there's no one else who can help. Dirk probably gave us up for the reward."

"You're already thinking you might be able to kill. You're already changing. Fight it. If you kill, it'll change you forever."

"I'll do my best. I can't promise anything else."

She signaled the dragons to fly then climbed into the smoky wind to become the heroine of her story.

CHAPTER 56

Welglen licked the gray ash away from the young ones' injuries, assessing the damage under Samote's watchful gaze. The sorcerer's lava had cut past scales to tender under-skin leaving gaping wounds on legs and wings. Forced to focus on those who stood a fighting chance, he cauterized the worst gashes with his healing flames. He reclined as exhaustion waved over his body.

Samote's voice fought through his thoughts. *Can you heal all their wounds?*

I've done what I can. Some damages will need time. There are too many smaller cuts and gouges for me to chance tackling them all. I must balance the energies I give away with what will be needed soon.

Samote faced him. *I can help.*

Not yet, young one. You'll need to learn to control your flames. If we succeed, there will be plenty of time to fully heal our brothers and sisters, time for you to learn how to heal others. You can serve the flight best with the chant to pull the spell. If that doesn't work, scatter the flight. Have you sorted the others into groups?

Samote nodded, her focus on the injured lying before her. *We have one plan for success and one plan for failure.*

Think of every dragon life saved as a success.

We need our human. Will she arrive in time?

We can't know. I can't hear her, though I sense she's close. We have each other. There's much we can do together.

One of the injured dragons squirmed against the rough surface, eyes closed.

Welglen's heart drew him back to the young dragons' sides. If he used the last of his strength to heal them, he would be too weary to fly the others to safety. They were nearly unconscious, which held the pain at bay. If they made it through the night, he could help.

The dragons quieted and a silence settled over the flight. The brief respite from the noise of the mountain unnerved. With the death of the young female in the lava, the news of the existence of the dragons would have traveled to the sorcerer, who could appear at any time.

Where are you, my Ellen? He called out to the abyss. *We need you.* He needed his human for their plan to work.

Welglen hunched over the injured younglings, soothing their jerky sleep with an ancient song designed to pull dragons closer to sleep and further from pain.

After a moment, Samote joined in.

It wasn't a song of words like humans learn. It was a song of instinct, protection, and love inborn.

The injured drifted from a light agitated sleep into a deep slumber. He motioned for Samote to rest. Within moments she was asleep.

Welglen allowed his muscles to relax, taking stock of his minor injuries, and recognizing his level of exhaustion. He closed his eyes and took in deep restorative breaths for a long period. He forced his thoughts toward hope.

An elongated ripple in the Earth sent Welglen back into high alert. He roused Samote. *Send the strongest to the sky.*

Samote moved between the uninjured, rallying them into the air.

An explosion erupted around the flight.

The land separated into islands of rocks surrounded by steaming heat, leaving the injured pair sleeping on a rock encircled by the sorcerer's lava.

Welglen soared, calling the others to fly higher. They flew in a chaotic pattern in several directions.

Samote. Lead them north.

Welglen lowered through the steam and smoke toward the sleeping dragons. Their rocky island bounced in the lava, ready to topple if one of the weights were removed. He would have to move them together, grabbing them with claws and teeth against their wounds.

He swooped down to their still forms, praying they wouldn't wake.

Welglen lifted his charges.

Their island inverted.

Lava splashed across the surface, sinking their temporary life raft. He pumped his wings in a slow pattern designed to keep the payload from swinging.

He hovered over an outcrop, ready to rest them gently to the ground and ferry them one by one.

A quick burst of air knocked him into the side of the mountain. His tender cargo wriggled in agony.

He thrust his wings and soared.

CHAPTER 57

The latest tremor sent a small cascade of sandy rock down the steep angle at Ellen's left.

She stabbed the point of her barbecue tongs into one of the patches of ice holding the gravel together and dragged herself forward. She tried not to think past the fact she'd left the only man who loved her, bleeding below, to trek to a battle she'd no idea how to win.

Her personal cheer squad fluttered above in the growing wind.

"I wish you babies could talk." She pulled a few feet higher, her foot in a fresh hold. "I'm sure that somewhere close is an easy path to the top for day hikers. Am I on it? No. My mom always said I did things the hard way. Let's not tell her about this, okay?"

Ellen paused at the next foothold, focusing on the act of breathing. Below her was a steep cliff.

A headache building in the back of her head grew with every foot higher.

"Jogging and twirling do not equal mountain climbing." She huffed. "All that work with Welglen, driving me.

I don't have to tell you he can be tough. That's the dragon way, I guess. He's warmed to me a little though, being partners and all."

The dragons landed above her to the right. They called down in a series of squawks from an outcrop large enough to lay on. "I'm coming." Ellen reached for the next catch.

A fresh quake knocked her against the rock, breaking her hold and sending her down in a slide.

She spread her arms and legs against the mountain and skidded to a spot when the barbecue tongs snagged a hold.

She panted with the building anxiety.

Her chin was raw, stinging. But she was alive. Bruised and scraped, it could have been worse. Much worse. The cliff below her feet had been a dangerous climb. It would be a deadly fall.

Ellen's heartbeat slipped from her neck back into her chest. The dragons surrounded her with anxious squawks. She tried to rally. "I'm okay, guys. Let's try that again."

She used her original holes to pull back to the outcrop. She slid onto her stomach on the large ledge and fished out the water bottle. When her heart rate slowed to a less fierce pound, she took in the hazy valley below, then turned to face upward.

"Crap." She checked out the wall of red-shaded rock above her. "Why is it every time I think I'm at the top of this thing, there's another top?"

Ellen, Welglen's voice entered her thoughts. She jerked around. *We need you.*

"Where are you?" She pulled the sword out of the tie on her pack and searched across the rocks.

Near the top. I have the spell if you can hold him.

"Almost there," she hoped. "Hold on!"

She holstered her sword, stabbed the ice above, and climbed.

"We need to have a talk, little dragons." She braced in the growing winds. "I don't know what we're walking into. I'm guessing it's bad. When the crap starts to fly, get out. Save yourself."

CHAPTER 58

The thin layer of icy snow crunched under the weight of the two injured dragons. Welglen settled them on a small plateau near the mountain's top. He circled above the flat, ringed by boulders and a climber's path. Ellen would arrive at that point.

If she made it.

The sorcerer could come from any side. The area with the thickest rock would be the safest.

Samote led the first of the flight over the ridge. *What do we need?*

Direct the others behind those large rocks. Welglen hovered, chanting the spell designed to shield the area from humans. *They must hover to remain concealed. If the spell doesn't work, scatter the flight.*

I'll stay.

Once the spell fails, go. Keeping your heart and the others safe is crucial.

The first dragons arrived and followed Samote's direction, disappearing behind the large boulders. *What of the injured?*

He checked the labored breathing of the pair at his feet. If he healed or transformed them, his energies wouldn't be enough for what lay ahead. *I'll have to protect them. Their connection to the earth will give the others away.*

The last of the flyers crested the edge. They hovered in a tight group above the ground. *I will take one. When the blue arrives, he could take the other. We are strong enough, together.*

Welglen nodded. The blue swooped in next to Samote. She motioned to the injured and they moved toward Welglen.

Steam burst through the Earth at Welglen's claws. *Hide!*

Samote and her partner slipped in with the others. Welglen flapped his wings at the ground, covering the injured in a cloud of dust.

The opening glowed deep orange. A bubble of heat-radiating lava gurgled out. It floated in the cool air like a small bat.

The shape stretched to seven feet. It darkened to garnet.

A head appeared first. Then arms.

Samote's chant filled his mind. *Oomm Rash O Woo. Oomm Rash O Woo.*

Welglen joined her call. The glow lightened, growing less opaque.

The form shrank slightly to the size of a man.

The height and build of Nilrem.

Facial features sharpened. A large scar deepened on the man's left cheek. Welglen hissed a long smoky breath.

Not Nilrem. The son had become the father.

Trigore.

Centuries of loss pulsed through Welglen's muscles. He craved the ability to kill. He hunched over the injured. Old instincts froze his claws in place.

Trigore tilted his head. His eyes opened.

His face was lined with age. His hair, streaked gray. His borrowed life, past halfway.

Trigore smiled. *Greetings, my friend.* He opened his arms wide. *I had hoped it would be you, though I'll admit to believing it unlikely you'd survived.*

The same voice Welglen remembered from his youth, though it had come from the father. *I expected Nilrem.*

Trigore dropped his arms, shoulders lifting in a shrug.

His gaze flickered to the injured beneath Welglen. *Father is ill, so he sent me. I'm grateful. Not only has my first trip through the Earth tingled most pleasantly, but we're also reunited.*

Why would he send you? Has trust erupted within the man for the first time?

I'm not a fool to believe him capable of change. Trigore rocked slightly from side to side, eyes on the small, exposed tail under Welglen. *I'm all that is left of the lives he created. He wishes to secure his dynasty, which means taking me with him.*

Trigore stepped forward. Welglen bent over his charges, unable to move back further without exposing them. The sorcerer's gaze traveled the length of Welglen's neck, then across his wings. *It's right that we've found each other. With you by my side, we can stop Father. Fight for me. I'll ensure you a long, full life at my side.*

Samote's chant echoed in Welglen's ears. *Oomm Rash O Woo. Oomm Rash O Woo.*

Trigore's head tilted to the ashy sky. His nostrils flared. Then he smiled wide, bearing long, wide teeth. *What a pleasure. Those you shelter aren't the only dragon hearts beating here.*

His lips moved in a whisper. He stepped toward the dragons' hideaway.

A flash of iridescent color flickered in the air.

Welglen repeated the spell to hide their nest, dimming the sparkling light.

Trigore raised his hands in the air and murmured words Welglen didn't understand.

A shimmer of dragon scales twinkled above the boulders.

Samote, scatter the flight!

The sound of dozens of dragon wings flapped into action. Brief glimpses exposed before they buried into the clouds.

Trigore sighed. Gray eyes settled on the snout of the closest young one.

Welglen shifted to cover his muzzle. He might not be able to pull the light completely from Trigore. The bond may block the ability to engage the spell by surprise.

You have injured. Let us end their suffering.

Welglen didn't need to reach into the sorcerer's mind to know he lied. To be here, he'd consumed the hearts of two dragons. Welglen repeated the chant he prayed would pull the light away. If there was time. *Oomm Rash O Woo. Oomm Rash O Woo.*

Trigore squatted to face the remaining babies tucked under Welglen's legs. *These you protect have suffered greatly. I'll receive what I need. They'll be free of pain, and we can stop a man intent on everything you detest.*

Are you not the servant of Nilrem? How would he respond to your activities?

Trigore stretched upward, chest expanding. *I am servant of no one. He thinks the groveling imp that scraped for any sign of love from a tyrant believes he's changed.* He drew a sword from his belt, pointing at the young one nearest Welglen's back legs. *I'm less patient than I'd thought. Speaking of the tyrant feeds my desire to end his reign. Release the young.*

Pride pulled Welglen's already alert muscles into a straightened position. He'd have groveled for the chance to give his own life to save his family.

He thrust open his wings and sprayed fire at Trigore's feet.

Trigore didn't move. *I'm not afraid of your flares.*

Samote's voice filled Welglen's brain with the chant. *Oomm Rash O Woo. Oomm Rash O Woo.*

Scatter, Samote! Go!

Welglen concentrated on Trigore. *I can't harm you, nor can I believe what you say. You fought against us the day my mate and most of my flight died. I suspect the same day you consumed your first dragon heart.*

Trigore raised his palms toward the gray sky. *You can't blame me, tormented all my life by an unloving father. He offered me a chance—if I fought with him, he'd recognize me as his son. He must have killed your mate since both of my hearts came from males. Join me. Fight against the man who took her from you.*

Welglen curled tighter against the young dragons. *Their fate is mine.*

Sorry to hear that. Trigore snapped at his fingertips, sending sparks out into the gray air. *I'm told this will hurt. Goodbye, old friend.*

With a quick flick of his hand, Trigore threw a shock of lightning from his fingertips. Welglen moved to block the bolt from the young ones. Burning whips of pain sliced across his chest and back, tying him to the ground. The searing agony turned his eyesight a stark colorless white.

Flames rumbled inside his soul. He fought to escape the ropes of fire that held him to the ground. His vision cleared. Trigore stood only steps away, sword raised.

Welglen clutched at the young ones, transforming all.

Shrinking into eagles, he slipped free and captured the injured eaglets in his claws.

He soared.

A lash of sparks grabbed at his neck. A whip of pain slapped him back to the ground.

The transformation broke. They were covered in burning whips, tied to the ground as dragons.

Trigore admired the power emanating from his hands. *You haven't lost your strength. Though you haven't saved everyone.* He looked at the injured dragons, exposed under Welglen's legs. *How lucky you've failed to protect the exact number I need.*

Welglen struggled to stay conscious during the pain to both protect the injured ones and attempt to free the light. Once this battle was lost, the others would be hunted down one by one. No hope left, but to chant. *Oomm Rash O Woo. Oomm Rash O Woo.*

The ties loosened.

Trigore stepped back. One hand squeezing the fabric over his heart.

The sorcerer's face contorted in confusion.

The spell worked. Welglen could fly the injured to safety. *Oomm Rash O Woo. Oomm Rash O Woo.*

One wing broke free.

Welglen rocked on his heels, tossed back his head. He snapped forward and let off a wall of flames.

Trigore stumbled back.

Welglen clutched the infants and strained upward.

Almost free.

A tug at his left slammed him hard atop the injured male.

Trigore's laughter raised to a higher pitch. He tugged the sleeping dragon free, then pressed another blinding surge directly into Welglen's head. *You're strong. I'm stronger.*

Welglen struggled to see through the white pain.

Red registered first.

Trigore cut open the chest of the dragon. He lifted the heart and tilted his head up to the sky, mouth open wide. Teeth bared.

Welglen sent off a fierce, narrow flame. The tiny heart disintegrated with a flash of fire before it could be devoured.

Damn you! Trigore shook his ashy hand against the heat. *I'll need the other heart. And yours.*

Electric flames shot from each of Trigore's fingertips, crisscrossing Welglen's back. They stabbed in sharp daggers retying Welglen against the Earth, unable to open his jaw.

Trigore wiped the infant's blood from his knife with great ceremony.

Welglen chanted in a prayer for the young one still breathing beneath him. *Oomm Rash O Woo. Oomm Rash O Woo.*

The flares from Trigore's fingertips dulled. The skin on his forehead creased into a scowl. He stared at his hands.

The ties loosened.

Welglen rolled atop the infant, hoping to grab him in his jaws.

He stretched upward.

Another searing shot pulsed through his body. The smell of burning flesh from his soft underwings met his nostrils.

They couldn't win. The spell merely slowed Trigore. Only life remained to give. *Hear me Ellen, save yourself.*

Trigore stretched on his toes. He raised the sharp point over the shoulder blade protecting Welglen's heart.

The lives Welglen had protected would be lost. He'd failed.

The tip broke through the first layer of scales.

Trigore cried out. "What?!"

The painful point released. Trigore spun.

Ellen stood at the top of the path, the Sword of Srekums high in one hand, flinging rocks with the other, and surrounded by a halo of tiny flying dragons.

CHAPTER 59

"Leave him alone!" Ellen screamed at a man in black who held Welglen down with a large knife. She'd tossed the last tattered oven mitt at the icy mountaintop. The backpack slipped off the sweaty grit on her shoulders. She let it fall, clutching the sword in both hands. She planted her feet flat on the ground, hunched her shoulders, and squinted—ready for impact.

The man spun to face Ellen. He smiled.

A calm power surrounded him—about six feet tall, a slight build, a sensual mouth, and a strong chin. A long scar shimmered down the side of his left cheek across pale skin. Nearly translucent, his original nationality could have been anything. Maybe vampire.

He wouldn't take her humanity without a fight.

A smear of red crossed the back of his hand. Ellen scanned Welglen long enough to confirm his body moved in breaths.

To his left, a small yellow dragon lay dead, covered in blood. She signaled to her babies. They disappeared down the path.

Ellen focused on the killer.

Dimples appeared at the corners of his lined mouth. "What do we have here?" he asked in a soft, sultry voice. Welglen growled. The sorcerer pointed a hand, and without looking behind him, released lightning out of his fingertips, binding her man-dragon to the ground.

Welglen's voice entered her head. *Engage your warrior. Fight for fairness.*

"Let my dragon go." She faked confidence at the sight of magic.

"Your dragon?" He nodded his head. "I'm afraid you are mistaken. Welglen is mine. We've been bonded since my infancy. Run along or stay. I'll deal with you soon enough either way."

"You must be Trigore. Welglen told me all about you. How he saved you from your father. You turned against him."

Trigore's eyes narrowed at Welglen. "Well, my old friend. I'm not sure how I feel about you betraying our bond in this way. Our stories are best left to us." He refocused on Ellen. "I would bet he hasn't told you everything. This creature is responsible for the current human problems. Their connection to the Earth has placed it in a disturbed state, awakening sleeping volcanoes. If he cannot take his place at my side, it would be in the interest of world peace that he perishes. He is, after all, merely a dragon. A creature which should have disappeared with the other dinosaurs."

Ellen's gut churned, deep and full of fear.

Welglen, what do I do?

He didn't answer, though she could hear his thoughts. *Oomm Rash O Woo. Oomm Rash O Woo.*

"You have no right to decide who lives and dies." Ellen prayed Welglen's words would break the sorcerer's powers over the Earth.

"Do you? I am Trigore, grand sorcerer of the Earth.

I have it in my power to protect the humans for eternity. Who are you?"

Ellen lifted her sword higher in front of her with two hands, mimicking the first time she'd held it, her balance foot forward, ready to lunge or run. "I'm Ellen the human, protector of all dragons, and have apparently been prophesized to kick your ass."

Trigore rocked back on his heels with a roar of laughter. "You are a bit of a human. You don't even have enough strength to hold your sword up without shaking."

Ellen's body did shake, but out of fear, not lack of strength. Perhaps Dirk's tactic would work. Welglen's chant echoed in her head. She had to keep him talking.

Trigore raised his shoulders, speaking softly. "Why do you care for these creatures? They are but lizards who have outgrown their nests."

"Dragons are beautiful beings. They exist to protect humans. They're not responsible for the lava. You did it. You'd kill them all!"

A red hue brightened his pale face. "I tire of you." A flick of his wrist sent a spray of electricity toward her chest. No chance for even a gasp, the white-hot light stopped a hair from her skin, pulling the hair on her arms outright in static.

He squinted, then threw multiple streams of lightning at Ellen. Every bright thread stopped before touching.

She released the air she'd held in her lungs.

Trigore nodded. "Ah, the Sword of Srekums protects. You are the one."

Ellen would hide her strengths. But she wouldn't play the weak female one more time in her life. "Let Welglen go."

"It's not so simple for you, my dear." Trigore shrugged off his long black coat, folded it into a neat square, and placed it at his feet. The slight color on his skin paled, like one who had spent all day inside playing video games trying to control imaginary worlds. Perhaps Welglen's chant worked.

"It appears true my magic can't reach you. I can, however, kill you as a human. What shall it be then? Strangulation? Stoning? Stabbing?" He smiled at her weapon. "Ah, swords."

He tapped the end of his knife to the ground twice. It transformed.

Into a *much bigger* sword.

Fear replaced courage. Ellen's fairness fairy flew away.

CHAPTER 60

Betrayed by shaking hands and sweat beading across her face, confidence hadn't reached the peak of the mountain with his Ellen.

The five newest flyers lifted from the path behind her in a protective circle.

Trigore smiled at the group, his tongue wetting his lips.

She followed his gaze, then cried out to the little ones, "Go, babies, go!"

The tiny flight raced above Welglen, squawking in distress at his bonds. They split into different directions, fleeing into the low blanket of smoke and clouds. *You have taught dragons to fly.*

Can he hear us? She asked, her focus on Trigore who watched the dragons sweep past. He didn't chase them. He didn't need them yet. He already had hearts tied to the ground.

This is our bond. He and I have another.

What did he do to you?

The sharp rocks sliced into Welglen's underside where lava had injured his scales. The ropes of energy that forced him against the ground burned his wings. *Focus on him. We have the spell.*

The fierce wind blew the tail of her hair around her face. She wobbled from foot to foot. He stopped resisting the force crossing his back. He focused his energy on the chant and the unfolding scene. *Oomm Rash O Woo. Oomm Rash O Woo…*

Trigore slowly circled Ellen in light steps. She turned with him, in a frightening dance. He brandished his sword in a figure eight. His flamboyant display of skill was clearly designed to frighten her.

Ellen twirled the sword over her head. Her leg buckled. She stumbled to the left.

Trigore smiled and watched her replant her feet.

The pressure on the bands across Welglen's wings loosened. He pushed against the ground. *Oomm Rash O Woo. Oomm Rash O Woo.*

Trigore pointed back without looking.

Strong iridescent color flew out of each fingertip and re-cinched Welglen to the ground.

Ellen's voice pressed against the pain. *Are you alright? I can feel the electricity through my body.*

Think only of the fight in front of you.

The Sword of Srekums trembled, outstretched in her pulsing right hand. She bent her elbow, grasping the hilt with both hands.

The weapon in Trigore's grasp would likely end her life if the spell didn't work. He would have experience. He would fight dirty. She needed the strength to stall him long enough for Welglen to pull away the powers.

With a flash of his blade, Trigore slashed from the right.

Ellen swung the sword. Her blade blocked his from hitting her head.

"Uh!" She shook her left hand out against the stinging vibration of the metal-to-metal contact.

Trigore swung again from the left. Their blades met again. Her face contorted in fear and pain.

"A fair defense." Trigore admired the length of his sword. Something changed. His flesh warmed.

Welglen repeated the chant in a constant rhythm. *Oomm Rash O Woo. Oomm Rash O Woo.*

Trigore barked out a laugh. "What if I were serious?" He lunged forward, chasing her backward.

Ellen slid on the shale knocked loose from the earthquakes and blocked his swings. Her footing slipped.

Her right arm dropped to steady herself on her knees. She swore in a long breath.

Trigore raised his sword. He swung at her neck.

Welglen released a spray of flames at Trigore's feet.

Trigore aborted his lunge. His blade dropped and sliced Ellen's right shoulder. She grabbed at her wound. A thin string of red blood outlined the cut through her gray shirt.

I couldn't stop his sword, though I tried to keep it from cutting too deep.

"Seriously?" Ellen gasped. *Get the light out!*

Trigore paused. He smiled at the blood. He moved to place Ellen between him and the possibility of flames, speaking to Welglen. "Kindly stay out of this fight. Yours will be coming soon enough."

Ellen rose and faced Trigore. Her eyes twitched in pain, though her stance was stronger. She needed to attack. *His right side is strongest. Show him what you've got while you still have strength.*

The veins in her flushed neck pushed against her skin. Blood dripped to her elbow. Her body moved with the confidence he'd seen in her baton practice.

She struck at Trigore's left. He blocked the full force, but the tip of her blade reached his cheek, drawing blood.

Trigore pulled back and dabbed at the thin cut. His eyes narrowed on the red smear on his palm. "Is that what you've been hiding? Let's play."

Trigore struck hard and fast.

Ellen matched his blows. Sweat dripped down her face.

Trigore stumbled, his heart open to her attack.

She paused, positioned to take the life of another.

Trigore kicked out a leg, slamming her down. Her head flipped sharply back against the ground.

The Sword of Srekums clanged on the rocks to the edge of the cliff near the path.

Trigore dabbed at his brow with his shirt sleeve. "You were quite entertaining. Though I'd expected the prophecy would have brought me someone not so squeamish about taking a life. How ironic that your downfall is your humanity. Still, all in all, you deserve to see what you've lost before you die."

"No," Ellen whimpered. *Welglen, stop him.*

The spell is not working fast enough. Run. Save yourself.

Trigore stepped past the dead young one. He tugged the unconscious red female out from under Welglen.

Ellen cradled her right arm against her side and scratched at the ground. She hurled rocks with her left hand and tried to regain her footing.

Trigore ignored the pelting at his back. Without fanfare, he stabbed his sword into the young dragon's chest.

A loud moan erupted from Ellen. *Oh God, it's my fault. My weakness killed this baby.*

Leave. Be safe.

She remained.

Trigore took several moments to pull the red dripping heart out of the dragon with great drama, making sure they witnessed every excruciating detail. His smile held traces of the young child Welglen had protected. The sorcerer's eyes, only inches away, had darkened to match his violent father. Trigore spun to Welglen. Flashes of hot lightening whipped around Welglen's head. His jaws clamped to the ground.

Trigore rested his sword at his feet. He lifted the small, red, pear-size heart to his mouth.

He sunk his teeth in.

Ellen's whimper carried across the rocks.

Blood dripped down his chin.

Trigore wiped his mouth on the back of his sleeve, smearing a line of blood to the right in an eerily crooked smile. He raised his arms to the sky and shouted, "I can feel it. The life grows quickly within me. Soon nothing can stop me."

A halo of light glowed around Trigore's head. It spun, then dissolved into glittery particles that floated into the air.

Ellen gasped. *He's immortal?*

A low growl released from Welglen's gut as he answered. *The energy builds inside him.*

Ellen stumbled, shaking her head. *You can kill him, Welglen. He's not human.*

Trigore picked up his sword and strode to Welglen. "It is right I shall enter eternal life with the one who saved me. I shall have the final course now."

CHAPTER 61

The baby's blood dripped from Trigore's hand. If Ellen had been stronger, the little one would be alive. She'd lose Welglen next.

The chant cut through Ellen's thoughts. It drove through her brain, then increased.

Samote's green scales flickered at Ellen's right. The young dragon hid behind one of the boulders, chanting with Welglen in a voice Ellen hadn't heard before. *Oomm Rash O Woo. Oomm Rash O Woo.*

A tiny glimmer twinkled from the edge of Trigore's lashes. A glistening followed. Light seeped out through his pores and evaporated into the air.

Ellen's thoughts were strained. *His color changes. Is he becoming immortal or is the light leaving?*

Welglen grunted as Trigore repositioned the sword above his scales. *My death doesn't matter compared to the safety of the others. Run away with them.*

He looked back at the knuckles gripping the weapon that would take his life. He chanted.

Trigore chopped at Welglen's back, panting against the effort. He angled the blade on its side and pried his way under a scale. The chant deepened into a groan. *Oomm Rash O Woo. Oomm Rash O Woo.*

Trigore climbed onto Welglen. He tucked the point of the sword into the tender gap created beneath the glassy plate. "This will do nicely."

Welglen's gaze met Ellen's. If he could keep fighting, so could she. She crept toward Trigore.

Run, my Ellen.

Ellen lunged. She rammed her body into Trigore's, knocking them into Welglen's side. The nerves running from her shoulder down her left arm screamed out. The hum of the chant vibrated from Welglen's chest, driving her forward. *Oomm Rash O Woo. Oomm Rash O Woo.*

She rolled to push at Trigore.

A blur of a fist slammed into Ellen's face.

She slid off Welglen's side, unable to see or hear past the striking pain. She inhaled deeply several times to force her vision back. She gingerly touched her face. Blood and ash smeared on her hand.

Trigore wrenched Welglen's horns to climb back on.

Run Ellen! He'll be immortal soon. His color changes.

I won't leave you! She held Welglen's wing and pulled to stand.

Trigore struck her in the side with the hilt of his sword.

"Ah!" Ellen rubbed at her ribs with one hand and wiped at the blood trickling out her nose with the other.

Trigore raised his weapon again.

Welglen's gaze met hers. Everything she'd ever wanted was in those eyes. Her dragon's eyes. *Go. I die either way.*

I can't. Ellen scratched at the gravel, pelting Trigore's head. He turned, roaring.

Ellen kicked Trigore in a frenzied attack.

She dragged at his elbow, his sleeve raising to expose the nearly translucent skin. She sunk her teeth into the salty forearm.

Trigore slammed a fist against her bleeding arm, pushing her hard on the rock. "If you won't run away," he pointed a long finger down at her, "lie still and wait your turn to die."

Ellen rolled over onto her knees, huffing for air. She had to save Welglen. She charged into Trigore's side head-first. A satisfying crack registering at the same time a massive headache erupted.

Trigore winced. "Uh! You annoy me, feeble human." He smashed her down with a shot to her left ear, the last unharmed part of her body.

Ellen turned over to face him, the ringing in her brain part of the background music for the last scene of her life.

Trigore's cheeks, once reddened from the heat of the lava, were white, crystalline as the inner wings of a dragon.

She struggled to sit.

He walked to her side. In slow motion, he leaned over her, cocked his arm back, fist ready, and slammed it against her head.

Ellen crumbled onto the edge of the cliff.

Trigore's voice screamed over the sound of her brain sloshing inside her skull.

CHAPTER 62

Welglen twisted toward Ellen. Blood smeared along her arm and one side of her face. Her breath heaved out in pants. She pushed to stand, but her knees buckled. She collapsed. Trigore bent for his weapon. The skin on his outstretched arm glistened.

The bonds that held Welglen loosened.

The light was leaving Trigore.

Ellen. The spell works. Oomm Rash O Woo. Oomm Rash O Woo.

A little more focus and he could save them all.

Oomm Rash O Woo. Oomm Rash O Woo.

Trigore wiped his blade against the side of his leg. He raised it high before her.

Welglen's wings broke free. He tried to fly.

A blistering pain radiated around his tied legs.

Oomm Rash O Woo. Oomm Rash O Woo. Trapped, Welglen hovered, wings spread wide. He roared in flame.

Trigore's cape ignited. He dropped to the ground, rolling. He pulled the fabric away from his red, welted skin.

Welglen released more fire. Trigore screamed in agony, his entire body in flames.

He writhed, then was still. Silent.

The last ties on Welglen's scales broke free. He flew to Ellen's side.

She buried her face in her hands and sobbed against him. "That was horrible."

I feared the spell would not work in time. If not for Samote, it may not have.

"I almost lost you."

A sound pierced through her cries.

Welglen rotated to Trigore's dark remains.

Tiny pinpoints of light shot out of the black pile. They merged into a fierce glow.

Ellen gasped. "What's happening?"

I was too late.

The hot pile moved.

A black arm shot into the air.

Glowing fingers unfurled; fierce orange petals reached for the light.

Ellen covered her mouth, unable to look away.

The molten hand curved into a fist and slammed against the ground, shooting the hot red color through the darkness. A back arched, followed by an outline of shoulders and Trigore's head, facing the ground.

The light brightened to a blinding white, radiating heat. Welglen lowered his inner eyelids, and shaded Ellen with his wings.

The light cooled. The full naked figure of a man appeared before them.

Trigore glowed nearly to the point of transparency before them, arms open wide. The color faded to blue, then returned to a pale whiteness. Hair, mouth, eyes, nose all returned.

Ellen grabbed at his wing. "What do we do? How can we stop him?"

We cannot. He is immortal.

Trigore's eyes opened. His voice scratched out toward them. "You would do that to your old friend? Pain beyond belief? That, will never happen again." Trigore swung his arms out in a white light that knocked Welglen into the air, then down to the ground. "You will only die once. I'll make this last."

Trigore whipped him with fresh slices of pain.

Welglen tried to call out to Ellen, crumbled on the rocks to his left.

He couldn't find the words past the torture.

Trigore swung his sword at Ellen's head.

A small flame ejected from Welglen's throat and hit the sword, turning it red hot.

Trigore dropped it. Immortal but not impervious to heat.

"Enough!" Trigore lashed out white-blue licks against Welglen's head and wings. "You shall distract me, no more."

CHAPTER 63

Ellen pressed a hand hard against her chest to force her pounding heart back into place. Trigore's sword lay between him and Welglen. The sword meant for her neck.

Welglen. Are you okay? What do I do?

Welglen's eyes were dark, the lids lowered.

Welglen! Please!

A slight movement of one wing proved he still breathed. *Run, Ellen. Run.*

Trigore picked up his weapon. Ellen struggled to gain enough coordination against the rough surface to stand, scratching for anything to throw. The Sword of Srekums lay yards away at the edge of the mountain.

Ellen flung a handful of rocks. "Leave Welglen alone!"

Trigore faced her, wearing only soot from the fire. "You," he hissed, "will die now."

"Probably. But I've written this scene many times and it never ends well for bastards. Because you're basically stupid."

Ellen dove for her sword.

Trigore swung around in a long kick. A hard bare foot smashed into her rib cage.

Ellen grunted. She rolled against the rocks. A sharp pain sliced into her side.

She reached out for the sword and a little luck.

Both were out of reach.

Trigore stood over her and raised his sword. "I said, wait your turn."

"ARRRRRG!" Ellen stared at the blade as her mind tried to place the sound.

Trigore's attention moved over his right shoulder.

Dirk scooped up the Sword of Srekums and raced toward him, screaming pirate style, "ARRRRRG!" He knocked Trigore's weapon to the ground.

"Bloody humans!" Trigore shot an electrical charge that slammed Dirk to his back. The Sword of Srekums flew out of Dirk's grasp, high into the air.

Ellen pushed against the rocks to stand. The sword appeared to stop, and through the haze of Ellen's pain, it paused thirty feet high before rotating down in a slow-motion vision. Her dreams flashed through her brain like an instruction guide.

She reached with her left hand, caught the tail of the metal dragon, and swung it around her head.

She twirled, kicking her baton skills into action.

"Go, Dragons, go!"

She lunged. The Sword of Srekums found little resistance in both the front and back of Trigore.

The carved-dragon hilt touched his ribcage. Trigore folded toward her, his face close enough for the smell of his hot breath on her face. "I'm not the last."

His dark eyes stared blankly. He glittered in an eerie translucence, light streaming out his pores. The weight against her arm lifted. He dissolved into different shades of crystals.

His light lifted to the sky. Dark particles fell to Earth.

In an instant, only the sword and a pile of ash remained.

A gust of wind spread the flaky pieces across the mountainside.

Gravel crunched behind her. Dirk stepped to her side. "Fantastic sword work. I particularly liked the cheer at the end. You'll have to explain the rest to me later."

A sharp contraction in her gut pulled her to her knees.

She vomited.

Good guy, bad guy, human, sorcerer, innocent or guilty, Ellen had ended a life.

"First kill, huh?" Dirk rested a hand on her shoulder after the retching stopped. "I could say it gets easier, but it doesn't. That's how you know you're one of the good ones."

Welglen pushed slowly off the ground. A deep groan amplified each breath that smoked out between his jaws. He stretched to his full height and spread out his wings, slashed with burns and cuts.

Dirk's voice rang above her. "Damn! That's one big dragon."

CHAPTER 64

Welglen wrapped his wings around Ellen, nuzzling her hair. Fabric and dust combined to scab her shoulder wound. Her knuckles were raw. Scratches and bruises covered any exposed skin. She had almost lost her life.

She dropped the sword to her side, wrapped her arms around him, and rested a swollen cheek against his cool scales.

Her voice was soft, low. "Will he come back again?"

I don't know. I know you have saved us all.

"Not all," she looked toward the fallen. "I choked. I should have killed him sooner, then the other baby would be alive."

We have asked you for so much. You gave it. Don't torture yourself with the timing of your gift.

Her weight slipped slightly. Welglen lowered his head against her uninjured shoulder and sheltered her with his wings. Her body wracked with sobs. He held her until her body relaxed and her breathing calmed.

She placed one hand on each side of his head. "I don't know what I would have done if anything had happened to you. You, all of you, have become my life."

Welglen bowed his head. *You will be forever remembered as our strongest warrior. You have reconnected the bond between humans and dragons, beginning with me.*

The man who had come to Ellen's aid cleared his throat. "Hi, I'm Dirk. So, what's the plan? When's the next battle?"

Thank you for your service.

Dirk clutched at his ears and faced Ellen. "How'd he do that?"

"It's a long story. But that's a good question, Welglen. Where to?"

I must return our dead to the circle of life.

Ellen's shoulders drooped. "I need to get Josh medical help. Where should we meet after?"

This human, who had given so much, deserved more than he could offer. *You must return to your humans and I to my kind. We cannot continue to ask you to risk your short life.*

"No!" she stroked his head. "You can't leave me. Not after all this. I've earned the right to be with you."

That you have. I must secure a safe home for the young ones. Afterwards, I won't return.

Ellen pressed harder against him. Her fingers grasped the edges of his scales.

He opened his wings slowly, sliding her hands away. He stepped to the bodies of the last little ones, grasped them in his talons, and hovered above Ellen's reach.

Farewell, my Ellen.

She slipped to the ground. "Don't go. Please don't leave me. Not yet."

You will always be in my heart. He lifted into the gray sky in a slow, low spiral. He waited for the remaining dragons to fly from their hiding places. They circled above her in farewell. Fresh tears glistened on her cheeks.

Ashamoor flew low and settled next to her human.

Ellen caressed the top of the young one's head. "I can't keep you with me. You belong with your brothers and sisters. They are your family. I'm not a dragon."

Ashamoor nuzzled into the hair at Ellen's shoulder, then joined the flight.

Welglen led the small dragons north, staying low over the treetops for cover until they were far from roads and homes.

Samote flew to his side. *Where will we go?*

To the deep forests on the mountain ahead. No visible roads, and the colors boast of a water supply. You should be safe there until you can transform, but beware. What is secluded now, will become either a destination or a path for humans. They don't stay in single places long. Eventually, they spread out.

What of you? Do you leave us?

I must carry our lost to the heavens. I can't see beyond the moment I meet with our ancestors. It'll be up to you to lead this flight in my absence.

Then let us fly longer together. You have much to tell. I have much to learn.

CHAPTER 65

Ellen's dragons disappeared into tiny pinpoints as late afternoon winds kicked up and offered glimpses of blue sky after days of gray. Only the pressure of Dirk's hands on her non-injured shoulder kept Ellen from falling to the ground in a weepy mess.

"Stay with me, girl." Dirk dug through his backpack. "You've been through a lot. You'll need to process. Important thing is to talk—don't go all mental. Let's get you put back together. Drink this."

Ellen's tongue absorbed the first sip of liquid. She drank deeply, rehydrating shocked cells.

Dirk splashed the cut on her shoulder.

"Ugh." Ellen moaned when muddy water dripped off her elbow on either side of a trickle of fresh blood. He blotted with a gauze pad. The sharp pain was a welcome distraction from the dull ache in her heart. He followed with a liberal squirt from an antiseptic tube and wrapped it tightly with a strip of tie-dyed cloth.

He stepped in front of her, the hair surrounding his belly button visible under the edge of the freshly cut T-shirt. "Thanks," she managed. "Sorry to ruin one of your favorites."

"I figure Jimmy wouldn't mind. Where's Josh?"

"Josh?" *Crap. Josh.* She tried to stand using Dirk's leg as leverage. He pushed her back to sit. "He's hurt. I had to leave him. He had a nasty cut on his head."

"He could be fine . . . maybe. Let's finish fixing you up to make it back down this frickin' mountain. You can tell me which way to go." He fashioned a sling from another strip of shirt and helped her up. A throb replaced the numbness.

Unable to do much more than walk, Ellen let Dirk carry both backpacks. She used the sword to balance against the steep face. He matched her slow pace.

Dirk didn't ask any more questions about Josh, or about why she'd left him alone, with a head injury. If he'd ask, she had no answer. It was a choice she'd made for her dragons. She hadn't even remembered to ask Welglen to fly Josh down to safety.

Dirk stopped for a swig of water, offering the bottle to Ellen first.

Her focus returned. "Not to be ungracious, but where the hell were you? We needed the water, gloves, and shoes."

He sat on a large boulder and patted the flat area next to him. When she refused to sit, he stood. "My fault. The stores were closed in fear of looting, which is probably smart since I broke into the back of the survival gear store to gather your list. Guess my breaking and entering skills are rusty because I set off a silent alarm. The cops caught me in the parking lot. I let Cay out to create enough of a distraction for me to escape on foot."

"How'd you get here?"

"I stole a truck from a farm and managed to scrounge food."

He'd tried harder for her than she had for Josh. She moved to the top of the next section of slides. "You did show up when I needed you the most. Let's get Josh and then you can find Cay."

Going down was much easier. Without earthquakes, they managed to slide far enough down to find Josh within minutes. He lay under the same outcrop, still, covered in black smudges and gray dust. Ellen stumbled toward him over the large rocks.

"Josh," she tried to call out, only managing a whisper. "Josh."

His head turned toward her, eyes opening in dry slits. "Thank God," his voice cracked over chapped lips.

Ellen slid into his arms. His voice rasped. "Don't ever do something like that again. I've never been so scared."

She cradled his face. His pupils were the same size. The makeshift stitches had held. "I came back for you. Dirk's here too. We can get you to help."

"I wasn't scared for myself." Tears spilled over his cheeks, leaving two clean tracks. She buried her face in his chest to hide the guilty pain lumped in her throat. Josh's hug pinched at her bruises, but she didn't move. Pain proved life.

Ellen didn't say sorry that she'd left him—sorry she hadn't given him a thought. He deserved the truth, though perhaps, not yet.

Dirk reached a hand down for Josh. "We'd better get to the truck. I know someone who can help."

Dirk supported most of Josh's weight on the trip down the mountain. The sliding shale rushed them down in a fast descent. An emptiness filled her that she couldn't deal with yet.

Ellen let Dirk tell Josh about the sorcerer on the mountaintop because she had no energy left for storytelling.

By the time they reached the truck, the entire sky had cleared to a dusky pre-sunset blue. The mountain appeared peaceful, as if nothing had changed.

Everything was different. Ellen and only two other humans on Earth knew it.

CHAPTER 66

Welglen clutched the lost pair in his claws, the air cooling with each upward thrust into the quiet sky. The heart of the young one, saved by his flight, rested on his tongue. Each inhale flavored his breaths with the blood of the lost.

His dragon's strength, fire, and spell hadn't stopped Trigore from killing his family. The sorcerer would have killed Ellen too, if not for the bearded human, placing his life before hers.

Welglen flew through the films of a cloud, turned, and circled in a slow glide. The familiar lightening proved the soul in this little dragon's heart reached the ancestors. Without the heart Trigore consumed, he couldn't reunite the other. He offered a prayer that the soul of the lost would return as dragon and would one day be able to rejoin the flight in life after death.

Goloo Glem Niks Kukar. Goloo Glem Niks Kukar.

Welglen released their bodies for a second chance at their stolen lives, his flames turning the lost into ash drifting on the currents.

Farewell, little ones.

The joy of rebirth didn't lessen the loss.

He shouldn't be their protector if he couldn't fight.

The answer wasn't in falling toward Earth.

Welglen turned upward.

His mouth dried against the cold air; his muscles cramped. He climbed.

Why have strength when it can't be used to protect? Why love only to have it pulled away?

A voice trailed across the void, filling Welglen's mind. *We play our part; we don't choose it.*

Slatetail? Is it you, my leader?

Welglen strained against the silence and cold muscles to fly higher, closer to the edge that separated life and life lived.

Slatetail flew at his right, his black scales opaque against the sky. *It is I. We're all here for you. You've done very well leading your small flight. We're proud of the dragon you've become in the face of so many obstacles.*

Welglen shook his head. *I failed. I've lost young ones. Without the ability to fight to save those I can, it's an impossible task. I had no strength against a sorcerer. If not for humans, I would have lost them all. I'm not enough for those who would rely upon me.*

Slatetail spread his wings, small lights twinkling through them. *These losses have stricken you, as they have me. But it's not our purpose to kill. It's our purpose to protect.*

How's that possible?

You've answered your question in your last battle. You've saved our own from extinction and the humans from eternal slavery. Don't you feel these accomplishments?

I did nothing that wasn't undone by the sorcerer. It was the humans.

Slatetail moved closer. Welglen could feel the air from Slatetail's wings move gently against his snout. *You did much. You brought the humans to our side. If not for how you worked together, dragons would be lost. Didn't you learn much from humans in your time as one?*

Welglen pictured Ellen's enraged face as she'd tried to save him from Trigore. *I'm gratified to learn of the character of some.*

Slatetail nodded his great head, still half again the size of Welglen. *It's a gift to discover faith and strength in another. No one controls what happens in battle. Because we fight, we're all at risk. It's not ours to fix the outcome.*

There were many more humans ready to kill us, either by force or by their treatments of the Earth. Living among them was torture.

A natural reaction to an unnatural situation. Slatetail hovered close. *I once took away your right to fight to the death. I'll not take such liberties with your freedom again. The choice is yours. You may return to Earth and rejoin the flight or remain with us in peace.*

Us?

Hundreds of dragons surrounded Welglen.

Roglir flew closest, his burned body healed.

Tacoma clipped past, still fast and agile; her eyes held the same challenging mischievousness.

He recognized nest mates. Those who'd fought alongside at the last great dragon battle. Just as Ellen had.

The warmth around him soothed the muscles between his wings. A calmness he hadn't felt in a very long time started in his mind and spread through his body.

A certainty of where he belonged.

CHAPTER 67

Ellen braced one hand against the hard, gray dash, and clutched the back of the bucket seat with her bandaged arm to avoid smacking against Josh's head. He cinched his hold around her waist to keep her still on his lap as they bumped off the edge of the dirt.

At the base of the highway on-ramp, beach and booze songs blared from Dirk's phone the instant his service restarted, relieving the silence that had pushed against the stolen truck's interior.

Dirk silenced his phone. "Want to go to the hospital? Or do I get my medic friend in on this? Less likely to arouse any suspicions. Your call."

Ellen touched Josh's warm cheek, wincing against the pain that shot through her shoulder. She'd dragged him into this mess. She had to be there for him. "No offense, but I'm thinking I'd rather take my chances at an overwhelmed hospital. Josh is feverish. He needs proper stitches."

"No worries. I'll drop you off and go back for your van. This truck is too hot to be in town for too long anyway."

Dirk inched through the traffic, thick with cars wrapped in painted protest slogans, and emergency vehicles.

A minivan crept up beside them, topped with bicycles and brimming with wide-eyed young children and bedraggled parents likely rethinking their family vacation to northern California. "This is unreal. On that mountain, all of this seemed so far away."

Josh sighed. "I can't wait to get back to normal."

Ellen focused on the minivan. *What's normal?*

Dirk followed a long line of cars exiting into the city of Mt. Shasta and crept toward the hospital. When they arrived, it was surrounded by an outline of orange construction cones. A young man dressed in dirty green scrubs tapped a clipboard against Ellen's window. "Extent of injuries?" he asked. His nameplate identified him as a hospital nurse.

Ellen pointed to Josh. "Head wound. We were on the mountain and got caught in a landslide."

The nurse clicked a penlight into Josh's eyes. "Any convulsions or loss of consciousness?"

Josh shook his head. "But she has a nasty cut on her arm."

The nurse noted their names and contact information. "It'll be hours before you can be seen. Likely too long for stitches. You can wait in this line, or we'll call you after the level one cases are under control."

Ellen leaned toward the window. "What's happening?"

The nurse handed Ellen a hospital contact card. "You name it. Two apartment buildings collapsed in the earthquake, and a couple propane tanks exploded."

Dirk pulled out of the line. "Time for Plan B."

They arrived at Dirk's cabin at the same time as a dark SUV. A young woman dressed in green camouflage pants and a black sleeveless shirt met them on the porch, carrying a canvas bag. She waved at Dirk.

"This is Stevie. She can fix anything."

Stevie touched Josh's face. "You have a fever. Let's get you inside."

She settled Josh at the table. "What about you?" she asked Ellen.

Ellen slipped onto a chair. "I'm good. Just take care of him." No particular spot hurt her more than another.

"It looks like someone kicked you in the face," Stevie said. "I'd send you both to the hospital if it wasn't overrun with earthquake victims. I can get you cleaned up. You'll need to see a doctor for antibiotics. You're both filthy." She gently lifted Josh's hat off and removed the blood-soaked sock. We're going to need to clean this first."

Stevie got Josh's health information, checked his eyes with a similar penlight that the nurse had used at the hospital, and offered a couple of aspirin for the fever.

Dirk tossed the remains of his T-shirt onto the bed and selected a similar option from a tall stack of folded tie-dye. "While you get to work, I'll get the van."

"Whose truck is that?" Stevie tugged on a pair of plastic gloves. "Where's the Jeep?"

Dirk tapped his hands on the top of the bar in a drum roll. "Gotta run."

Stevie shook her head. She moved Josh to the kitchen sink. She cleaned out the wound on his scalp using a green soap from her bag. "That's some pretty interesting sutures here."

"It's all I could think of."

"How long has it been like this?"

Ellen looked out the window. The light was nearly gone. "I'm not sure. Several hours at least."

Stevie used a small razor to cut away the clotted hair. She pulled out a suture kit. "This is going to hurt a bit. I'll be quick."

Ellen's stomach lurched with each of the three stitches Stevie tied in Josh's head.

Josh moaned but held still. Stevie covered her work with antiseptic and gauze, then helped him back to the chair. "How ya feeling?"

Josh touched the area outside of the bandage. "Better, now that you're finished poking through my brains."

Stevie laughed. "You'll be fine." She changed her gloves and motioned for Ellen to sit in the chair. "Just get in to see a doctor to ensure infection doesn't have a chance to grow. That was a nasty cut. Rocks leave pretty jagged edges, so take it easy on those stitches."

Stevie cut away the T-shirt scraps from Ellen's arm. "Hmm."

"What?" Ellen asked.

Stevie shrugged; her expression was covered by the mask.

The cold pressure of a wet cloth dabbed at Ellen's arm before a strong soap stung her open wound. A strong odor filled her nose.

"Hold this tight." Stevie lifted Ellen's opposite hand to hold a wad of gauze against her cut. Stevie opened another fresh kit of needles.

"You come prepared."

"Always." Stevie pushed the needle through Ellen's skin.

Ellen gasped, then let out a long exhale.

"We'll need to do that about eight more times," Stevie said. "Your cut is longer than Josh's. I guess the same rock that hit him missed you."

"I don't know. There was a lot happening."

Stevie added another stitch. "Looks like it."

Ellen turned to Josh. He raised one eyebrow.

Stevie finished her necessary torture, re-cleaned, and wrapped Ellen's arm. "What else?"

"That's it."

Stevie lifted Ellen's chin and leaned close. She touched a few points on Ellen's jaw that drew moans that rippled along her aching rib cage. "I don't think that whatever hit you broke anything, but you're going to want to ice your face. Tomorrow it's going to be twice this size." She motioned for Ellen to lift her shirt.

Ellen waved her hands and moved forward to get up. Stevie placed a firm hand on Ellen's shoulder.

Ellen lifted her shirt. A thick dark bruise covered her sides from underwire to hip, a clear shape of a footprint outlined on one side.

Stevie clicked her tongue. "Are you going to tell me a rock did this one too?"

"It was a crazy day. Hard to say exactly how everything went down."

Stevie's touch at her ribs looked light but hammered along her nerves. She pressed a stethoscope at several points along Ellen's back and had her breathe deep, painful breaths. "It looks like you got lucky here. You should have full-body x-rays. As for your cut, I wouldn't mention it unless it gets infected. Knife wounds require police reports."

Crap. More to deal with later.

"You can snip these out in a week yourself or ask a friend to help out."

Dirk returned and spoke with Stevie in front of the cabin for several minutes before she drove away. "I can take you home."

Ellen held her hands out for the van keys. "Thanks Dirk. You've already saved us twice today. It's my turn to take care of someone."

CHAPTER 68

Ellen rocked the old chair hard against the wooden floor, searching out the window for her dragons. She hadn't been fast enough to save some of the babies, and she'd dragged Josh into a life-and-death situation. She longed for a second chance to protect the others, but her part in the adventure had ended.

Beams of afternoon sunlight streamed through the dusty window onto Josh's face. Ellen leaned forward to block the rays before they woke him. He opened his eyes to her. "Have you been in that chair all night?"

"I dozed next to you for a while, but I kept waking up. I thought I would be better here."

"The animals are quiet."

"Your uncle fed them this morning. He said he'd take care of them this afternoon too, so you can rest. He's worried about you. He wants you to call and let him know you're really okay."

Josh sat against the pillows and patted the spot next to him. Ellen climbed into his open arms. She nestled against his cool cheek, relieved his fever had broken.

He petted the top of her head. "Sadness seeps out of you. It has to be a natural reaction to all this. Tell me about it. Sharing what happened could help you."

A large lump developed in Ellen's throat and tightened her emotions. She couldn't talk about Welglen. She didn't have the words yet. She didn't know if she ever would. It was easier to talk about Trigore.

"He looked like a man. A tall, skinny, angry man. I fought him with my sword, but he had actual skills. He cut me, smacked me around, and stomped on my ribs. No matter what I did, he still came after us. He killed two baby dragons and threatened to kill me, Welglen, and anyone else that got in his way."

Josh's face whitened and his lips pursed. He took her hands into his.

Ellen choked on emotion as she described Trigore's first death and resurrection. "It was . . . horrific. When he returned, the sorcerer had already left his humanity behind. My sword went through him. He dissolved. Nothing remained. No blood. No gore. He just blew away in a fine dust."

Josh rubbed Ellen's palms in a light, circular pattern. "When you needed me most, I panicked. Then you left. I didn't know if you were alive or dead."

"Leaving you probably made me the worst person in history. I don't expect you to forgive me but know I worried for you too. I had to go. I was drawn to help the dragons."

Josh dried her cheeks with the edge of a blanket. "I had a lot of time to think about it. There's nothing like a head injury on a mountainside while the one you love is battling sorcerers with dragons to bring out the introspection. I understand why you left me two years ago. I wasn't the right man for you. I couldn't give you what you want. I couldn't see that. I do now. I can be who you need me to be. We can be together. You can write to your heart's content.

We'll adopt some kids and I'll take care of them. How hard can it really be? I take care of the animals already. I'll take care of you. If you'll let me."

Ellen's eyesight blurred. Everything she'd always wanted dropped in her lap. She tried to speak but couldn't generate the words. Josh pulled her back against him. She sobbed. She'd lost the loves of her life. But she wasn't alone.

At dawn, they woke to the sound of hungry animals.

Josh groaned. "Was that the goats or is my stomach growling?"

Ellen stretched stiff muscles. "You start our coffee. I'll take care of the critters. And call your uncle."

Ellen bent for her shoes.

Pain shot through her ribs, and she moaned.

"Are you okay?"

"I will be," Ellen let out a short exhale. "It's just going to take a while." The physical pain would heal.

A pair of birds took off from the trees into the clear sky at the sound of her footsteps on the porch. They traveled in the same direction she'd watched her dragons fly days ago.

Sounds escalated from the barn. Goats and chickens wouldn't wait for her pity party.

Ellen filled feed buckets and water troughs. She opened the gates to let the animals outside, comforted with the ordinary, real-life activities. This could be her life. She'd write her dragon adventures. She'd have to sell them as fiction. No one would believe they were true. On this peaceful morning, she almost didn't believe.

She bumped her sore arm on the barn doorway.

"Ow!" She rubbed the area below the bandage.

"Are you okay?" Josh walked toward her with two cups of coffee. He looked rested, normal. He was going to be fine. He held the mug out to her. "Ready to go down to the clinic after breakfast? I figure we should go early since there's likely going to be a wait."

She stared into his clear eyes, unable to move.

His smile faded. "You're leaving me again."

Ellen struggled for words. "You've offered me everything I've always wanted. I love you."

"But it's not enough."

"It's not about enough. I guess it's timing. There's a hole in my life. I thought you could fill it. I realized this second that I need to figure it out for myself. And there's something you should know. I found out I couldn't have kids when I lost a baby. Our baby. I didn't know I was pregnant until it was too late. Once it happened, I froze. I couldn't write. I couldn't think. Nothing seemed possible anymore."

Josh placed the cups on the dirt and hugged her. "I'm sorry you had to go through that alone. But if you want kids, there's always adoption. And that surrogacy thing. It's not the end."

She faced him. "You're right. It's not the end. I'm just not sure what the beginning should be."

"Don't make any permanent decisions. You've had an unbelievable week full of mythical creatures. Stay here, I'll take care of you while you take some time to process everything that's happened. I can help."

There was only one other soul who could help. He wasn't available to her. She had to do this by herself. "I need to go home."

"I hate to think of you alone." He cupped her face in his hands, avoiding the bruise that stretched from ear to chin.

"I'll have my stories. They'll keep me focused." Her voice caught in her throat. She forced the emotions into a space in her heart she'd open at home. She couldn't mourn the loss of her man-dragon with the human who loved her.

Welglen had stripped away her normal life, then didn't stay around to help her build another. She needed to chip away at that chunk of loneliness alone.

"Take however much time you need. However, this time, we're going to stay in touch. No more radio silence. I need to know you're okay."

Ellen slid back into his arms and listened to his steady, comforting heartbeat. She couldn't stay in his warmth until she tackled her loss. "I will. I promise."

She would dive deep into her writing and chronicle her adventure. At the other end of the story, she hoped to find peace.

CHAPTER 69

An icy winter wind gusted into Britta's Brews. Ellen's favorite two regulars pushed through the double doors, settled onto their stools and the topic of the evening: whether the cold snap or the lack of rain was damaging local trees.

"Evening, Ellen," they said in unison, and ordered wine from Britta.

Ellen smiled at Jeff and John. She'd made a point of getting to know them. Invisibility hadn't done her any favors.

She gazed at her screen at the final page of the dragon adventure that had poured out in the last months between fits of crying and anger. She attached the draft to an email for her agent with a note including a full outline of a seven-book young-adult series. She would write the tales to educate kids about the world of dragons. There would come a time when belief would be required, and if she started with the children, she could influence a generation of believers.

She was going to be busy writing for a very long time.

Ellen hit the send button and waited for the expected relief to wave over her.

Nothing.

It didn't make sense.

She had a mission and a good living. She'd saved her career. She stayed in shape practicing her sword. She'd visited her parents for Christmas and expected Josh back for another visit in a few days for New Year's Eve. She had made sure to fit in with humans since Sonoma life had returned to normal.

Except normal didn't fit.

And she didn't belong with the dragons. They'd left her.

Britta set another pint of grapefruit lager in front of her.

"What's going on?" Britta crossed her arms over her chest, staring down. "You've been acting weird for months. If I didn't think you and Josh were tight, I'd suspect you're nursing a broken heart."

Ellen shrugged. They'd had this conversation before. Her heart was broken but she couldn't talk about it to another human. Her adventure warranted therapy, except explaining what happened to a mental health professional would probably wind up with her commitment in a special home with padded walls. She settled for liquid counseling and tried to process the traumatic days with her dragons. "It's just a story. I'm trying to figure out which way to go."

"I find my first instinct is usually the right one."

Ellen shrugged.

Britta moved to a young couple sitting at a table near the same window Ellen had first seen Welglen.

She closed her laptop.

Writing wasn't her passion. It had never been. It was always dragons.

Ellen craved action. Her world required her to sit still and type.

Welglen had flown off to his Dragon Neverland. For all she knew, he'd left the little ones scattered to fend for themselves. The same way he'd left her. Not knowing if they were safe came in close second to the anger of being the one left behind.

Ashamoor had been ripped out of her life after only a week. Gone without the luxury of a lingering adolescence, painful high school years, or a launch to college. What would happen when the next sorcerer arrived? Trigore said there would be more. What would they do without her and her sword?

Ellen left the second hard cider untouched. She packed her laptop, dropped cash at the bar, and tugged the new backpack straps to redistribute the weight.

Jeff called out, the tuft on top of his head waving, "Careful walking through the park tonight. Some of those trees have been dropping limbs."

John's frizzy hair stood out as if absorbing electricity from the air. "Probably damaged during those earthquakes."

"Or it could be disease brought on by long periods of drought," Jeff added.

John turned to his friend. "We should have rain by next week."

Jeff nodded. "When I was a kid, it rained every day from October through April."

Britta smiled over the top of the two, now competing with stories. Ellen waved and stepped outside.

A couple passed arm in arm in thick coats. Winter had come in the new usual of cold and dry. A thin wisp of smoke trailed across the street to the backs of two men, entering the dark park. She followed, careful to keep her distance.

The first month alone, Ellen had fantasized Welglen watching over her on her walks home. She wouldn't allow that comfort anymore. It wasn't healthy to dwell on the impossible. Calling Josh to ask if he'd come a day early would be a step forward. He'd seen the dragons. He knew what had happened.

Bundled on the outside with a fleece parka, and on the inside by a pint of Britta's brew, she didn't have to worry about a fairness fairy alter ego anymore. They were one and the same.

Not that it did her any good. She pictured the remainder of her life without heroics. Without her dragons.

Repressed anger fought for the surface. She longed for another fight with a sorcerer. This time she'd fight without hesitation.

The dark shadows of the sidewalk between light posts shaded her face. She picked up her pace. She'd promised to call Josh tonight.

The leaves crunched beneath Ellen's shoes on the concrete path across Plaza Park. The sound reminded her of being a little girl, daydreaming about dragons on the walk to school. She kicked at an empty soda can on the sidewalk, flinging it into the side of a tree with an unsatisfactory clank.

A rapid popping sound came from behind her.

She whirled around. Conscious of once again being a woman in the normal world, she laced her keys between her fingers.

Fear should be registering. Instead, she wanted to kick a little ass.

Orange construction tape sectioned off an area of downed limbs. Charged up, she held her breath and stepped into the shadows, allowing her eyes to adjust. She circled the trees.

No one in sight.

She slowly exhaled. Looking for trouble was careless. Being disappointed at not finding any—worse. Time to go home before she completely lost it.

At the edge of the park, she stepped off the curb. A groan of wood about to snap pierced the air.

She pictured a battle against a sickly tree. *Great. I'm lonely, angry, and paranoid.*

Ellen jogged across the street and down the block to burn off some of the negative energy that filled her. Angry tears threatened to freeze on her face. She wiped them away and jogged, increasing speed block by block. She was in a full sprint when she reached her house.

She burst through the front door, tossed the backpack onto the couch, and searched for something to hit or break. She found a can of beer in the refrigerator, popped the top, and after one sip, threw it into the sink. It foamed and splattered against the backsplash.

The soft voice behind her shot against the walls. "What'd that beer do to you?"

Ellen swung toward the sound, grabbing a paring knife.

Dirk leaned against the wall, a beer in one hand, and a Jimmy Buffett 2018 tour T-shirt stretched tightly over his now muscular torso.

"Dirk!" Ellen dropped the knife, pinned her visitor in a hug, and planted a large kiss on his lips.

"Babe," Dirk drawled against her mouth. He squeezed his arms around her.

"Oh!" Ellen pushed away and touched her cheek, the skin on her face radiating heat. "Sorry. I'm not sure what came over me. You saved my life, and I never thanked you. Yeah, that's it."

"You're welcome." He took a long draw from the can, crushed it into a flat disk, and set it on the counter. He pulled a piece of paper out of his pocket. A check. "Here's the second half of the money you sent. I don't take money for dragon ops. Less expenses, of course."

"Of course." Ellen glanced at the check that had a tie-dyed background and set it on the counter. "But a little out of character."

She avoided eye contact and wiped at the splattered wall with a dishtowel. A hundred questions filled her mind.

Mostly why his face made her completely happy. "How did you get in?"

Dirk sat at the small kitchen table. "Not easy. Your neighbor peppered me with questions when I knocked on the front door. When she left, I circled around back. In my new line of work, I don't like to announce myself."

"That's Mrs. Delalo. You must be rather good to get past her." Ellen sat across from him, excited someone knew all the craziness and characters of her favorite tale. "What's the new line of work? Giving up illegal farming?"

"I found something better. I'm a dragon warrior."

"I guess I am too." She'd leave out the pathetic parts of her current life. "I'm writing dragon stories designed to illustrate their real history and purpose to children. Not exactly exciting, but it's all we have left of them now. Want another beer? I think I have another. I'd love a chance to talk about our dragons with someone who won't think I'm nuts."

Ellen dug through the refrigerator and found a light beer behind a stack of old takeout containers.

"I'm thinking more in the present tense."

Ellen closed the door with her elbow and handed Dirk a can. "Meaning?"

"As in, I'm fighting for the dragons . . . still." He popped the tab.

Ellen's heart fluttered. "What? What does that mean? How can you—" she sunk into the chair and rested the unopened can in front of her. "You've seen the babies?"

"I wouldn't call them babies anymore. They're nearly full grown."

The words caught in her dry throat. "Ashamoor?"

"A wee bit smaller than the rest, but still a good deal taller than you."

Worry melted out of her pores.

Jealousy filled the void. She leaned toward him over the table. "Welglen scattered the flight. They couldn't be together. You can't be with them."

He took a long drink before answering.

Ellen needed all her strength not to toss her can at his head.

The edges of his mouth turned slightly, drawing out the suspense. She walked to the fireplace and lifted her weapon off the display hooks.

She placed the Sword of Srekums on the table between them, the point toward Dirk. "You have two seconds to tell me everything."

Dirk choked a bit. He wiped his mouth on his dark forearm hair.

"After I sprung Cay from the pound, I went back home. I thought life would continue as normal." Dirk chuckled. "It turns out normal isn't my thing. I missed the crazy fire breathers. It marked the first time I'd worried about something other than myself in a long while, and I liked it. I listened for any odd notices of unusual activity around farm animals—missing critters, sudden drops in the snake populations. Stuff like that. I started hiking the mountain trails, following my instincts."

Ellen traced the dragon tail on the sword's hilt with one finger as Dirk told his story.

All this time alone wishing she could see them again and he'd taken action.

Sweet enough to make her want to vomit.

"I expected a handful of small flying lizards, but I came face to face with a couple dozen large animals, not thrilled I'd tracked them. The rascals pinned me to the ground. I thought they'd tear me in half." Dirk downed the rest of the beer and smiled at his fond memory of near death.

"Welglen planned they would fly far away, then scatter."

"Plans change."

Ellen leaned further over the table, nearly nose to nose with Dirk. "I'm supposed to believe you know where my dragons are?"

Dirk shrugged. "I kind of thought that would be your response. So, I didn't come alone." He walked around her to the back door and reached for the knob.

The blood pulsed in Ellen's neck and launched her across the room. She pushed him aside and rushed out.

Ashamoor perched on the empty chicken coop, the familiar purple, blue, and green scales reflecting the house lights. She drifted down and nuzzled the top of Ellen's head,

"Oh," Ellen stammered. She wrapped her arms around Ashamoor's neck, emotion clogging words in her throat as the unexpected feeling of happiness surged through her. "I worried nonstop."

"That's ironic," Dirk said. His voice surprised her. She'd already forgotten him. "Ashamoor's broken nearly every branch hiding in the park trees to keep an eye on you. It's what brought us back here."

"One of the reasons." Ellen swung around at the sound of a second male voice, and stared into the face of Welglen, the man. His familiar brown hair curled a bit longer over his wide shoulders. "Ashamoor has bonded to one specific human. One woman, who needs her."

Afraid to let go and find out her imagination had taken over again, Ellen clung to Ashamoor. The words tumbled out. "You said you'd be gone forever. You said you'd scatter the flight. Yet you turn up with him," she pointed in Dirk's direction.

"I had the opportunity to live among the souls of my ancestors. But as Roglir and Tacoma had fought their last fights, I found my journey wasn't over yet." He stepped closer and she instinctively stepped back to save the remains of her crushed emotions. "I returned because the flight needs to start over. They need each other. I need to teach them the old ways."

"Why are you here?" She dropped her arms to her sides and moved a step toward him. "Here. At my house."

"As I said, the family needs to stay together. We missed one member."

Ellen touched her hand to her chest, her rapid pulse increasing. "I'm part of the flight?"

He nodded.

"I've missed you, Welglen."

"And I you." Welglen opened his arms.

She slipped into his embrace, wrapped her arms around her strong dragon-man, and squeezed.

He squeezed back.

Dirk slapped a hand on her back and one on Welglen's. "Now that we've got the band back together, we need to make some plans."

"Plans?" She reached one hand out to Ashamoor. She wanted to touch them both.

Welglen's voice vibrated against her cheek, still pressed to his chest. "There has been a great deal of activity in the east I believe could be tied to the birth of another set of dragons. We'll need to travel soon."

"Me too?"

"If you choose to join us."

Ellen tried to think seriously about sharing her life with the dragons—the dangers and the loss of normal relationships. A smile tugged on her face that she couldn't control. She'd need to pack her sword, laptop, and a baton.

And she needed to shop for new oven mitts.

She rubbed at a growing burning sensation in her stomach. It wasn't butterflies.

She stepped back, confronting the trio in her backyard. "How do I know you won't just leave me again?"

"A fair concern. I'd planned to stay away, forever. You nearly died protecting us. I didn't want to ever place you back in danger. Yet there were many questions as I wondered how your wounds healed and how you survived the blow of having to take a life in the defense of others. I could not stop thinking of you."

"I appreciate the thought behind that. I'm thrilled you're here, but I have to be in charge of my own life." Ellen took a deep breath with a long exhale. She tried to see past the emotional indigestion. "Being cut out of the flight tore me apart."

"I have placed you in danger and caused you pain."

Ellen squared off in front of Welglen, hands on her hips. "You were given a sacred duty from Slatetail. Guess what? Me too. While you were sent away with the eggs, I carried the history in my dreams and let's not forget, the sword. But without asking my opinion, or what I needed personally, you dropped my character from the story. You can't keep making my life decisions."

Welglen rested his hands on her shoulders. "I have the remainder of my time on Earth to protect the world from sorcerers. Your lifetime is much shorter and therefore more precious than mine. I can promise you, there will be dangers. New fights, and new enemies. We'll need the help of our warrior. If you stay with us, we'll stay with you. Partners?"

Ashamoor nuzzled Ellen's hair, the warm breath tickling her neck. "Okay, okay. But remember. No one writes my life story but me."

Acknowledgments

To my writing support group: Bonnie Lee Petri, Patricia Lynn Henley, and Carole Kelleher.

To the inspiring group of Left Coast Writers led by Linda Watanabe McFerrin.

Thank you to Haley Kvasnicka for her wonderful dragon art.

About the Author

TAMI CASIAS lives in the mountains of Northern California with her husband, and a black bear intent on smashing all barriers between his stomach and her pear tree. Her other works include *Crystal Bound,* and *My Affair with Mickey.* Subscribe to www.tamicasias.com for upcoming events.

CPSIA information can be obtained
at www.ICGtesting.com
Printed in the USA
JSHW081056160423
40382JS00001B/86

9 780982 973547